SECOND NATURE

Alice Hoffman...

"A rich and satisfying concoction . . . [A] modern fairy tale, full of insights into the battle between instinct and upbringing, desire and conformity."
—*BOOKLIST*

"Hoffman is a prolific and fine-tuned writer . . . Everywhere within the larger structure of this book, in niches such beauty flourishes."
—*WASHINGTON POST BOOK WORLD*

"Iridescent prose, taut narrative suspense, alluring atmosphere, vivid characters."
—*BOSTON SUNDAY GLOBE*

"A phenomenally romantic tale."
—*GLAMOUR*

"Another page-turner . . . *Second Nature* is first-rate storytelling."
—*CLEVELAND PLAIN DEALER*

continued on next page...

"Beautifully written, suspenseful and thought-provoking."
—*LIBRARY JOURNAL*

"Hoffman gets inside her characters and manages to make them all sympathetic and often downright touching . . . a riveting novel."
—*NEWSDAY*

"Lyrical . . . richly ambiguous."
—*THE NEW YORK TIMES*

"Once again, Hoffman stirs up the unlikely with the ordinary and seasons it, expertly, deliciously, with our darkest desires."
—*KIRKUS REVIEWS*

"A wise and gracious reminder that maybe what we really want is simpler than we think."
—*CHICAGO SUN-TIMES*

"Hoffman is an endlessly fascinating writer."
—*DAYTON DAILY NEWS*

"Alice Hoffman takes seemingly ordinary lives and lets us see and feel extraordinary things."
—*AMY TAN*

"She is a born storyteller."

—*ENTERTAINMENT WEEKLY*

"Showing the magic that lies below the surface of everyday life is just what we hope for in a satisfying novel, and that's what Ms. Hoffman gives us every time."

—*BALTIMORE SUN*

"Hoffman's novels get better and better."

—*SEATTLE TIMES*

"With her glorious prose and extraordinary eye for the magic of the mundane . . . Alice Hoffman seems to know what it means to be a human being."

—SUSAN ISAACS, *NEWSDAY*

"A reader is in good hands with Alice Hoffman, able to count on many pleasures. She is one of our quirkiest and most interesting novelists, and her skills and talents increase with each new book."

—JANE SMILEY, *USA TODAY*

continued on next page...

TURTLE MOON

PRACTICAL MAGIC

"One of her most lyrical works . . . Hoffman is at her best."

—SAN FRANCISCO CHRONICLE BOOK REVIEW

"Charmingly told, and a good deal of fun."

—THE NEW YORK TIMES BOOK REVIEW

"Written with a light hand and perfect rhythm . . . *Practical Magic* has the pace of a fairy tale but the impact of accomplished fiction."

—PEOPLE

"A sweet, sweet story that, like the best fairy tales, says more than at first it seems to."

—NEW YORK DAILY NEWS

"[Hoffman] has proved once again her potency as a story-teller, combining the mundane with the fantastic in a totally engaging way."

—BOSTON SUNDAY HERALD

"[A] delicious fantasy of witchcraft and love in a world where gardens smell of lemon verbena and happy endings are possible."

—COSMOPOLITAN

"Hoffman's best . . . readers will relish this magical tale."

—PUBLISHERS WEEKLY

SECOND NATURE

Alice Hoffman

BERKLEY BOOKS, NEW YORK

This is a work of fiction. The events described
are imaginary, and the characters are fictitious and not
intended to represent specific living persons.

SECOND NATURE

A Berkley Book / published by arrangement with
Property Of, Inc.

PRINTING HISTORY
G. P. Putnam's Sons edition / February 1994
Berkley mass market edition / April 1995
Berkley trade paperback edition / February 1998

The Penguin Putnam Inc. World Wide Web site address is
http://www.penguinputnam.com

ISBN: 0-425-16163-3

BERKLEY®
Berkley Books are published by The Berkley Publishing Group,
a member of Penguin Putnam Inc.,
375 Hudson Street, New York, New York 10014.
BERKLEY and the "B" design
are trademarks belonging to Berkley Publishing Corporation.

PRINTED IN THE UNITED STATES OF AMERICA

10   9   8   7   6   5   4   3

To Tom

*"Nature never deceives us;
it is always we who deceive ourselves."*

—JEAN-JACQUES ROUSSEAU

SECOND NATURE

Alice Hoffman

ONE

BY APRIL MOST PEOPLE HAD
already forgotten about him, except for some of the nurses on
the floor, who crossed themselves when they walked past his
room. The guard stationed outside his door, who had little to
do but read magazines and drink coffee for more than three
months, bragged to his friends that on nights when there was
a full moon he needed a whip and a chair just to set a dinner
tray on the other side of the door. But in fact, the guard had
never even dared to look around the room, where the metal
bed was made up with clean white sheets every week, though
it had not once been slept in.

The man who occupied the room had no name. He refused
to look anyone in the eye or, even after months of work with
the speech therapists, to make any sound whatsoever, at least
not in the presence of others. Officially he was listed as patient
3119, but among themselves the staff called him the Wolf
Man, although they were expressly forbidden to do so. He was
underweight and had a long scar along the inside of one thigh
that had healed years before but still turned purple on cold or
rainy days. For two months he'd needed to wear a cast on his

reconstructed foot; otherwise he was in surprisingly good health. Since he had no birthday, the staff at Kelvin Medical Center had assigned him one. They'd chipped in to buy him a sweater, blue wool, on sale at Bloomingdale's, and one of the cooks had baked and frosted an angel food cake. But that was back in January, after he learned to use a fork and dress himself, and they'd still had hope for him. Now, they left him alone, and when he sat motionless, and sunlight came through the bars on his window, some of the nurses swore that his eyes turned yellow.

The evening before his transfer upstate, the barber was sent to his room. There would be no need to sweep the floor after his shave and haircut; the raven that had been perching on the window ledge was waiting to dart through the bars and gather up the hair to wind into its nest. One lab technician, who had been brave enough to look through the glass window in the door, had once seen the raven eating right out of his plate while the Wolf Man calmly continued with his dinner. Now, the raven watched as the attendants strapped the Wolf Man into a metal chair and held his head back. The barber wanted no chances taken; a human bite was the most dangerous of all. In the interest of speed, he used a razor rather than scissors, and while he worked he quickly recited a blessing.

The following morning, two attendants helped the Wolf Man into a black overcoat, which would be taken away once he settled into the State Hospital, since he'd never need it again and another patient could make use of it. The cook who had baked the angel food cake for his birthday wept. She insisted he had smiled when she lit the candles on the cake, but no one believed her, except the guard stationed at his door, who had been made so anxious by this bit of news that he took to biting his fingernails, close enough to the skin to draw blood.

The cook had discovered that the Wolf Man would not eat meat unless it was raw. He liked his potatoes unbaked as well, and would not touch a salad or a pudding. For his last meal, an early breakfast, she had simply passed a hamburger patty over a flame for a moment. So what if uncooked meat was bad for you, and most of the patients liked cereal and toast, she wanted him to have what he liked. She had an impulse to hide a knife or a screwdriver inside the folded napkin, because she knew that as soon as he'd eaten his breakfast, he would be handcuffed, then released into the custody of a social worker from the State Hospital for the ride along the Hudson. By afternoon he would be signed into a ward from which no one was ever released. But she didn't follow her impulse, and after the Wolf Man had his meal, the attendants dressed him and helped him into the black overcoat, then clasped the handcuffs on him, quickly, from behind, before he could fight back.

Outside the door, the guard turned his Walkman up to the highest volume, and he slipped his sunglasses on, though the April sky threatened to storm. His friends liked to hear stories about the Wolf Man—how he crouched and circled three times before he curled up to sleep with his back against the wall, that five strong men were needed to hold him down each time they drew blood or inoculated him against measles and tetanus—and the guard was always happy to oblige. But what he never mentioned, as he drank cold beer with his friends, was that on nights when there was thunder he often heard a whimpering behind the door, a sound so pitiful it turned his bones cold and his heart inside out.

That was the sound the trappers had heard on the last day of December, when the snow was ten feet deep and deer stuck in the drifts and froze solid. There, at the edge of northern Michigan, much of the land had never been charted and trees were so dense they blocked out the sun. Beneath the ice, streams were filled with green water. Bears in these mountains grew to seven feet, and their hides were so thick a whole hive of bees couldn't sting them. It was dark as night on winter afternoons; trappers had to carry flashlights and leave lanterns hung on their snowmobiles in order to find their way back. Most of these men never poached enough to get caught by the rangers, and anyone looking for them would have had a difficult time. In the spring, moss appeared overnight and covered any footprints completely by morning. In winter, no one but a maniac or an experienced hunter would venture into the forest. For those men who didn't fear the woods, there was little chance of legal action against them. Trapping was, after all, a criminal act without a witness. There was no one to hear a shotgun fired, or the peculiar cry made by a fox when a piece of cyanide-laced lamb takes effect.

The men who found him were an uncle and nephew who had worked the forest for more than ten years and who were not nearly as greedy or cruel as some of their neighbors. They worked in silence, not with poisoned meat but with steel traps, and they were always particularly careful to stay together, even when it made sense to split up, since they had seen, several times, huge paw prints, three times as big as a dog's. In these mountains all sorts of things were said on winter nights, some to be believed, some not. A man they knew, over in Cromley, had a wolf-skin rug on his living room floor, head and all. He told everyone he'd shot the wolf, a male of more than a hundred and ten pounds, head-on, but his wife had let it slip that he'd simply found it the spring before, dead of natural causes, preserved all winter long by the cold. Wolves were rare, even this far north; you could probably count on your fingers the ones that had come down from Canada and stayed.

Still, their tenuous presence made for good talk and real fear. An old trapper who hadn't been caught once in sixty years of making a living liked to scare some of the boys who were just starting out by swearing that it was possible for some wolves to become human. He'd seen it himself on a night when there was an orange hunter's moon. A wolf was crouching down with the pack one minute and standing on two feet like a man the next. That happened with old trappers sometimes—they had killed more animals than they could number and, now that they were senior citizens who couldn't eat anything but oatmeal, they suddenly started to have some kind of funny regret that mixed them up so badly they didn't even notice people were laughing at them.

The uncle and his nephew didn't listen to stories and they didn't take foolish chances. As far as they were concerned, they weren't breaking the law so much as taking care of their families. They were interested in deer for the meat, foxes, and raccoons for their skins, but they got much more than that on the last day of December. This was the season when the sky turned black at four-thirty and the cold made breathing painful and sharp. They were inspecting the traps they had left out the day before when they heard the howling. Normally they would have backtracked, but they had worked all day with nothing to show and still had one trap left to check. As they walked forward, it wasn't the cold that made them shiver, and their brand-new parkas from Sears couldn't help them one bit. The nephew's teeth were hitting against each other so hard he thought he'd chip the enamel right off them.

It was hard to tell from the howling exactly how many wolves there were until they saw them. What sounded like a dozen turned out to be three, up above, on the ridgetop. All three were silver, brothers by the look of them. They seemed to be waiting for the uncle and his nephew, because as soon as they saw the men, the wolves stopped their racket. Yet they stayed where they were, unprotected up there on the ridge. When the uncle saw a pool of blood, he thought the wolves were after a deer or a fisher caught in the last trap, and he figured it might be best just to let them have it. The temperature had begun to drop and the sun would soon be going down. The uncle would have turned back then if his nephew hadn't grabbed his arm.

The last steel trap was a good one; kept oiled and cleaned, it would last another fifty years. When they heard the whimpering sound, they assumed they were simply suffering from the cold. Hallucinations occurred in severe weather; they sprang up from the ground fully formed. Jack Flannagan insisted he'd been visited by his dead mother one day in the woods, when the temperature was ten below zero. A friend of the nephew's would not hunt after dark, convinced that a deer he had shot one snowy day had cried real tears, just like a baby. So the wailing they heard might have been caused by twilight and ice. The notion of going home began to feel about right, even necessary. Then they saw the thing in the trap, struggling and bleeding, its foot partially crushed, and they might have shot it then, to put it out of its misery, if they hadn't realized, all at once, that the struggling thing had the shape of a man.

The wolves took up their howling again, while the uncle labored to open the trap. The nephew fired his gun in the air, even though he knew it was bad luck to shoot at wolves, and they took off, across the ridge and through the pine trees. It took almost two hours to get the poor creature out of the trap and carry him back to the snowmobiles. A trail of red blood burned through the snow. The drifts were now much higher, so that a mile seemed to go on endlessly. The nephew wondered aloud whether they'd be charged with murder if their unintended victim should die. He was already unconscious and his skin had turned blue. How had it been possible, the nephew asked his uncle, for him to have survived through the winter, wearing only skins on his body and wrapped around his feet? Why had they never seen him before, when they knew every man for a hundred miles around?

The uncle didn't bother to answer, he was too busy tying the limp body onto the snowmobile with thick brown rope. Clouds were moving in fast, threatening more snow. They had to get to the rangers' station, where a helicopter ran an airlift to St. Joseph's Hospital in Cromley. The uncle's breathing was ragged. He knew for a fact that the trap had shattered the left foot; bone jutted through the skin. As the uncle was positioning the head onto a blanket he realized how young their victim was, younger than his nephew. Once he looked at the pale face, with its high cheekbones and knots of dark hair, he couldn't look away, even though he had removed his gloves to lash the rope to the snowmobile and his fingers were freezing. If he'd seen anything like this face before, it was in the chapel at St. Joseph's, where he'd waited while his wife was being operated on for something wrong inside her stomach a few years back. To the right of the pews, in a dark alcove, there had been a statue made of white wood with a countenance so calm it had made him weep.

He pulled his gloves back on and started his snowmobile. In less than three hours, work would begin in the only operating room in St. Joseph's as an orthopedic surgeon repaired the bones the steel trap had shattered. Two weeks later, the patient would be flown to Kelvin Medical Center on East Eighty-sixth Street in New York, a hospital that dealt exclusively with victims of traumatic stress. There he would stay, in a locked room, for the next few months, while some of the best doctors in the city tried to ascertain what they were dealing with. But the uncle knew what they had right then and there. It didn't matter what people said on winter nights this year or the year after or the one after that. It didn't matter what people believed. The uncle knew exactly what it was they were dealing with, on this night and forever after. They had caught themselves a wolf.

Robin Moore was stopped for speeding every time she drove through town. It made no difference whether she was going thirty-three miles an hour in a thirty-mile-an-hour zone, or if teenagers in Trans Ams were revving their engines and passing her by. She could tell when it was going to happen, she'd get a funny taste in her mouth, as if she'd eaten a lemon or a spoonful of salt, and then she'd hear the siren. Robin always pulled over to the side of the road calmly, then rolled down her window and waited. "Is there a problem, Officer?" she'd say in a voice so sweet you'd never guess at the depth of her bitterness or imagine that she knew every local policeman by name. She'd had coffee with their wives, and invited everyone over to the house for barbecues; she'd fixed onion dip and guacamole on nights when the men had sat in her kitchen playing poker.

The problem was that she was divorcing Roy, and either he thought it was amusing to have his buddies stop her for minor infractions—an inspection sticker overdue, a broken left taillight, the alleged speeding—or he believed this harassment would make her realize she needed him. Either way, Robin's glove compartment was now chock-full of tickets, none of which she'd paid. She had fallen for Roy when she was sixteen, the same age their son, Connor, was now: a dangerous and stupid year when boys jumped into fast cars without thinking twice and girls drank themselves silly down at the beach near Poorman's Point and sometimes did enough damage to last a lifetime.

She couldn't keep away from Roy back then. The more trouble he got into, the more her family despaired, the more she had to have him. His father, Neil, had worked for Robin's grandfather and drawn up the sketches for the arboretum when the land was nothing more than cattails and scrub pine. In Nassau County, Roy's father was known as the Doctor, since he could cure almost any tree, whether it was a dying elm or a willow hit by lightning. Roy had started coming around with the Doctor during the summer Robin turned sixteen, although it was clear he didn't give a damn for willows and elms. He started throwing rocks at the patio whenever she was out reading in the hammock. He began to wait for her outside the kitchen door, near the rosemary and the Russian sage. He kissed her for the first time beneath the arbor where the wisteria bloomed. Not long after this kiss, and hundreds more like it, Robin's grandfather made his declaration that under no circumstances could she marry Roy, which pretty much sealed her fate.

And now, although they had a legal separation, Roy was somehow convinced they were still together, even after their final fight, a nasty display of distrust on the corner of Delaney. That night Robin went home and dragged all of Roy's clothes out to the driveway, and when he got home and saw his clothes flung across the concrete, he must have known where they were heading. Yet almost a year later he continued to appear at the house unexpectedly. He was there, he said, to check Connor's homework—something he'd never done when he lived with them—or to make certain the hot water heater wasn't on the fritz. Once, he had arrived on a Saturday night and had done everything possible to try to get her into bed. He came up behind her and whispered, the way he used to: *Just this one time, one little fuck, come on, baby.* She thought he was kidding until he shoved his hand into her pants, and she had to push him away. The next day he'd come back, sheepish and polite, with a peace offering: a truckful of manure, which he said the Doctor had asked him to deliver, highly unlikely, since Robin had just seen her father-in-law that morning and he hadn't mentioned a word about cow shit.

When Robin was starting out, the Doctor never viewed her as competition; surely there were enough gardens on the island for them both. He sent her customers and called nurseries out on the East End to get her a discount. He taught her to hang jars of beer from fruit trees so that wasps could drink themselves to death, and to circle herb gardens with a ring of salt, which slugs wouldn't dare to cross.

It was true that Robin spent too long with each client, poring over books, plotting out designs for perennial beds in watercolor and ink, but that wasn't the reason her business was ailing. Lately, everything she touched seemed to die. Robin attributed this to the anger she had carried around all winter, ever since her breakup with Roy. If she pruned a rosebush in the morning, by midafternoon the canes would begin to wither; by evening they would turn black. Just last night, she'd discovered that every bulb in the pot of forced tulips on her dining room table had decayed only minutes after she'd torn off some of the yellowing leaves. All week there had been good weather for gardens, with a light rain turning the cold earth squishy and warm—perfect conditions to begin spring cleanup for her regular clients—but Robin didn't bother to return any of their calls. Whatever bad luck she was having might seep through the old leather gloves she wore when she cut back brambles and raked mulch off the season's first liliesof-the-valley.

This stretch of sour fortune wasn't the reason she was driving in to see her brother, although it now seemed as if just getting out of town would take all day. Already she had been pulled over twice, once near the King Kullen supermarket by that moron Woody Preston, who grinned as he wrote out a speeding ticket—four miles over the limit—and the second time only a mile from the bridge, where George Tenney at least had the decency to look embarrassed as he wrote out the ticket for failing to signal when she changed lanes. Robin had tossed the ticket into the overflowing glove compartment right in front of him.

"You're going to have to start paying those," George said of her growing collection.

"I don't think so," Robin said. She hadn't bothered to dress up and was wearing her rain slicker, a pair of jeans, a khaki-colored sweater, old green boots. She had small callused hands and beneath each fingernail was a line of dirt that seemed never to wash away, not even if she sat in the bath for hours and used her good soap from Italy.

"You could give Roy another chance," George suggested. He was a large, soft man who loved poker and almost went nuts when his own wife left him. For months afterward, Roy brought him home for dinner on Tuesday nights, and George ate steadily and slowly, asking for the peas or the rolls in a wounded voice.

"Are you a marriage counselor?" Robin asked him.

"Well, no," George said. "I can't say that I am."

"Okay, George, just tell me this. Was Roy fucking around the whole time we were married, or just at the end?"

"Robin," George said in that wounded voice. "That's not nice."

"No, it's not," Robin agreed. A fine rain had begun, and Robin turned on the windshield wipers, then gunned the engine of the pickup so it wouldn't die on her as it often did in damp weather. "Do you want to come over for dinner on Friday? Vegetarian lasagna, but you won't be able to tell there's no meat."

"You know I can't," George said. He'd known Robin forever and he hadn't had a home-cooked meal for months, but it wasn't a good idea to socialize with a beautiful woman who happened to be Roy's not-quite ex-wife.

"It's not like I'm asking you for a date, George," Robin said. "But hey, I guess it's good to find out who your real friends are."

She said this just to ride him, since she knew that anyone connected with the police department had to side with Roy. People simply couldn't stand it when your marriage broke up; they took it personally. Even Robin's oldest friend, Michelle Altero, who had never liked Roy, and had cried at their wedding, real sobs, not just polite tears, had suggested she give him another chance.

"Can I go now?" Robin asked George.

"Sure," George said. He wasn't too happy about standing on the side of the service road in the rain, getting involved in someone's private affairs. "Where is it you're going, anyway?" he asked. He truly believed he was being casual.

"Who wants to know?" Robin said.

She could be real fresh when she wanted to be, which George figured came from growing up with the notion she'd be rich someday. As it was, he knew for a fact she'd been hours away from having her electricity cut off the month before. Roy had thought that might bring her back to him, but it hadn't worked out that way. The electric company had given her a five-day extension, and before Roy could persuade them otherwise, Robin had paid off her bill.

"Come on, Robin," George said.

"Tell Roy where I go is none of his business."

"How do you think Old Dick would have liked what's happened between you and Roy?" George asked. "Did you ever consider that?"

Robin hated to hear her grandfather referred to as Old Dick, but she kept her mouth shut. This is what happened when you grew up on an island, people assumed they had a perfect right to pull you over on a service road and give you marital advice. Maybe Robin's brother had been right; when he and Kay broke up, Stuart moved into Manhattan. He couldn't pass a single street corner in town without being reminded of a dozen things he'd done or said. It was like living with ghosts: he couldn't have a cup of coffee at Fred's Diner in peace without having some phantom settle down on the stool beside him.

"My grandfather always despised Roy," Robin announced. In fact, there wasn't a man in town her grandfather hadn't loathed. "He refused to come to our wedding."

"Old Dick would never have favored a divorce," George insisted, but he let her go and watched mournfully as she pulled her truck onto the service road, then headed toward the bridge where the willow trees grew. Once she crossed over, no one on the local police force could stop her; she'd be out of their jurisdiction, driving as fast as she pleased.

Beside the wooden bridge, the thick twisted roots of the old willows coiled through the muddy earth. Anyone who approached the island for the first time at dusk could easily believe that these willows had once been men; they seemed to cry out loud and their thin branches tapped against the hoods of passing cars. No one knew when the trees had been planted, but they were already old when Richard Aaron first came to the island in 1923. They'd frightened off everyone but the bravest fishermen and the cats that someone had once brought across to drown in a burlap bag but that had escaped to breed in the marshes, living wild on bluefish and sparrows.

There was no bridge back then, and Aaron had to put on black hip boots and wade through the water to the other side, stepping over hermit crabs and moon snails. He'd paid thirteen thousand dollars cash for the island—a good deal even then, one he'd managed because the previous owner believed that warm air rising from marshes caused malaria and scarlet fever. On the north side the first big Queen Annes were built, with stone fireplaces and fish-head shingles; on the south side were workers' cottages for the stonemasons and carpenters, some of whom stayed on after their work was through. Off to the west, Aaron built his own house, with bricks carted over the bridge, and panels of stained glass that were tied to the masons' backs with thick rope, then covered with white muslin to protect them from cracking. He kept five acres of black pine and beach grass and *Rosa rugosa* for himself, most of which was to become Poorman's Point after his only son squandered everything on a real estate venture in Florida that went wrong because of hurricanes or bad economic times or simple carelessness.

Old Dick was not dead, as many people on the island assumed, although he was always talked about in the past tense. He was ninety-one years old and had outlived his son and his sisters and brothers and just about everybody else he considered to be worth two cents. The main house had been closed down for more than twenty years, and Old Dick lived above the garage with his housekeeper, Ginny, who was eighty-four. He couldn't get out of his bed unless he was lifted, and he hadn't seen sunlight for years, but when Robin went to visit him he was still able to muster the strength to scream at her. She went only once a month, on the last Sunday, making certain always to bring an apple pie. A good apple pie was the one thing Old Dick wouldn't scream about, and Robin sneaked slices to him, on paper plates, since Ginny didn't allow him any sugar or salt.

And that's what Robin was going to see Stuart about. Trying to get Stuart on the phone was always so frustrating, and this was too important, she couldn't wait. Ginny's health was failing and her daughters wanted to send her to a nursing home in New Jersey, and then what the hell would they do with Old Dick? Stuart had been all but supporting him, since Social Security was barely enough to pay Ginny's weekly salary, and there were food and heating bills and medicine to consider. The truth of it was, Stuart had been helping Robin out, too, since she didn't want to ask Roy for any more than the pittance she was legally allowed. Thank goodness for Stuart, who was so practical, he liked to joke, that he applied to medical school when he realized he needed a twenty-four-hour-a-day psychiatrist and decided it was cheaper to become one than to engage one at the going rates. When he and Kay divorced, Stuart had insisted she buy a Volvo, after checking every import's safety record; he heartily disapproved of

Robin's old pickup, which, as she now approached the Midtown Tunnel, skidded as it always did when she was in a hurry and the asphalt was wet.

There were no meters free, so Robin had to park in one of the expensive lots, on Eighty-fifth, then run through the rain over to Kelvin Medical Center, but at least she was wearing her boots. By the time she reached the building, her hair had unwound from its elastic band and her rain slicker was dripping wet. The storm had now begun in earnest, the kind of downpour that flooded gutters and whipped umbrellas into the air. When Robin got out of the elevator on the fourteenth floor, her ears ached with the drop in air pressure. She was on her way to Stuart's office, thinking about Medicare and lasagna and a new mildew-resistant variety of aster, when the Wolf Man was led into the hallway. Because he was handcuffed, the attendants assumed he was harmless; they left him in the corridor while they went to sign for his transfer. The air was so murky and still that the mice grew confused, and believing it was midnight, they dashed out of the heating vents. A few nurses and attendants who had the day off had come in just to get a glimpse of the Wolf Man, and they were disappointed when he kept his eyes downcast. Patients on crutches struggled to their doorways in their hospital gowns so that someday they could tell their grandchildren they'd been there, right in the same hospital, breathing the very same air, but most of them mistook the Wolf Man for a maintenance worker and looked right past him.

"Is that him?" Robin asked one of the nurses. "The Wolf Man?"

"We're not supposed to call him that," the nurse told her,

but of course Stuart called him that all the time, at least in private.

Stuart had talked about this patient constantly when he'd first been flown in from Michigan. All the cases of children raised by animals had been dubious, records had been tampered with, fears reported as fact, medical histories obscured, so that one never knew whether ill children simply had been abandoned out in the woods, where no one was likely to find them, by families too poor or overwhelmed to cope. Not one of these children had ever gained enough language to tell his own story, and Stuart's hope was that this patient would change all that. If they were lucky, he had been able to speak before he was lost, and with help he might remember all he once knew. But by the beginning of March, Stuart no longer discussed the Wolf Man with Robin, and by the end of the month the arguments he offered to his colleagues about keeping the patient at the medical center sounded weak, even to him. Through all the hours of therapy, the patient had not spoken one word.

"Well, he doesn't look very fierce," Robin said to the nurse.

"Oh, really?" the nurse said archly, as she started down the hall. "He'd bite your head off in a minute. He'd slit your throat and never think twice."

The Wolf Man was hunched over on a wooden bench in his black overcoat, which was two sizes too big. His hair had been clipped so short Robin could see his scalp. There was a gash in the back of his neck, left when the barber's hand had begun to tremble. Robin took off her yellow slicker and shook out the rain; she would have continued on to Stuart's office at the end of the hall if she hadn't seen a mouse scurry along the bench.

Behind his back, the Wolf Man closed his fist over the mouse before it had the chance to dart away. Then he looked at Robin, suddenly, as if he knew he was being watched.

Robin stayed exactly where she was, dripping rain onto the linoleum, even after the Wolf Man turned his back to her. Slowly he opened his hand, and the mouse ran in circles, as though dazed by the scent of human flesh, before scurrying off to hide in a heating vent. For weeks the Wolf Man had been thinking how easy it would be to tear out one of his doctors' throats during their sessions together. The doctor would reach for a pen, or turn to look out the window, and he wouldn't even know what was happening until his shirt was drenched with blood and clouds filled his vision. It was the same with a deer. Even if it was still struggling, you knew it had given up the fight when its eyes turned white, when it saw something so far away it wasn't even in this world.

The thunderstorm had moved in quickly, across the river, from New Jersey. The windows were rattling. Alone on the bench, the Wolf Man began to shiver. If he hadn't, Robin would never have gone over to him. When she reached out and touched his arm, the heat from her fingers went right through his black coat and into his skin. She was the first person to touch him who didn't have to. He still had blood blisters all over his hands and feet, and on rainy days like this the scar that ran along the inside of his thigh ached horribly. Lately, he had been remembering things that seemed to belong to someone else: forks and spoons set out on a kitchen table, slices of an orange on a blue china plate.

"It's just thunder," Robin said.

It's raining, it's pouring, the old man is snoring. He knew that by heart. They thought he understood nothing, but he had heard them talking, right in front of him. The attendant who had kicked his shins while the handcuffs were clasped on was coming down the hall, tossing a set of keys in the air and catching them in the palm of his hand. The Wolf Man looked at the woman next to him; the heat from her touch moved upward, into his throat, until at last the words came out on their own, like birds rising.

"Don't let them take me someplace," he said.

When you spoke after so many years, the words actually hurt, each one a crooked bone, a fishhook, a burning star.

Robin dropped her hand from his arm; her rain slicker fell at her feet. Something made her skin feel hot, and although it might have been pity, it might just as easily have been something else.

The Wolf Man had known enough to keep what was inside him secret, and now he cursed himself. He should never have said a word. He looked down at the linoleum tiles on the floor; he tried not to breathe. The edge of the handcuffs cut through the skin above his wrists. In only a few hours, they'd transfer him and he'd be gone forever. Already, he was starting to disappear. Soon he would forget that the upturned leaves on the trees predicted whether or not it would rain, and that a rabbit dared not move if you covered its eyes. That was how they decided what to take down, at least he remembered that. They went after whatever was frightened and gave up easily. Anything that had the courage to stare you down, you let pass by.

And so, in spite of the thunder, he raised his eyes. As soon as he saw her looking at him that way, he knew he hadn't made a mistake. By then, Robin was telling the attendants that she'd been sent to pick up their patient. Later, in the hallway near the elevator, she would inform the social worker from the State Hospital that the transfer had been canceled. No one had reason to doubt her, not even when she insisted that handcuffs were no longer necessary. And although there was now lightning streaking the sky and the clouds were the size of black mountains, the Wolf Man smiled, exactly as the cook who baked his birthday cake vowed he could, when the attendant handed over the key.

T W O

THE EVENING HAD TURNED sweet and blue. Mockingbirds appeared in the gardens to pull worms from the rich, damp earth, and all through the island you could hear their stolen songs. It was the hour when deer ventured out of the pine woods to feast on ivy and potted geraniums, when raccoons in the marshes scooped up mouthfuls of mullet and snails, and the blue air made people dizzy and thankful for all that they had.

Commuters returning from the city were so anxious to get home they bolted from their trains and ran for the wooden bridge, their umbrellas unfurling behind them like black wings. How lucky to live here, far from the soot and the savage business of the city, where dogs needn't be leashed and children could ride their bikes for miles, stopping to collect driftwood and smooth beach stones. Cemetery Road wound along the marsh and into town, past the hardware store, which sold hurricane lamps and wicker furniture, as well as pipe and paint, past Fred's Diner, where the omelets were always served with home fries dotted with paprika, past the post office and the five-and-dime and the town green, where three ginkgo trees had been planted for summer shade.

It was told that the owners of the original houses had all sunk to their knees when they first crossed the bridge; they kissed the earth until their lips were sandy and cracked. Even now, most people felt the same way. Gardens were tended carefully, stone fences repaired, children taken by the hand and walked to school, though it was safe enough for even the young ones to be out on their own in cheerful groups on warm evenings, turning flashlights onto the old pine trees to scare the owls. Croissants and brioches and Blue Mountain coffee beans could be had at the bakery, but Richard Aaron had made certain to leave acres of open land. Half a mile from the driveways and front porches seemed like untamed territory, wilderness really, compared with the rest of Nassau County. This past February, a fox had wandered into Miriam and Jeff Carson's window well, and after they'd tied up their basset hound in the backyard, everyone on Mansfield Terrace came to see it, bringing tidbits of meat and bread, until the Animal Rescue League arrived. People had banded together when a developer from Roslyn proposed a mall, just east of Cemetery Road. Miriam Carson, who was so kind-hearted she fed her dog cereal and cream for breakfast, and Patty Dixon, who had plenty of time on her hands now that her son Matthew was off to college, organized a core group of demonstrators who made the developer so wary he walked away from the project, leaving Cemetery Road as overgrown and neglected as it was meant to be.

Good deeds were not uncommon on the island. Every Christmas, baskets of apples and pears were delivered to senior citizens, with the exception of Richard Aaron, who had once dragged himself to his bedroom window in order to throw the holiday fruit into the snow. The school library was crowded with volunteers on Wednesday afternoons. Alcoholics Anonymous meetings were held in the basement of the Episcopal church on Thursday nights, with French-roast coffee and blueberry bread free for everyone, and a big potluck supper was held each spring. When Roy moved out in October, Robin's neighbors began to keep an eye on her house, and also, it seemed, on her. Did she need sugar or salt, or maybe just a shoulder to cry on? Robin might occasionally confide in her friend Michelle, who was a guidance counselor at the high school and had a way of getting people to confess things they might later regret mentioning, but she certainly wasn't about to say much more than good morning to her neighbors. Still, they insisted on offering help. Patty Dixon, whose yard backed onto Robin's, suggested that Connor might want to borrow the weights Matthew had left behind, just to make sure Connor stayed out of trouble now that there was no man in the house; Jeff Carson advised new rain gutters, and he phoned when he spotted some loose shingles after a storm.

On this evening when the sky was clear and the roads washed clean by cool rainwater, Robin wished she lived in a place where people minded their own business. There was Jeff Carson, taking his dog for a walk before supper as he always did, fair weather or foul.

"Damn it," Robin said when she saw him.

She waited at the corner of Mansfield Terrace, giving the pickup some gas when it idled roughly, until Jeff had turned onto Cemetery Road, pulling the basset hound behind him. By now, Robin had the distinct impression that everything she did—rounding the corner, parking in her own driveway, getting out quickly so she could usher the Wolf Man through the side yard—was a criminal act. She was a grown woman with a teenaged son and mortgage payments, yet her hands were shaking as she opened her own back door. She refused to consider the possibility that what she was doing was crazy, that she was off her rocker, as Roy had often suggested when they were breaking up. She was stubborn, that she admitted, and she didn't like unfair advantages. This was particularly true when she was younger. The children at school used to harass Stuart in the playground; they thought he was highfalutin and snotty although their grandfather was already bankrupt, and they tied his feet together with twine and threw mudballs at his clean white shirts. When Robin was in first grade, she would run over to those big boys and kick them in the shins, hard enough to leave purple bruises before they could shove her away.

"Don't do that," Stuart always said when she defended him, but on the way home he held her hand.

An unfair advantage, those handcuffs, that terrible haircut. And now the Wolf Man was following her into her kitchen, obedient and silent, his overcoat smelling like wool and rain. Well, she'd feed him and let him have a good night's sleep, then get rid of him before Connor ever knew he'd been there.

"Why don't you sit down," Robin said. "Please."

The Wolf Man was standing in the corner, almost as if he were stuck there, his hands deep in the pockets of his overcoat. When he went to the table, Robin heated the pot of vegetable soup she'd made the night before and poured some into a bowl for him. For herself, she fixed a lukewarm cup of that morning's coffee, though she was jittery enough without it. Her face was burning; she would have liked to dash cold water on her cheeks. There was the faint possibility that Roy was right, that she'd become so intent on having things her way she'd stopped thinking altogether, driven by something as untrustworthy as pure emotion. She now had, after all, a man in her kitchen who could easily murder her and sneak out the back door without leaving any footprints behind. If need be, she supposed, she could scream, and one of her neighbors would come running, wielding a shovel or a rake.

The Wolf Man hadn't said another word since his plea in the hospital corridor; he carefully kept his eyes averted. When he heard footsteps on the stairs, the muscles in his arms and legs grew tight. A white thing with a long tail came into the kitchen. It crossed in front of him and mewed.

"Homer, you silly cat," Robin scolded the thing. "He thinks he owns the place," she said as she scooped the cat up, opened the back door, and set him outside.

The Wolf Man remembered how to spell it, but not what it looked like. Cats drank milk, he knew, and they teased mice, even when they weren't the least bit hungry.

"I thought you might be starving," Robin said when she came back to the table.

He had not touched his soup, but because she expected him to eat, he took the spoon and slowly began. The food burned his mouth, still he continued to eat. He knew to take what was offered. If you were hungry enough, you would turn over a rock and eat beetles, snapping their shells with your back teeth.

"Would you like something to drink?" Robin said. She was ridiculously nervous; she was having trouble holding on to her coffee cup. "Apple juice? Milk?"

"No, thank you," the Wolf Man said.

Someone, a long time ago, had taught him well. Not only please and thank you, but excuse me whenever he pushed. He finished all his soup, quickly, so that heat blisters rose on his tongue, then followed Robin when she signaled to him. As she led him up to the guest room, Robin explained that he must stay in his room when her son came home.

"We'll figure out what to do with you in the morning," she said.

She fumbled with the lock, which was there to keep the cat from making the guest room his own. The room was small, with a sloping ceiling, and had not been occupied in more than a year, since Stuart camped out after his divorce, complaining about cat hair and mildew and dust. The house's previous owner had been one of the original workmen brought in by Robin's grandfather. In his old age, the woodcarver had sat in this room every morning, drinking the coffee his wife brought him, watching purple finches and starlings on the lawn. The scent of wood shavings and espresso clung to the wallpaper, violets on thin green shoots all along a cream-colored border.

While Robin made up the bed with clean sheets, the Wolf Man went to the window. There was a redwood fence around the backyard that he could take easily, with one leap. But where, exactly, would that get him? All along he'd had a single plan, one he had thought about every morning and every night. Get free and get back home. If anything, getting free seemed the hardest part, since all the doors at the hospital were locked with metal keys and it was impossible to dig out or under the walls. He had tried the first few days, scraping at the concrete until his fingers bled.

It was not until he'd actually been freed, and led onto the street, that he realized how horribly flawed his plan was. Terrified by the buses and the crowds, he'd followed behind Robin so closely he'd stepped on the backs of her boots. At home, he could travel as much as thirty miles in a day and find his way back in the dark. He could cover two hundred miles in a single season and still distinguish one pine tree from another. But here, his sense of direction failed him completely. He stumbled on the sidewalk and shied away from the hordes of people with their raincoats and black umbrellas. And even later, while they were driving, he didn't make his move. It would have been so easy. He could have grabbed the woman by the throat and forced her to pull over. He could have thrown the door open and leapt out onto the road when they passed a stretch of woods. The black coat wouldn't have slowed him down, nor would the heavy shoes they made him wear; not even the thunder could have stopped him. If only he had known the way back home. He wasn't even sure that the same constellations rose in the sky here.

"Extra blankets," Robin said to him.

Two woolen blankets had been placed at the foot of the bed. Before he could stop himself, the Wolf Man looked at Robin. He had an odd feeling, almost as if he were hungry. He sat on the edge of the bed, not that he planned to sleep on it, or in it, or whatever it was that men did. He forced himself to look away from Robin. Instead, he stared at his own hands; with their calluses and broken fingernails and ropes of blue veins, they could not have looked uglier.

When, at last, Robin left him and closed the door behind her, the Wolf Man got off the bed. After he'd heard her go down the stairs, he opened the window. The sweet air made him restless, and he paced the length of the room three times. Even a room as small as this might be dangerous. He looked in the closet, to make certain nothing was there, then went to the corner. He carefully crouched down next to the bureau the wood-carver had fashioned out of cherry. Since they'd found him, he'd taken to sleeping this way, with his back to the wall, protected from any surprise attack. Outside in the yard, the birds were calling; the white cat sharpened his claws on the bark of a magnolia tree. Lately the Wolf Man fought sleep; he'd become afraid of it. But all the night before, he'd stayed awake, waiting for the attendants to come for him, and now his eyes began to close. He dozed off to the sound of the birds, and once he'd begun, he couldn't stop himself from falling deeper and deeper asleep.

He could sleep safely for hours, but then, when the moon was in the center of the sky, the dream would surface. There was no way to stop it. He was back on the ridgetop, shivering. All the trees were black, but not as black as what was within him. He was beside a pool of dark water, but he would not look at his reflection. Still, he knew something deep inside, and the knowledge broke him apart and filled him with terror. His brothers were calling to him, but he had lost the power to answer. He wanted to run with them, to sleep beside them and dream the same dreams: mice and owls, blood and bones, acres of tall, sweet grass. He threw his head back and opened his mouth, but nothing came out. In his dream he stayed this way for a long time, terrified and mute, until his voice finally tore out from him and he could answer his brothers.

On Mansfield Terrace, at a little before midnight, many of the neighbors thought what they heard was the Carsons' basset hound, Marco Polo, who always howled at the moon and scratched at the screen door, begging to be let out. But Connor Moore, on his way home, late for his curfew and woozy from six bottles of beer, knew this was no dog, for there was Marco Polo, out in his driveway, silent and puzzled, as he, too, listened to the howling.

The hair on the back of Connor's neck rose up and he walked faster. The clouds moved quickly, sweeping past the moon, and anyone who had the least bit of sense was already in bed asleep. At sixteen, Connor was a big, beautiful boy who could have really enjoyed himself if he hadn't been cursed with a conscience, and for this he blamed his mother. He had grown six inches taller than Robin, quite suddenly, and now he felt condemned to protect her. When offered a dare, Connor still accepted. He jumped off the bridge at low tide fully clothed, he drank six-packs of beer at a sitting, he knew which girls would accompany him to one of the old fisherman's shacks on the north beach, late at night, when not another soul was around. But somehow, the easygoing boy Connor had once been had disappeared; he had become a worrier, and he was uneasy now, as he walked along the wet pavement, headed for home.

Maybe what he was hearing was a night heron, whose sudden screams could sound like a baby's frantic cries, or a man who'd discovered his lover had been unfaithful. Nothing worth worrying about. Connor could see the light go on in his mother's bedroom and her shadow against the window shade. Odd, since she was the one who insisted they use candles after nine at night ever since their run-in with the electric company, when they'd been hours away from having their power cut off. Connor felt bad for his mother, but it seemed his father couldn't help himself. When Roy talked to women he came on to them, even older women he had no interest in whatsoever; it was a bad habit, like smoking, and he'd been doing it his whole life. But all that sweet talk had led to something more: a series of girlfriends Connor had known about before his mother found out and dragged his father's clothes into the driveway for all the neighbors to see. It wasn't as if he had caught his father with another woman, the way his mother finally had, in a parked car over on Delaney, but he'd sensed something was wrong, and he'd worried. When, at last, he'd been called into the living room and told about their separation, he could hardly pretend to be surprised.

He just couldn't shake this feeling of dread; he was like an old woman, waiting for disaster to strike. Watching Adam Lubell goofing around after school, foolishly perched on the handlebars of his bike, Connor grew so disturbed he actually experienced some sort of relief when Adam finally fell and broke his two front teeth. Connor, who could ace all his classes with a minimum of work, now fretted on the days exams were to be handed back. He supposed that if you figured out the probabilities for catastrophe the results would be double any possibility for good fortune. In the fall, when his parents were still in the middle of breaking up, and he became accustomed to hearing them argue, sometimes he couldn't sleep without the rhythm of their quarrels. His worrying got so out of control he started to read the obituaries in the *Island Tribune,* just to make certain no one he knew had died in the night.

And then, in early November, when the trees were leafless and black and the twilight turned purple, he had a strange taste of grief. He'd gone over to the police station to ask his father for an advance on his allowance, for beer of course, though he didn't plan to mention that, and found he'd taken a wrong turn in the hallway. Only days before, a five-year-old had disappeared while trick-or-treating. Because the little girl still hadn't been found, several of the detectives had agreed to meet with a psychic from New Jersey, an ordinary-looking woman who wore a navy-blue wool coat and a silk scarf patterned with lilies. Connor happened to look through the glass partition to find the psychic staring right at him, or through him, and he felt himself get all cold, as if he'd stepped inside a freezer. He slipped into the office; it was possible that the detectives were used to his hanging around, and that's why they didn't notice him, or perhaps, like Connor, they were completely focused on the psychic. She described the sewer pipe that brought rainwater into the Sound and the usually shy hermit crabs, which had gathered around, drawn to the scent of candy. Connor listened until he couldn't bear to hear more, and when he left he ran all the way home. The following day, Connor couldn't bring himself to read the *Island Trib-une*. He didn't want to know that the little girl had been wear-ing a witch's hat or that Milky Ways and candy corn had been scattered through the eelgrass.

Everything was dangerous, that much was clear to him. Strangely, no one else seemed to realize this, so he kept his worries secret, especially from his parents. When he saw his father they usually went to McDonald's or to Harper's, the bar Roy liked, which served great cheeseburgers and tacos.

"It's not like this is permanent or anything," Roy had told him after he'd moved out. He was living in an apartment in a big old house on Third, and he hadn't yet gotten any furni-ture, except for a mattress, which he left on the floor.

"Right," Connor had said, and he kept his mouth shut. But sitting there, eating Big Macs out of the bag, Connor held no hope for his parents' reunion. He could already imagine the furniture his father would soon have: a gray-and-white-striped couch, a brass pole lamp, and black-and-white rug.

And now, tonight, on his own street, with enough beer inside him to make for a wicked hangover in the morning, Connor had that feeling all over again. Something wasn't right. He ran past Marco Polo, and cut through the hedge of lilacs that separated their front yard from the Carsons'. Every-thing still looked the same: the slate path around to the side door, the perennial beds filled with tender new shoots, the bike he had left propped against the pear tree. But what he saw could be deceiving; if he blinked, just once, it could all dis-appear.

Inside, at the end of the hallway, Robin was already at the

Wolf Man's door. When he cried out, she'd been washing her face. The warm tap water had immediately turned cold. She had been rehearsing exactly what she would say when she phoned Stuart in the morning. There was no other choice. She would simply admit to her brother that she'd acted on impulse. Now, having realized she'd made a mistake, she'd be more than willing to drive the Wolf Man back to Kelvin if Stuart would promise to review his case. But when Robin heard the cry from the guest room, she forgot Stuart completely. She went into the hallway, grateful that Connor had broken his curfew, because even after there was nothing but silence, she was afraid to open the guest room door.

When she went into the room and found the bed empty, Robin felt as if she had imagined him completely. Such a thing was possible, after all; the roses in the garden would not bloom for another month, yet their fragrance had somehow been left behind from other seasons. The air through the open window was chilly and damp; in only a few weeks the crickets would begin to call, and their song would wake people in the neighborhood and make them toss and turn in their own beds. In the corner, the Wolf Man rose to his feet. Then Robin knew she was not about to call her brother in the morning. It was much too late for rational acts; plain logic had been surrendered hours before.

"You're not asleep," Robin said when she saw him. For some reason she was whispering.

He was still wearing the black overcoat, and although he wanted to go closer, he forced himself to stay where he was. He didn't know what he might be capable of; he didn't want to find out. When she took a step toward him, he realized that he was having trouble breathing. He held his hands up, the way he had when the doctors first came at him.

"Go out, now," he said. "Lock the door."

In the garden, beside the rose trellis, the white cat came out of the bushes and rubbed against Connor's legs, then streaked inside as soon as the side door was opened. The refrigerator hummed softly and a grid of moonlight came in through the window above the counter. The cat mewed and jumped up to lap water out of a blue bowl left in the sink. Connor took off his sneakers before he went upstairs; a pulse at the base of his throat was driving him crazy. If he were smart, he'd concentrate on hightailing it into his room to make certain his mother wouldn't find him in the hall and interrogate him on where he'd been on a school night. He'd throw himself on his bed, and sleep late, and mind his own business.

Instead, he went on down the hall. That damn pulse was still there, as if he had swallowed a clock and it had lodged in his throat. He knew every corner of this house, every creak the floorboards made, but tonight there were shadows he'd never seen before, and for some reason he felt like a thief, in his very own home. When he saw that the guest room had been bolted shut he stopped and leaned against the wall. On any other night he would have been merely curious, he would have slid the lock open to see what was inside. It was his house, after all, there was nothing to be afraid of. But on this night Connor took a step backward. For the first time in his life he considered that his mother might have a few secrets of her own.

36

When Robin unlocked the door and brought him his breakfast, she warned him not to be seen. He was not to go outside
or stand by the windows while she was out, and most important of all, he was to make certain to be back in the guest room
before her son came home from school. She was nervous about
leaving him while she went to pick up groceries for dinner and
flats of ivy, and she might not have gone if she hadn't already
committed to an appointment with a new client, about a job
she needed if she was to pay this month's bills. Still, she asked
three times if he'd be all right alone and didn't seem to believe
him when he promised that he would be.

He planned not to leave his room for any reason, but after
Robin had gone, he opened the guest room door and studied
the hallway. In spite of himself, he was curious about the way
men lived. He used the toilet, the way he'd been taught in the
hospital, then went downstairs, trailed by the white cat. While
he investigated the living room, he remembered that some
chairs went back and forth when rocked. Someone had once
told him never to put his feet up on the couch. He studied the
photographs on the mantel and the framed posters on the wall,
but he avoided mirrors and was afraid of the blue light the TV
sent out when he turned the set on.

He had already eaten soup at the table, but he found the
kitchen even more disturbing. Everything made noise; even
the water seemed to explode when he turned on the tap. There
was food everywhere, but he didn't dare eat, although the
white cat jumped up on the counter, where a bowl of fishy
paste had been set out. He thought about leaving and went so
far as to open the side door, but the dog in the next yard
barked at him, and he didn't chance stepping outside. Later,

he crept up to the attic, where he found a trunk full of tiny clothes and an oak box of chisels and knives the wood-carver had left behind. He took the sharpest of the knives, a small fierce piece with a handle that fit his palm. You never knew what you might need when you were dealing with men, that was the way he saw it, and later he hid the knife up in the guest room closet, deep in the pocket of the black coat.

The house was not as uncomfortable as he would have imagined. Still, he did not feel right in an easy chair, beneath a bright light, and he found himself drawn to the cellar, where the walls were damp and cool and jars of raspberry jam sat on a metal shelf. He was there, exploring the cellar, when Connor came home unexpectedly, having decided that no one would notice if he cut his last class.

It was a wet, windy afternoon; on the clothesline in the backyard, the white shirts Robin had hung out early that morning flapped and scared away the starlings. Before he went into the house, Connor stopped and looked up into the guest room window. Nothing. Of course. He'd let himself get spooked for no reason at all last night. He had to stop letting things get to him, inventing the possibility of trouble when there was none. He should be concentrating on enjoying himself, and that's what he planned to do now, just grab his skateboard and meet his friends in the parking lot behind the market. But as soon as he went down the rickety basement stairs, Connor was no longer interested in finding his skateboard. The Wolf Man didn't hear Connor until it was too late. Now he averted his face and stared at the floor; his back was flat against the wall.

"What are you doing here?" Connor said.

There was a baseball bat under the stairs, and if Connor was quick enough, he might be able to grab it and defend himself. But instead of attacking, the Wolf Man crouched down in the corner and hid his face in his hands.

"Jesus Christ," Connor said. "Who are you?"

They both heard the door upstairs open. The Wolf Man flinched, and as soon as he did, Connor grabbed the bat and held it out. He felt as if his head was going to explode.

"Mom?" Connor called up the stairs. "Don't come down here."

Robin ran to the cellar door; potatoes and pears fell out of the grocery bag she carried. Connor swung the baseball bat just to let the intruder know he wasn't dealing with a kid. He expected his mother to scream, but instead she slowly came down the stairs. She was looking at the man against the wall in some strange way, as if Connor weren't even there.

"Mom?" Connor said.

Later, he realized she would never have told him. She would have left him in the dark, a child sent to bed after supper. He was already a man, but his mother refused to accept that. If he hadn't stumbled into the basement, she would have kept this stranger a secret from him. Connor was furious. Why did she feel she always had to protect him? He slammed out of the house, then walked into town and talked Sal Penny into buying him a fifth of Irish Mist, which he drank at the arboretum beneath one of the last remaining elm trees.

When he came home it was already growing dark. Homer mewed, greeting him, then wound around his legs while Connor vomited into the kitchen sink. It was a little after seven but felt much later, one of those damp April nights that made it seem as though summer might be years away. When the front doorbell rang, Connor went into the living room, still weaving from whiskey and anger, his face pale, his shirt messed and half unbuttoned. He stopped when he saw that his mother was sitting on the couch, in the dark, just listening to the doorbell. She looked up at him, then looked back at the door.

Connor sat down beside her on the couch, and together they waited for the bell to stop ringing. At last it did, and Connor went to the window. He lifted the curtain and saw it had only been Mrs. Dixon, armed with one of her petitions for a moratorium on building on the island. He watched Mrs. Dixon cross the lawn to the Carsons' house next door, scooting as best she could around Marco Polo, who lay belly down in the damp grass, letting forth his great rolling bark without bothering to move. It wasn't until Connor let the curtain drop that he suddenly understood why his mother had not told him about the locked guest room. If Connor was a man, as he presumed himself to be, this moment had to come, when his mother looked to him not knowing what to do next, and he would be forced to become completely and instantly sober, whether he liked it or not.

Each day, after Connor left for school, Robin came up to the guest room with armfuls of old children's books. Later, she brought a tape recorder and a few books that had their own story tapes, so he could try to read along when she wasn't there. She truly believed that once he could read and write he could decide his own fate; no one could come after him with handcuffs.

"They wouldn't dare," she told him. "Over my dead body," she whispered as she shifted the pile of storybooks on her lap.

He knew when he made progress, because each time he did, Robin clapped her hands and smiled. He wanted to please her, maybe too much; he couldn't get enough of that look she had whenever he did something right. But more important, he felt certain that if he learned to read he could figure out his way back home, and this made him an excellent student. Sometimes whole words jumped out from the page. *Cat* and *dog, my* and *no, eggs* and *ham.*

Robin was proud of him, and that was good, but often he frightened himself by how much he knew. When he was given a pad of paper and a pencil one afternoon he realized that he'd already been taught to imagine he was drawing a snake when he wrote the first letter of his name.

"What are you doing?" Robin asked when he began to write. "What is that?"

He hadn't known himself until he had spelled it out completely. *Stephen.* That's what he'd been called.

Robin had been delighted. She'd tossed a book high into the air and called him brilliant and suggested he practice writing every day. He did as she asked; he knew it was in his best interest. But the funny thing was, each time he printed out a word on a piece of lined paper, he felt as though he were losing something, as though the lines on the paper had somehow shifted, dividing him in two.

With every word he wrote, with each book he read, he remembered more, as if he had to be reminded of the story of his own life. They had been up in the sky, that much he knew, when the flight from San Francisco to New York veered so far from its route that the plane wasn't sighted until three months after its disappearance. Another month had passed before the search party reached what was left. By then, the remains of the passengers that hadn't been carried off by foxes and hawks were so decayed even the tracking dogs refused to go close. The search party assumed there were no survivors, but in fact there was one. He was three and a half years old and had just learned how to whistle and spell his name; he could recite all of *The Cat in the Hat* by heart.

Stephen planned to be a fireman when he grew up and own a white-and-black spotted dog. He was cheerful and good-natured and tended to see the sunny side of things, but he knew something wasn't right when the clouds all around him began to move too quickly. As he looked out the window, he found himself believing that the sky was a dish without a lid. It was possible to rise forever, but once the fall began, the bottom was only inches away. It took a long time before he managed to get out from beneath the crush of bodies on top of him. The metal all around hissed and grew hot. Stephen recognized his father's brown shoe and the pink baby blanket the little girl in the next row had used to play peek-a-boo. "I see you," she had called to him. When he found his mother, he sat hunched over right beside her, waiting for her eyes to open, almost believing his cries could bring her back to life.

He was an only child, well loved and well cared for. Every morning, his mother had served him oatmeal with honey. Every night, he'd been tucked into bed at seven. They lived in an apartment where pigeons roosted on the window ledges; he liked the cooing noises they made, he liked to hear them flap their wings. When he climbed out of what was left of the plane and looked up, he was amazed to see that the sky he had fallen from was filled with light. There was nothing like this in the city, where a grid of metal meshing covered the windows. What was above him was so beautiful and surprising he couldn't look away. It was as if he'd never before seen stars.

When the big dog came up behind him she was so quiet he hadn't known she was there until he turned and saw her face, near his own. She was gray with a silver muzzle and yellow eyes. Stephen's mother had always warned him to stay away from strange dogs, but without thinking he reached out and touched the dog's nose. She pulled her head back, startled, then pushed against his chest with her nose. She didn't have a collar or a leash like the dogs that were walked around his block, but she made a little barking noise. Stephen's face was still hot and red from crying. It was late September, but cold as a December day in New York; when he breathed out, there were puffs of smoke. Behind him, in the dark, the twisted remains of the plane made a sizzling sound. The big dog stared at the wreckage; she tilted her head, listening.

"My mommy's in there," Stephen told her.

The dog quickly looked back at him when he spoke.

"We fell down," he said, and his face felt even hotter.

It was dark out in the woods, and the trees looked as if they might come alive and swoop him up in their arms. Stephen had been glad that the big dog had come up to him. He had seen Lassie on TV; he knew dogs could always find the way back home. But he must have blinked, because the big dog had suddenly disappeared into the darkness. He looked and looked, but she wasn't there. Then he heard a whimpering, and she was back. She walked away again, stopping after a few paces to look back at him. He followed her then, and each time she disappeared, Stephen found that if he just kept going she'd be waiting for him.

After a while he could no longer hear the fiery sound of the plane. The woods were still, except for the wind, which called out numbers and names in a hollow blue voice. The moss was so thick Stephen stumbled, and his shoes slipped into badger holes. He was getting tired, but each time he stopped, the dog came out of the darkness and pushed against his back, and they kept on this way until they came to the base of a ridge. His feet hurt by then, and he was hungry. He wanted oatmeal with raisins, or chocolate chip cookies, or a big, red apple, peeled and cut into quarters by his mother. The sky was still filled with lights, but he couldn't see them anymore because the pine trees grew so close together, and they were so tall, taller than the brick buildings on his block. That was where he had thought they were heading, but now he had the funny feeling that the buildings and shops and sidewalks that he knew were so far he'd never be able to walk all the way there. His throat became dry just thinking about the distance, and his thirst was so bad he started to make little choking sounds that were almost like crying.

When the two other dogs came out of the shadows, Stephen had leaned against the big dog's side for comfort. One dog was even bigger, and black, so that all Stephen could see of him were his eyes and his teeth. The other was gray and white and he looked over at the black one, waiting for some sort of sign: flattened ears, hair standing on end, a rumbling sound deep in the throat. The black one was crouched down as he came toward Stephen, but he stopped when the big dog came between them. Her tail was straight up and she showed her teeth, and the black dog looked at her bewildered, then moved aside.

Stephen held on to the big dog's fur as she led him toward the base of the ridge, where a cave had been dug. It was even darker here than it had been outside, but Stephen just kept following, though he'd had to crawl part of the way. The cave was surprisingly warm, so warm his eyes were closing as he followed her. The big dog stopped, and when Stephen's eyes adjusted to the dark, he had seen that two puppies were waiting. As soon as the big dog flopped down, they scrambled over to her, and Stephen had heard them drinking. He was just as thirsty as they were, and when he went to join them, and found they were drinking right from the big dog, he did, too, and his eyes continued to close. As he drank he was saying good-bye, to feather pillows and ABC books, to cool lemonade on June days and potted hyacinths along the windowsill. On all other nights, he had worn blue pajamas and slept with a stuffed panda his father had brought home from a business trip; he had stretched out beneath his quilt and listened to the sound of traffic out on the street, like a river winding along the avenue. But on this night, all he heard was the big dog's heart beating as he curled up beside her, and all night long he dreamed he was home.

She told the butcher that they were no longer vegetarians, in order to explain why she was now one of his better customers, stopping in twice a week. She told her best friend, Michelle, whom she had never once lied to, that she couldn't afford their nights out on Tuesdays, not even a movie or a Greek salad at the diner. She was not a particularly good liar; she stuttered and coughed when she amended the truth, but nobody seemed to notice. One night, as she brushed her hair a hundred strokes, Robin realized she was no longer even considering that she might take him back. She had begun to call him by his given name, and that alone had changed something. He was taking up more and more of her time, so much that she had begun to forget simple things: dishes in the sink, Connor's lunch, the cat's needing to be fed or set out at night, the name of the variety of hollyhock that grew beside her own garden gate. The last Sunday of the month she forgot to take an apple pie to her grandfather, and Old Dick refused to be consoled.

"I didn't have time to fix the crust," Robin told him. "The market was all out of Mrs. Smith's."

"Bullshit," he spat back. He still looked formidable, even in bed, beneath a tartan blanket. "I want my pie," he insisted.

"Ssh," Robin whispered. "Do you want Ginny to hear?"

"I hear everything," Ginny called from the dusty living room, where she was watching her program.

"I'll bring you two pies next time," Robin offered.

"Not a good deal for me," her grandfather said. "I could be dead. You don't look well," he added. He reached for his bifocals, which hung on a string tied around his neck. "Let me see your face."

Robin was sitting in the big chair by the window; she lifted her chin to him. Her hair was piled on top of her head, caught up in a silver clip, and she was wearing old clothes, a gray thermal undershirt, jeans, worn riding boots splattered with mud. As a child, she'd been stubborn and willful; she considered her grandfather's land to be the whole universe, and anyone who stepped inside the iron gates had to play by her rules. Even Michelle was always a foot soldier or a lady-in-waiting, always second in command. When Poorman's Point had belonged to her grandfather, she believed she could do exactly as she pleased, and her grandfather had encouraged it; he didn't mind if there were burrs in her hair or if she slogged through the marsh grass in her socks. Ginny would throw up her hands and shriek, but she couldn't stop Robin from inviting squirrels to the tea parties she held on the porch. Robin was never satisfied until those squirrels ate their salted peanuts off the china plates and sipped lemonade right out of the cups.

"You're lying about something," Robin's grandfather said. He was still sharp, and he drove a hard bargain; it was impossible to get away with much in his presence, whether or not he was wearing his glasses.

"Don't be silly," Robin said, but she stumbled over the word "silly" and her face grew as pink as a cabbage rose. As soon as she could she put away the groceries she'd brought him, vacuumed the living room under Ginny's direction, and got out of there, taking the stairs two at a time, running down the gravel driveway to her parked truck.

Of course, that was the thing about lying, once you began, you had to do it again and again. After fifteen years of decreeing the difference between right and wrong, Robin had turned Connor into a liar as well, and had even advised him on what lies to tell. When Stuart called, Connor insisted that Robin had a bad case of laryngitis, which made it impossible for her to speak on the phone. He asked his father not to come to the house but to meet him instead at Harper's, for dinner or lunch; they needed time alone, man to man. Roy fell for this line and was pleased, and he didn't seem to notice that, when they did meet, Connor didn't say a word. At the hardware store, Connor told Jack Merrill they were having problems with the electric company again; he even managed to act embarrassed as he paid for the box of white utility candles. But of course, it wasn't the electric bill that was the problem. Lamps cast shadows and drew the attention of anyone who might be walking a dog or riding a bicycle along the street after supper. At twilight, they closed the curtains and double-locked the front door. If an unexpected guest should arrive—a school friend of Connor's, or Michelle's younger daughter, Jenny, selling mint cookies to raise funds for a class trip—they wouldn't answer the doorbell. Instead, they sat in the dark. They listened to the wind and the echo of footsteps on their front porch, and if they counted slowly to one hundred, whoever it was who had come to visit would be gone.

Every evening, before daylight was gone completely, Connor played checkers with Stephen. Stephen definitely liked to win, and he showed no mercy. One day, after only a few games, he was double-jumping so much that Connor decided they should leave checkers behind and move on to chess. Robin wasn't home yet, so after he set out the pieces on the board, Connor went to the kitchen and got beers for both of them. That evening, he heard Stephen laugh for the first time.

As it turned out, Stephen was a natural at chess, a bit better at offense than defense.

"Your little horse," Stephen said, triumphant, as he took Connor's knight.

Connor grinned right along with him. When his mother had told him the little she'd heard of Stephen's history from her brother, he'd thought living in the woods sounded exciting. Now he reconsidered, and he wasn't so sure.

"Were you actually with the wolves, or just kind of in the same vicinity?"

Stephen stopped smiling; he turned his gaze back to their game. "The same vicinity," he answered.

"What did you do to get food?" Connor said. "Did you have to kill the things you ate?"

Stephen took Connor's bishop and placed it on the coffee table.

"Deer and things like that?" Connor said.

"Things like that," Stephen said. He nodded to the chessboard. "Your move."

Connor carelessly moved a pawn. "Did you cook them, or just eat them? Like raw or something?"

One more move and he could put the boy in check. He knew the right maneuver instinctively, just as he knew the moves to make before a kill. This board of black and white squares was nothing compared to a dark night and tall grass. There was a strategy always, a place for each of them, to the left and the right, in a fan shape, deep in the sweet grass. It took forever, and no time at all; once you were running, you could taste what you were after.

"Holy shit," Connor said when Stephen captured his queen. "I sure screwed up."

Stephen held the white queen in his hand. He should not be in this house and he knew it. The nights had become more difficult for him. He paced the guest room, wearing out the carpet. It had been so long since he'd been able to run that he could actually feel his muscles growing weaker. The calluses on his hands and feet were no longer as thick; if he pricked himself with a thorn, he would probably feel it now. On some nights, the scar on the inside of his thigh caused him great pain, as if to remind him of who he'd once been. But the truth of it was, he'd been locked away for so long that when a butterfly came in through the open window one evening, he'd been startled.

They should have finished him off after he'd been caught; they should have left him where he'd fallen. Yellow leaves would have covered him, and frost, and the long, brown feathers of the hawks above him in the sky would have fallen across his back like a blanket. He put aside his beer and shook Connor's hand when congratulated on his win. After the chessboard had been put away, he said good night and went upstairs. If he was downstairs when Robin came home, she would look at him and ask what was wrong, and he wouldn't know if she really wanted an answer. He'd already realized he could not begin to understand the things men did; now he saw women were even harder to figure out. Sometimes it almost seemed as if they were thinking one thing and talking about something else completely, and you didn't know what to believe: the thing they said or the thing they didn't say.

A long time ago he had given up speech because it had

ceased to matter. Year after year, he had named his brothers and sisters with words that had less and less meaning, until he had stopped naming things altogether. Things were, with or without names. The snow always fell and then melted. There was no point in questioning why, just as there was no reason to ask why the moon turned orange after the first frost or why white flowers appeared each time the earth grew muddy and warm. Ask one question, and a thousand would follow. Doubt, and who were you? Nothing but a creature who paced all night long, who watched the night from behind a screen window. Do what you must; he'd learned that at least. Hang clothes in the closet, unlace sneakers, don't look in mirrors, try not to think.

Up in his room, Stephen rewound one of the story tapes Robin had given him and read along with a flashlight. It was a silly children's tale in which rabbits and bears were not flesh and blood but partly human things who wore suits and could talk. As Stephen followed along, the sound of his own voice disturbed him, but he kept at it. He heard the truck in the driveway when Robin came home; he heard her footsteps on the stairs and, later, the sound of the shower running. Once, he had had the ability to hear a single drop of rain on a single green leaf. Now the sounds all ran together, and he had to force himself to concentrate in order to read.

And when, finally, his eyes grew weary, and the words on the page ran together in a jumble, he put his book away. He tried his best to ignore the moonlight. Instead, he concentrated on all the things he must learn, inconsequential things he could forget as soon as they allowed him to go home. How *i* came before *e,* except after *c;* how orange juice was poured into a cup, and bread must always be sliced with a knife. How a book began at the beginning, and ended at the last page; how to sit, motionless, in a chair by the window, while out in the driveway a deer that has wandered down the road chews the new shoots of hollyhocks. How to spend the night in a locked room, when what he wanted was right down the hall.

THREE

     EVERY MEMORIAL DAY THE Dixons had their big party. They hung red, white, and blue streamers from the branches of their maple trees and started barbecuing chicken and ribs at noon. Their little poodle, Casper, was locked in the utility closet early in the day to make certain he wouldn't bother the guests or steal chicken bones off the paper plates. Various neighbors were enlisted to prepare huge tubs of potato salad and cole slaw, and the first of the season's lemonade was always served, made with real lemons and cold spring water.

This year the Dixons really had something to celebrate. Matthew, whom they'd always worried about—his lack of friends for one thing, his weight for another—was home from his first year at Cornell. Matthew was a sweet-faced, hulking boy who had spent his entire high school career locked in his bedroom with a computer. But now it seemed to have paid off. He'd made dean's list at Cornell and had been allowed to register for graduate seminars; next fall he'd be teaching a section on computer languages to freshmen. As guests arrived, they fished beers out of a trash barrel filled with ice, then stopped by the barbecue, where Matthew was turning peppery ribs with metal tongs, and they patted him on the back, congratulating him and welcoming him home.

The young people congregated in the rear of the yard, sitting cross-legged on Indian bedspreads, drinking lemonade and beer. The sunlight was honey-colored and thick. Summer was close enough to make everything seem charged, the blades of grass, bare knees, the lazy sound of ice in a paper cup. Lydia Altero, who was seventeen and had brown hair to her waist, sat with her girlfriends and watched Connor duck under the branches of a maple on his way to get himself a drink. He was so tall and so uncomfortable with the neighbors who greeted him that all his movements looked tender and silly. Lydia felt herself grow angry when Josh Torenson bumped into Connor as he approached the rear of the yard and lemonade spilled onto Connor's white shirt. Without bothering to think what her girlfriends would say, Lydia went over and handed him a paper napkin.

"Josh is an idiot," she said. She judged people smartly and quickly, and often found herself in a huff. "Lemonade doesn't stain," she told Connor.

Connor stared at the napkin as if it were something delivered directly from the moon. Lydia Altero hated him, didn't she? At least that was what he'd always been led to believe. Because their mothers had been best friends for so long, he and Lydia had always been thrown together, with unpleasant results. Lydia was only a few months older than Connor, but she had specialized in pinching when they were babies, and graduated to snubbing him completely by the time they'd entered junior high.

"Well?" she said to him now. She held one hand over her eyes to block out the sun. "Aren't you going to clean your shirt?"

It seemed impossible that Connor had known her his whole life and had never once noticed how beautiful she was.

"What?" Lydia said when she saw the look on his face.

"You," Connor said, before he could stop himself, and then he got all flustered, and pretended to dab at his shirt, which had already dried in the sun.

Lydia chewed a piece of ice and acted as if she didn't know what he meant, but there were goose bumps up and down her arms. She'd fallen in love with him so slowly she didn't even know it herself, until it had all but smacked her in the face last week when she'd seen him talking to a red-haired girl before gym class. She'd actually taken sick with jealousy and had to be sent home by the school nurse.

"Who's that with your mom?" she asked.

Connor whipped his head around as though he'd been shot. Over by the long picnic table, set out with pies and cakes, his mother was introducing Stephen to the Carsons and the Simons. Robin was wearing a blue dress and a strand of old pearls that had belonged to her grandmother. It was amazing to see how calm she looked; how young, really, as though she weren't even Connor's mother. Robin arched her neck when she laughed at one of Jeff Carson's jokes, then poured two glasses of lemonade. When she saw Connor staring, she waved, then turned back to Miriam Carson. This was the date they'd been aiming for. They'd anxiously planned for Stephen's introduction to their neighbors back when it seemed they had all the time in the world, and now it was here, and

Connor wondered if he was the only one who was worried. Stephen's bad haircut had grown out, and he was wearing the clothes they'd picked out for him at Macy's. Standing beneath a mimosa tree on a beautiful hot day he looked like any handsome young man you might meet at a party. There was an official story they were supposed to tell, with facts Connor had helped them invent, but looking at Lydia he became undone. Could it be that he'd never noticed that her eyes were blue? Lydia turned for a moment, to wave away her little sister, Jenny, so she couldn't eavesdrop, and when she turned back to Connor, he could feel his pulse quicken.

"He's just some guy who's living with us," Connor told her. His face was burning hot, and he held his glass of lemonade up to his forehead.

"He's gorgeous," Lydia said, and when she saw Connor's face fall, she almost laughed out loud. He felt the same way that she did, whether he knew it or not. "For someone his age," she added tactfully.

Miriam Carson was pretty much saying the same thing to Robin as she sliced a pecan pie.

"His cheekbones," Miriam whispered. "Those eyes." She turned to Stephen and handed him a fork and a plateful of pie. "Slavic blood?" she guessed. "Ukrainian?"

Stephen balanced the plate in one hand and looked to Robin for help.

"The Midwest," Robin said. "Napkin?" she asked Stephen, because the pie was still warm and the filling dripped over the edge of the plate.

Stephen had already begun to eat the pie, since it seemed

56

that Miriam wanted him to. It was disgusting, pure sugar, but he had to chew what was already in his mouth and swallow it.

"I baked that," Miriam told him.

"Ah," Stephen said.

Robin forced herself to keep a straight face. As soon as Miriam went to look for more paper plates, she pulled Stephen aside, behind the mimosa.

"If you don't like something you don't have to eat it," she said.

"No, thank you," Stephen said, hesitant.

"Exactly," Robin agreed.

Most of the neighbors were already there, including Stuart and Kay, who always surprised everyone with how good-natured they were toward each other since their divorce. George Tenney and Al Flynn were organizing a softball game, as they did every year, insisting the young people move their picnic blankets to give the ballplayers most of the yard, shouting at Matthew to fan the smoke from the grill in another direction.

Robin smoothed down the hem of her dress; she was actually a nervous wreck. In the past week, she and Connor had taken Stephen on several dry runs, to the bakery and the market and finally all the way to Westbury, where the fluorescent lights and the jostling crowds in Macy's had driven Stephen into the try-on room in the men's department. It had taken Connor twenty minutes to talk Stephen into coming out from behind the curtain to continue the search for a sports jacket. They all realized that it was Stuart who really mattered. If he didn't recognize Stephen, if he accepted him as just another guest, then they had done their work well. Someday, long after

Stephen disappeared, Robin planned to tell her brother the truth. The young man he'd met at the Dixons' and the patient who'd been handcuffed and forgotten were one and the same. He had stood beside him in the sunlight, and Stuart hadn't suspected a thing.

And now, just when it all seemed to be going so well they could almost relax, Robin saw her soon-to-be ex-husband's shadow fall across the lawn. One thing she had never figured on was that Patty Dixon would invite Roy, but there he was, headed straight for the barrel of ice and beer, until he spotted Robin.

"Bad luck," she said to Stephen. "Roy."

He looked great, even Robin had to admit that. His dark hair was combed back; he had the same blue-green eyes as Connor and, to anyone who'd never been married to him, just about the best smile in the world. He joined them behind the mimosa tree and looked Stephen over carefully.

"Terrific party," he said to Robin, and then, almost as an afterthought, "Who's this?"

"Stephen." The first introduction and it had to be with Roy. "He's an exchange student."

"Oh, yeah?" Roy said. "A little old for that, aren't you?" Roy reached out to shake hands, and Stephen had to shift his plate of sticky pie. "Roy Moore," he said.

His voice sounded friendly, but Stephen had the urge to back away from him. Stephen lowered his eyes, but that didn't mean he wasn't ready if he had to be.

"He's studying horticulture with me," Robin said.

"With you?" Roy laughed. "That's a good one. My father will get a kick out of that."

"Why don't you get yourself one of those hamburgers?" Robin suggested to Stephen, but he didn't move. "Why don't you get one for Roy, too," she urged him, wanting to keep him as far away from Roy as possible.

"You're sure?" Stephen asked her. "That's what you want?"

Of course it wasn't, but Robin nodded, and then she smiled when Stephen looked confused.

"With ketchup," Roy called with a big grin as he watched Stephen walk away. "Lots." He turned to Robin. "You wanted to talk to me alone," he said. "Should I be flattered?"

"I need money," Robin said. "You know I hate to ask you."

Roy took out his wallet and made a show of giving her all the cash he had. "Life would be a lot simpler and cheaper if I moved back," he said.

Stephen was waiting his turn at the barbecue; there was a mourning dove in the tree above him, a spoiled foolish bird, used to eating bread crumbs and crusts. If Stephen slowly moved one hand in front of the dove, he could snatch it up in a second, before it could hop to another branch or spread its wings.

"Chicken or burger?" Matthew Dixon said. He was wearing a white apron which didn't quite fit across his wide body and there were smudgy charcoal streaks on his arms.

Stephen held his plate out, but he was staring past the barbecue. Robin was leaning up against the trunk of the tree now; she tied the strand of pearls she wore in a knot. Fat dripped into the flames, and when the smoke turned black Stephen couldn't tell whether or not she was smiling.

Robin had turned to wave to Michelle, who was on her way over with Paul and their twelve-year-old, Jenny. Robin had been avoiding Michelle for weeks, and now Michelle raised her eyebrows and pointed at Roy, as if there was a chance in hell they'd gotten back together.

"No way," Robin told her, and they both laughed while Paul and Roy exchanged a look.

"How do they know what they mean without talking?" Paul said.

"Well, you know women have ESP," Roy said.

"Extra spending power?" Paul joked.

Roy laughed and took the bottle of beer Paul offered him. "Whatever they've got, it's definitely extra."

"Is that cute guy the one who's living with you?" Jenny asked Robin.

Roy turned to Robin; his face had gone so white he looked as if he didn't have a drop of blood inside.

"Excuse me?" Robin said. She would have liked to give Jenny a good shake; instead she smiled and reknotted her pearls.

"The guy at the table," Jenny went on. "He's living at your house."

They all turned to look. There was Stephen pouring ketchup on a hamburger bun. When he glanced up and saw them all staring, he immediately put the ketchup down. Maybe he wasn't supposed to pour it straight from the bottle; maybe it was like mayonnaise, which Connor scooped out with a knife or a spoon.

"That's what Connor told Lydia," Jenny said. She took a step backward when Robin glared at her. "Is it supposed to be a secret?"

Robin quickly scanned the yard. Connor and Lydia were

beside the forsythia. They hadn't even noticed the bees swarming around them.

"Robin?" Michelle said.

"He's a horticulture student," Robin explained.

No one seemed convinced that this was an answer.

Roy nodded to a secluded corner of the yard. "I want to talk to you."

"Well, I don't want to talk to you," Robin told him.

"Well, too fucking bad," Roy said.

Michelle put her hands over Jenny's ears. "Do you two mind?"

"Let me guess," Robin said coldly to Roy. "You're trying to charm me."

"Don't do this in public," Michelle whispered to Robin.

"He's living with you?" Roy said. "Am I hearing this correctly?"

"Are you speaking to me?" Robin said. "Or are you interrogating a witness?"

This was not at all the way she had planned it; everything she said sounded suspect and weak. Michelle seemed insulted, as if Robin had somehow intended to cloud their friendship by keeping Stephen from her. And Roy simply wouldn't let it go. People were starting to stare at them. Stuart and Kay were being drawn over by their raised voices. George Tenney had stopped in midswing, and was holding up the ball game so he could see what was going on. Stephen had already begun to walk toward them, carrying the hamburgers; even from this distance Robin could see how cautious he was.

"What I do is none of your business," Robin informed Roy.

"Go get ice cream," Michelle told her daughter. "Now."

"See, that's where I think you're wrong," Roy told Robin.

Stuart came up behind Robin, and when he touched her arm she was startled, even after she'd turned to him. He seemed so rumpled and middle-aged it took Robin an instant to realize this was indeed her brother, the boy she used to protect in the schoolyard.

"You two sound like you're married," Stuart said cheerfully. "We could hear you over by the dessert table."

"We are married," Roy said darkly.

"Well, there you go," Stuart said, less cheerful now. "There you have it."

"You don't need to be rude to Stuart," Kay said to Roy. She had just come back from a vacation in Mexico, and Robin noticed that she looked ten years younger than she had when she and Stuart were still married.

Stuart beamed, genuinely happy to be defended by his ex-wife. "Oh, don't pay any attention to Roy," he told her. "Nobody else does."

"Let's get ice cream," Paul whispered to Michelle.

"And here he is," Roy said. He was truly smooth when he wanted to be. There was that smile, for one thing. "The man who's living with my wife."

For a brief moment, Robin had the sense that something horrible could happen. Stephen's eyes were hooded and cold; along his neck a line of veins rose up. He was face to face with Roy, and although his mouth was curled, he didn't appear to be smiling.

"Hamburger," Robin said. She took one of the plates from Stephen and shoved it at Roy. "This is Stephen," she told Stuart. "He's studying landscape design."

Robin had drawn Stephen over to her brother, but he was still looking at Roy.

"Will you be working with the Doctor?" Stuart asked. "Roy's father plotted out the arboretum for our grandfather."

"I'm working with Robin," Stephen said.

"You should come see the moon garden Robin did for me," Kay suggested. Hers was an all-white garden: white hybrid tea roses, masses of white lilies and bearded iris, Miss Lingard's icy phlox, clematis that opened to look like a handful of snow.

"Thank you," Stephen said. Robin nodded at him, so he knew he was doing well, but his heart was pounding. "I will," he told Kay. He could still feel the bad thing between him and Roy; if they were honest about it, they'd be circling each other right now. But men weren't honest; they sipped beer and smiled and didn't show their teeth.

"When did you plan to tell me about him?" Michelle whispered as Paul tried to guide her toward the dessert table.

"There's nothing to tell," Robin insisted. "Really," she swore, but by that time no one was listening to her.

"Is the cat driving you crazy?" Stuart asked Stephen. "When I stayed at Robin's the damned thing used to jump on me in the middle of the night. I'm convinced the sole purpose of its existence is to shed."

"The cat doesn't bother me," Stephen said carefully. This was it, this small encounter was what they had practiced for. The true test, Robin had said, the real McCoy.

"You're a tolerant man," Stuart said. "Lemonade?"

And that was when Stephen knew they had actually accomplished it. Stuart had no idea that he'd talked to Stephen dozens of times in that room with bars on the windows. *Just*

blink your eyes if you want to answer yes. Shake your head for no.
All Stuart saw now was the sports jacket from Macy's and the
Nike sneakers and the sunlight, and what he saw he believed.
Tell me anything at all, say one word, Stuart had pleaded, while
Stephen sat across from him, in a hard-backed chair, consider-
ing how easy it would be to break his neck, then steal the ring
of keys from his belt.

Bees buzzed around the pitchers on the table, and out in the
rear of the yard a bat cracked against a ball and sent it flying.
Robin glanced over at Stephen, pleased, as if their accomplish-
ment had turned him, all at once, into the person he appeared
to be on this one fine day in May. People all around them were
talking, they sounded like birds, or water in a stream, unintel-
ligible and constant. There were women in cotton dresses, and
boys running through the new grass, and here he was, dressed
like a man, accepting a tall glass of lemonade beneath a clear
blue sky, more than a thousand miles from home.

In that first week of June, when the tide was so low that children went far out across the mud flats, collecting baskets of
mussels, the roses bloomed all at once. People stopped at their
own gates, openmouthed, surprised by the profusion in their
own gardens. Everywhere on the island, roses spilled over
lawns and climbed over rooftops, a glorious infestation.
Thorns and brambles choked lawn mowers, allergy sufferers
went crazy with sneezing, little girls complained they couldn't
sleep because the bees began buzzing long before dawn.

"It was the rainy winter," the Doctor told Robin when he

stopped by for a cup of coffee. The bed of his parked truck was filled with branches and canes; wasps hovered above the pick-up. "The ground never froze," he went on. But still he seemed puzzled; there was no real explanation. Usually, roses demanded more care than other plants; they were tricky and cantankerous and had to be coaxed into growing with bone-meal and lime. "So how's business?" he asked.

"I'm sort of behind," Robin said.

In fact, she'd hardly worked all spring, and if she wasn't careful she'd have to borrow money from Stuart or, far worse, ask Roy for help again. Stephen was out in the yard now, practicing what she'd taught him about pruning back roses. She was afraid to do the job she knew so well; gardening was a gift, after all, and what was given might be taken away. She didn't believe in bad luck or curses, but just in case, each time she found a toad in someone's garden she made certain to set it free.

"It seems that I have a black thumb these days. I don't know what to do about it."

"It's the divorce," the Doctor said as he spooned sugar into his coffee. "Planning a divorce can kill a garden."

"That's a dreadful thing to say," Robin chided him, although she secretly believed he might be right.

She made a face at him, the way she used to when he was working for her grandfather and she would annoy him until he shooed her away. It was, indeed, a dreadful thing to say, but the Doctor didn't give a damn. He had recently celebrated his sixty-third birthday, and although he could still lift a magnolia out of the bed of his truck with no help at all, he figured he was now old enough to say whatever he pleased, whether or not it was true. As far as he was concerned, Roy had made a lot of mistakes in his life, and now he had screwed up the one thing he'd done right. "Have pity on him," the Doctor suggested.

"I don't think that's what you're supposed to feel for your husband," Robin said.

The Doctor laughed and went to the sink to wash out his coffee cup. He would never have let a girl like Robin get away from him. The problem with Roy was that he was too good-looking. His mother, the Doctor's wife, had been that way, too, and in the years before she died, she grew colder and more distant, shocked that the world hadn't offered her everything she'd wanted just because she was beautiful.

"The boy's doing a good job," the Doctor said as he watched Stephen through the window.

Robin came over and lifted the edge of the curtain, then made herself look away.

"He's not a boy." She laughed.

The Doctor put his cup on the drainboard. His point exactly.

"How's my grandson?" he asked on his way to the door.

"Sixteen," Robin said. A word synonymous with moody, and getting moodier all the time. Connor had taken to going out by himself at night. He needed to think, he said. He needed to be alone, and there was no point in her waiting up for him. There was no need to worry about him drinking, he'd stopped completely, she could trust him on that. Occasionally Robin would catch him grinning, and when she'd ask what was so funny, he'd clam up. Whatever it was, it was a serious business, but one that delighted him all the same.

"Your punishment for having once been a teenager your-self," the Doctor told her. "Everything we do comes back to haunt us."

Later that day, when the Doctor was working over at the Morrisons', he saw Robin's truck go by. He felt bad about throwing the breakup with Roy at her. He should have told her there was no such thing as a black thumb; if you believed something would grow it would, plain and simple. Anyone who knew gardens knew that. The Doctor let Angelo and Jim finish up the yard work so he could go to the curb and watch where his daughter-in-law was headed. The Feldmans' place, one of the first of the old shingled houses. This was a job the Doctor had turned down, since Cheryl Feldman took no one's advice but her own, and that was hardly worth heeding. Robin somehow managed to tolerate even the most obnoxious clients, but then, she'd had plenty of practice with her grand-father. If a client insisted on pansies or gladioli, Robin would nod, then go ahead and plant one or two in among the masses of lilies and cornflowers she'd suggested in the first place. The Doctor had taught Robin well, and he was proud of her. As his helpers raked up the cut grass, he decided that he'd better have a long talk with his son. He'd better do it soon, maybe as soon as tonight, because even from this distance, the Doctor could see that fellow who was staying with her didn't mind the thorns on the Feldmans' roses. He wouldn't notice the blood on his hands.

"Floribunda," Robin said, pleased to discover the rose Stephen handed her didn't wilt as soon as she touched it. She'd been foolish to think she'd been cursed. Some plants died and others lived, and human touch had nothing to do with it. "The

old name for it," she explained to Stephen. "From the Latin."
She pulled her hair back into an elastic band. "We have to cut
this all back. Pronto."

It was good to work with Stephen; he worked hard and he
didn't say much, and at noon he walked down to the bakery to
get them both lunch. They had agreed he needed as much
practice as possible going to stores, making small talk, waiting
for the light to turn red before he crossed the street. But sitting
on the Feldmans' lawn, waiting for him to return, Robin realized that she was almost sorry he was such a good student. He
had learned to read more quickly than she'd ever imagined
possible; he was already on chapter books. A few days ago he
had asked for an atlas, and it wasn't until she had brought one
home from the library that she understood why he'd wanted
it. She'd had the urge to take the atlas right back, but then he'd
been so grateful when she gave it to him she'd felt silly and
selfish. She opened the book and showed him the blue curves
of Michigan and watched as he ran a finger over the lines that
signified rivers and roads.

He brought back two tuna salad sandwiches and two bottles of spring water, and handed her the change, which he had
tried his best to count. They unwrapped their lunches and
didn't speak as they ate. They moved only to wave away the
bees. Robin tilted her face toward the sun and closed her eyes.
Of course he wanted to go back; at night he was memorizing
all the routes leading west, he was sounding out the numbers
and the names. The mission had always been to let him decide
his own fate, but that didn't mean Robin had to think about it.
She didn't have to think about the atlas, left open on the oak
dresser in his room. She would not think about how close they

68

were sitting, or even allow herself to wonder if, by this time in her life, she shouldn't have a little more sense.

Michelle Altero rarely got angry, and when she did, those who knew her could tell something was wrong after one look. Her face puckered and grew flushed; her mouth formed a hard, straight line. The students she counseled at the high school thought she was a pushover; they liked her generous spirit and knew she wasn't in the least bit dangerous, unless someone was bullied or mistreated and that angry look of hers took over, which meant there'd be a price to pay.

Working in a high school meant never hearing anything straight-out; information just sort of filtered down. Who was dating, who was flunking out, whose father had missed his AA meetings, whose mother had hit the roof over a Master-Card bill or a dented fender. Snatches of conversations drifted through the hallways, whispers arose in the study hall, messages were scrawled in lipstick on the bathroom walls. And so it happened that Michelle was hearing the latest gossip with half an ear, not paying much attention until she realized that the girl everyone was talking about was her daughter Lydia. Lydia was madly in love, that's what they were saying. She was sneaking out at night, when her parents were already in bed asleep, down to one of the shacks on the beach. One rainy morning, she had walked over the bridge and taken the bus to Great Neck and gotten herself a prescription for the pill, then hitchhiked back home before anyone knew she'd been gone. Michelle locked herself in her office and canceled all her appointments. Lydia was just seventeen. She never had to be reminded to wash the breakfast dishes; her grades were straight A's. Was this the sort of girl who would lie to her parents, hitchhike, pull off her underpants in a cold shack the fishermen had abandoned when Richard Aaron bought the island, start off so early in ruining her life? Of course she was not, and that was why Michelle did exactly what she always cautioned parents about. She assumed she knew where to place the blame.

That evening at dinner, everyone knew to avoid Michelle. She didn't take a single bite of the Boston cream pie she'd bought at the bakery. She slammed the clean dishes into the cabinets after supper, chipping the edges of the plates.

"Uh-oh," Jenny whispered to her sister. "Watch out for Mom. Red alert."

But the explosion never came, and as darkness fell, they all thought they were safe. Paul went into the den and turned on the TV; Jenny trooped upstairs, flopped on her bed, and finished her homework. While Lydia carefully chose her clothes for the next day, Michelle put on a sweater and walked down Mansfield Terrace to Robin's house.

"Oh, boy," Robin said as soon as she opened the door. "Who are you mad at? Paul?"

Michelle went into the kitchen, but she was too fired up to sit at the table or have a cup of tea.

"Lydia's sleeping with someone," Michelle said.

Connor and the student they had living with them were playing chess in the living room, so Michelle kept her voice down, but her face was getting more and more puckered.

"Lydia?" Robin said. "No. She's much too young."

"Really?" Michelle said. "How old were you when you started with Roy?"

"That was different," Robin said. "I was stupid. And look where it got me."

"Precisely," Michelle said. "Lydia has been talked into it. That's what's happened. She's been tricked."

In the living room, Connor was looking at his watch, missing the opportunity to put Stephen in check. Clearly he wasn't paying attention, but Stephen had already learned this was a game without mercy, so he made his best move. They were playing by candlelight, and one moth hovered above the flame. Michelle watched them through the doorway; she had her back to Robin, she didn't want her to see there were tears in her eyes.

"I have to find out who it is," Michelle said. "Then Paul will talk to the boy. God, will he talk to him."

"You want my advice?" Robin said. "Stay out of it."

Michelle turned to her then. "Easy for you to say. Isn't it? Your son's in there playing chess. Why should you worry?"

"You're right," Robin said. "Don't listen to me. I'm an idiot about these things."

Robin smiled, but she was looking past Michelle. In the living room, where he'd just put Connor in check, Stephen was looking right back at her. When Robin finally turned away, she laughed, for no reason at all. Michelle buttoned her sweater; there were chills up and down her arms. She was in her best friend's kitchen, and yet she had the sense that she was unwelcome. What is happening here? she thought. As she walked home in the dark, it suddenly seemed as if Mansfield Terrace was the very end of the earth. One step, and there was the edge. What did we know about those closest to us, really? No one ever dared to speak plainly about desire; no one said the word out loud.

By the time Michelle got home, Lydia was up in the bathroom. She smiled at herself in the mirror and began to brush her hair. Her whole life had changed, and you couldn't even tell by looking at her. She could barely remember who she was before, or what on earth had been important to her. When there was a knock on the door, Lydia's stomach flipped over. Could it be that she really had a mother and a father and a little sister, who was right now rifling through her jewelry box, searching for dangling earrings and bangle bracelets?

"I'm in here," Lydia called. "Stay out."

Michelle came in anyway and closed the door behind her. Not a week went by that she didn't counsel a junior or senior about birth control; she believed she never once made a moral judgment. But this was different. This was her daughter.

"Mom!" Lydia said. "Can't you wait?"

"I want to know who he is," Michelle said.

Lydia eyed her mother coolly. "I don't know what you're talking about," she said.

"The boy," Michelle said. "Don't lie to me."

Lydia bit her lip. Just thinking about Connor, imagining the goofy look he had on his face the first time she took off her blouse, made her smile. They hadn't planned to keep their love secret; it had just turned out that way. They didn't want to be bothered with nosy families and friends. The last person on earth Lydia would consider sharing her news with was her mother.

"Get that smirk off your face," Michelle said.

Before Michelle could stop herself, she smacked Lydia. Lydia's head reeled back; her blue eyes were wide and they stung. She looked at herself in the mirror and saw the red hand mark on her face.

"Oh, my God," Michelle said. "Lydia, I didn't mean that."

They were staring at each other in the mirror. For an instant, Michelle looked so crumpled, so very far away from being young, she hardly recognized herself. Hadn't she just been the one who was seventeen?

"Oh, yes you did," Lydia said. She felt something burst inside her, as if she'd just been granted her freedom. She raised her chin, and her eyes were perfectly clear. "You meant it," she said.

That night Lydia didn't bother climbing out her window. She put on her boots and a heavy sweater and left by the front door. It was after eleven, and Paul had already fallen asleep, but beside him in their bed, Michelle was wide awake, and she heard the door open, then close. She could have jumped out of bed and chased Lydia down the front path; she could have phoned Roy down at the station and had him pick up the boy Lydia was off to meet and give him a good scare. Instead, she kept her head on her pillow and listened to her husband shift in his sleep. She knew then why parents often came to her office distraught, torn apart by what was really only a minor transgression. She knew why she'd been beside herself with worry. There came a moment when quite suddenly a mother realized that a child was no longer hers, and for Michelle that moment had already come and gone. Without bothering to ask, or even give notice, her daughter had just grown up.

FOUR

OLD DICK HAD LIVED FOR almost a century, but even that wasn't nearly long enough. Common knowledge would certainly lead anyone to believe that more than thirty thousand mornings and afternoons spent lugging flesh and bones around would tire a man out and leave him begging for eternal rest. This was not true. It was absolute bullshit. At the age of ninety-one, Richard Aaron had never found the earth more beautiful or more distant. Some nights he dreamed he was flying, and in his dreams he reached out his arms. There was so much he wanted. But he was moving far too quickly to walk on the grass or touch the newly spaded dirt or kiss the girl who was waving to him from below, and when he woke up, and discovered his body was old, he swore at his housekeeper, and had the curtains drawn against the sun, and threw his pathetic breakfast of cooked cereal and weak tea on the floor, all of which led everyone to assume he was tired of life, as if that could ever be the case.

He'd been remarkably smart as a boy, surprising even himself. Not with lessons learned in school; he hadn't bothered with that. Human nature was what he understood, and he'd made a good deal of money in ways he wasn't particularly proud of, all because he knew what men wanted or, maybe more important, what they wanted to believe. It was the possibility of paradise, here on earth. With guidance, such a thing could be found on city streets in Manhattan, in the dredged swamps of Florida, over in New Jersey, where all a man had to do was take a deep breath and he'd know he was there. Old Dick's mistake wasn't that he convinced others what they dreamed could be had, for very little cash down, it was that he'd believed it himself. He'd heard about the island during a poker game, played for high stakes with several of the building inspectors he regularly bribed. The land was mud and straw, he was told, and the air wicked and muggy; a man who walked through the marshes would take ill by morning. Since he never listened to anyone, Aaron went out to see for himself. He was already past thirty, with a wife and new baby, a straightforward man who never acted on impulse. He didn't even know he was looking for something until he walked across to the island and realized he'd found it.

Another man might have been bitter when his fortune disappeared, when his wife and son died much too young, when his grandchildren were shuttled into his care in what was already his old age, but not Richard Aaron. He'd gotten what he wanted, he had it still, even though he no longer owned it on paper; his only regret was that he now had to look at the island from his dusty bedroom window. What he wouldn't give for more time and strong legs. So there it was, a joke, really: Once you had paradise, what good did it do you? The mattress he slept on was filled with hundred-dollar bills, all worthless to him now. So he yelled at Ginny, who'd helped raise his grandchildren and never listened to him anyway, and he waited for the last Sunday of the month, when his granddaughter brought him his contraband pie, laced with brown sugar and cinnamon, and he found some interest in living long enough to see who his great-grandson would turn out to be.

Old Dick was in his bed next to the window, scanning the *Island Tribune*—he could read only the large print of the headlines, even with his glasses—when he heard Robin's truck pull up. It was the end of June, and everything was perfectly green, the way it was before the heat of summer came and turned the edges of the leaves paper-thin and brown. Old Dick had jimmied his window open a crack in spite of Ginny's vow that he'd catch pneumonia; he liked to hear the birds calling and the crunch of the gravel in his driveway when his granddaughter came to visit. Robin and Connor got out of the truck; she was wearing shorts and sneakers and a pale blue shirt, and yes, she had the pie. Old Dick could feel his mouth water; disgusted with himself, he wiped his lips. He hadn't seen his great-grandson for long enough to be surprised by how tall he'd grown; Connor had inherited his height from Old Dick, who'd passed six feet when he was fourteen, then grown a bit more, as if he'd needed the extra height to accomplish all his plans. Someone else was in the truck, behind the wheel, but as far as Old Dick could tell, he wasn't much of a driver. When the truck was pulled over by the garden, where hundreds of yellow tulips had once grown, it bucked, then stalled out. Old Dick rapped on the window and Robin looked up, then waved.

"Who's there?" Old Dick called. His voice was shaky; the truth was, he wasn't talking much these days, and it took all

77

his strength just to scream at Ginny. Afterward he'd have to take a good two-hour nap.

"Us," Robin called back.

"Maybe he doesn't remember us," Connor said. "Hey, Gramps," he shouted.

"In the truck." Old Dick signaled. "Bring him up."

"I told you this was a bad idea," Robin said to Connor.

"He needed the practice," Connor insisted.

Connor wouldn't let go of his plan for Stephen to schedule a road test with him in the winter. For the past two weeks they'd been teaching him how to drive, and as far as Stephen was concerned, reading was simple compared with parallel parking.

"My grandfather wants you to visit," Robin told him through the open window of the parked truck.

Stephen got out, but he hung back, worried.

"He'll do all the talking," Robin said. "If he yells, just ignore him."

They passed beneath the arbor where the wisteria grew, then followed the path to the door of the garage apartment. Across the lawn was the big house where Robin and Stuart had grown up. They had tried to donate it to the county or the state, but nobody wanted it; the house was too expensive to keep up, or even to heat, and now a whole section of the roof had blown away. Egrets were roosting in the chimney.

"Hide the pie," Robin whispered when they heard Ginny's heavy footsteps approaching.

Connor slipped the pie box between some magazines they had brought along. Robin actually felt giddy, like the naughty child she used to be. On the drive here, George Tenney had pulled them over, and this time he'd had a good reason: Stephen had driven right through an intersection, ignoring the stop sign on the corner.

"You didn't stop!" Robin said, as George got out of his patrol car and walked toward them. She and Connor and Stephen were wedged into the pickup, and Robin wished there were room for her to change places with Stephen so that George wouldn't find him at the wheel.

"I could see no one was coming," Stephen said. "The road's clear."

"Doesn't matter," Robin had told him. "The rule is, you have to stop."

"It doesn't make sense," Stephen said. "And you still do it?" Why did he need a sign? He had good eyesight, he could see in the dark on a moonless night; if a rabbit had darted into the road, he would have spotted it in time and stepped on the brakes.

"Now you're getting it," Connor told Stephen. "There's a rule for everything."

"Problem, Officer?" Robin said when George came up to the driver's window.

"I thought this was your vehicle, Robin," George said. "Maybe your friend would like to show me his license."

"He'd love to, George, but he's learning to drive. Don't give us a hard time." She held up the apple pie she'd bought at the store, then warmed in the oven, so her grandfather would think it was homemade. "Old Dick's waiting for us."

Stephen noticed the gun George wore near his waist, but he forced himself to stare straight ahead and keep his hands on the steering wheel. He knew what guns did; they blew into you so that whatever you had been once seeped into the ground. He'd had brothers taken that way: men always appeared suddenly, and they called out some sort of curses before they fired the first shots. When that happened, Stephen knew, you had to run, and even then you might not get away. The muscles along Stephen's jaw tightened. He wished he were wearing the black coat. Then, if this man reached for his gun, Stephen could pull out his knife. He could do it so quickly that the gun would never be fired.

"I hope your friend's got his learner's permit," George said. He was usually the last one to hear gossip, but even he knew that Roy had reason to be bitter. This guy didn't even have anything to offer her, that's what got to Roy most.

"Come on, George," Connor said. "Give him a break."

George wrote up a warning, which Robin tossed in the glove compartment.

"We can go now," she told Stephen. George had already driven off, but Stephen hadn't pulled back onto the road. "Stephen?" Robin said.

He slammed his foot on the gas pedal and the pickup skidded onto the road.

"All right!" Connor said as they careened toward Poorman's Point.

"Slow down," Robin told him. "There's a speed limit."

Stephen had broken into a sweat. He was thinking about that gun, and the way blood froze when it fell onto the snow. He was thinking about the maps in his room, and the cool, clear taste of water up high on the ridge, and the way Robin always stood outside his door to say good night before she went to bed. Now she was sitting so close he could feel her leg against his. She smelled like apples and soap.

"Thirty-five miles an hour," she told him.

Stephen had believed he was making progress, but as he made the turn into the long gravel driveway, he wasn't so sure. Was it progress to learn to pretend to be something he wasn't, because that's what he'd have to do to be a man. Even the way they killed, from a distance, with a piece of cold metal, belied who they were in their hearts. Thinking about this, he could feel himself closing up. He kept his head bowed as Ginny opened the door and threw her arms around Robin and Connor, then tilted her head to study him. Ginny's white hair was pinned up on her head and she used a cane to help her navigate the stairs and the cluttered hallways.

"Your grandfather had a hard night," Ginny warned Robin. "His heart is murmuring. I'm not certain he's up to three visitors."

"You're not my watchdog," Old Dick called from his bedroom. "Send them in."

"He probably won't even notice you," Robin whispered to Stephen. "If he says anything rude, just smile. He'll think you're stupid and he'll leave you alone."

They filed into the bedroom and blinked until their eyes adjusted to the murky light. Old Dick was propped up, his head resting on three feather pillows. He'd had difficulty sleeping and now he was more ill-tempered than usual.

"I didn't mean you," he said to Ginny. "I can see you anytime. I see you too much as it is."

"There you go," Ginny announced, before she went to the kitchen to fix tea. "He must be feeling better."

"You're so nasty," Robin said to her grandfather.

"My pie," he said.

Robin put the pie on the bureau and sliced it into pieces. "This is Stephen. A friend of ours," Robin told her grandfather as she handed Connor a plate of pie.

"What are you staring at?" Old Dick demanded.

Stephen was in the doorway, and just seeing him, Old Dick was reminded of a thousand things he'd been trying to forget. His hunger for his own youth left a terrible taste in his mouth. Old Dick didn't need facts to know that this man in the doorway had everything he wanted. He could run for miles, he could fuck a woman all night, he could probably see the smallest newspaper print with no trouble at all.

"That's right!" Old Dick said. "I'm old. Take a good look at me."

"Grandpa!" Robin said. "That's enough."

Old Dick sat up as best he could; he was shaking from the exertion. The newspaper he'd struggled to read fell into a pile on the floor.

"Come over here," Old Dick shouted at Stephen. "Look at me!"

"What's wrong with him?" Connor whispered to his mother.

Robin put her arm around Connor and drew him to her.

"Look at what I've become," Old Dick believed he was saying. But in fact, no words had been spoken. Old Dick had simply lost the ability to do what most people did every day of their lives. He couldn't pretend there was enough time. He was crying in front of them all, and it didn't seem to matter.

Stephen glanced at Robin, then approached the old man.

He should have been hesitant, but he wasn't. As Old Dick wept, Stephen was remembering the most terrible winter he had known, with nights so cold he thought his blood would freeze. Day and night were both white, thick with falling snow; to get one drink he'd had to lap at the ice covering the green stream below the ridge. Deer were nothing more than hide and bone; owls were silent. And then, just when it seemed winter was over, and the bears had already emerged from their dens, there was a sudden early-spring storm. The black wolf, nearly crippled by arthritis in his legs and spine, froze to death half a mile from home.

When they found him, the big dog pulled at her own fur until she bled. She paced back and forth in front of the black wolf's body until the ice cut the pads of her feet. She took off, by herself, and didn't come back till morning, though her new pups, now fatherless, whimpered in their den and went hungry. When the big dog returned, she seemed confused. Every evening at dusk she went off, they could hear her singing, but the song was so lonely no one dared to answer. For days she didn't eat or drink, but she continued to nurse the new pups, three silver males whose hunger was never satisfied. The big dog was old, though she was the same age as Stephen; her teeth were worn down to nubs and she limped. After only a few months, when the air had turned blue and summer was at its height, she lay down in a patch of sunlight and stopped moving altogether.

That evening Stephen went off by himself. He climbed high on the ridgetop, and when his brothers down below called to him mournfully, begging him to return, he just climbed higher. He had never once cried, not when he was cut or hungry or sick, but he cried now and he could not stop. It did not seem possible for the world to exist without the big dog, and yet it did. He waited for the world to end, nearly starving, tearing out his hair, and in the morning he went back to his brothers. Suffering did not stop the clouds from appearing in the east, it didn't change the sound of the wind in the trees, or the hunger you felt, or the thirst you would always have.

When Stephen reached the side of the bed, Old Dick covered his face with his hands. Stephen sat down anyway, in the chair beside the window. The glass was smudged, making it impossible to tell the true color of the leaves on the trees. Stephen raised the window higher. At first the green leaves seemed tinted yellow, but it was only the bees; they could hear them now, a low constant hum. Ginny had rushed back to the bedroom. When she saw Old Dick crying, she threw her hands up.

"Look what you've done!" she said, but Robin motioned her to be quiet.

A sparrow had come to the window ledge. Its song was so common that Robin had never listened before. She had never even heard it. Old Dick peeked out from behind his hands. Every breath he took was a shudder, every breath hurt. Stephen put his palm down flat on the ledge. The sparrow had flown the length of the island just that morning; its nest was in a cherry tree, in the tallest branches. If the sparrow knew that nothing lasted forever, would it still sing? Would it still build its nest with the same exact pieces of twine and straw? Old Dick, who could not read past the newspaper headlines, suddenly saw that there was salt on the bird's wings. Its beak was stained red from the cherries it had eaten only minutes before. The sparrow hopped onto the back of Stephen's hand, and then it flew away so quickly it was back in its nest, way on the north side of the island, before Robin had served her grandfather his first piece of pie.

People in town got used to the sight of him running. Every evening, as she walked home from the recreation center where she was a counselor in training, Jenny Altero waved to him as she turned the corner onto Cemetery Road, and he always waved back. Dogs out in the backyards began to bark all at once, and their fierce echo could be heard across the island. How fast Stephen ran was a matter of debate. Boys on bicycles couldn't keep up with him. Cars stopped at red lights had no chance of overtaking him once he'd hit his stride. Roy often followed in his patrol car, close enough to keep an eye on him but not so close that Stephen would notice. But of course Stephen knew anyway, and he paced himself accordingly whenever Roy tailed him, never revealing his true speed. When Roy told his buddies Stephen wasn't nearly as good as everyone was saying, and practically limped after a quarter-mile, he thought he was telling the truth, and got white with anger when no one believed him.

Stephen had given up any hope of ever learning to drive. The last time he'd tried he'd plowed right into a parked car, denting the front end of Robin's truck. There were too many rules and regulations, but with running he could just let go. At first, the foot that had been shattered in the trap seemed to have trouble keeping up with the rest of him. The sneakers on his feet were uncomfortable and the asphalt was harder than dirt, but after a while these things didn't matter so much. He concentrated on the road to Poorman's Point, where the trees were twisted by the wind. He listened to the sound of the gravel driveway as he passed by the place where the tulips once grew.

Ginny left the door open for him; that way she didn't have to go up and down all those stairs. She often set out a snack on the dusty cherry-wood table that filled up the whole dining room, though she never would have admitted that the cookies or shelled pecans were for Stephen. Usually, Ginny was fast asleep in front of one of her programs at this hour, a pot of cold tea on the table beside her. Stephen took off his shoes at the front door, so he wouldn't wake her or track mud inside. Sometimes the old man was asleep, too, and Stephen would sit in the chair by the window and read the newspaper until he woke up.

"What are you? A cat?" Old Dick would say when he opened his eyes to see Stephen's bowed head as he read editorials and comics. "Don't you announce yourself? Don't you ask before you steal a man's newspaper?"

Stephen would fold the newspaper then, and pretend to put it away, until Old Dick suggested that since he was fiddling with the *Tribune* anyway, he might as well read it aloud. Old Dick, who could grumble about almost anyone and anything, never once criticized the halting way Stephen read. Birds often came to the window, as if to eavesdrop, but perhaps they were there only because Old Dick had taken to leaving crumbs along the sill. Old Dick had lived longer than anyone else on the island; he was the first to choose a place for himself in the cemetery, on the highest knoll, with a view of the north beach and the marshes. More and more headstones were raised each year, and still Old Dick's piece of ground continued to wait for him; the grass there grew taller, wild asters bloomed. To Stephen, it didn't matter that Richard Aaron could no longer move from his bed or that he needed his food softened by boiling. Old Dick knew things someone younger couldn't begin to imagine. Every day, as the light began to fade and the shadows across the lawn grew longer, Stephen tried to ask him what it meant to be a man, and every day his tongue wrapped around itself so that he could not ask.

"What?" Old Dick sometimes said for no reason at all, when he drowsed off, then woke suddenly. "What is it?" he asked.

And still Stephen could not ask what he needed to know. Instead, he readjusted the old man's pillows and closed the window, to make certain the night air wouldn't chill him.

"Don't think you have to come back here," Old Dick often called out when Ginny brought his dinner in on a tray and it was time for Stephen to leave.

"Pay no attention to him," Ginny whispered, even though it was clear that Stephen paid more attention to the old man than anyone had for years.

Stephen always took the same route back, but it was more difficult for him to pace himself on the way home, and he often ran flat-out. His plan was the same as it had always been, even now that he knew how great the distance was. With the use of a magnifying glass, he had found Cromley on a map, but Cromley was a town, with a hospital and a post office, and where exactly he'd come from he had no idea. His sense of direction was based not on miles or lines drawn on paper, but on the land itself: the rock in the shape of an eagle, the meadow bordered by streams, the place where the rabbits hid in late summer, where the brambles grew taller than a man.

He couldn't rush it, he knew that now. He had only just learned to look both ways before crossing a street, especially at night. Last week, he'd narrowly missed being hit when he was running down the road and a set of blinding headlights had appeared before him. After that, he stayed close to the curb. He was so fast now that nothing could have stopped him if he had known the way back home. Or maybe he still would have taken the same old route to Robin's.

It was always dark by the time he reached Mansfield Terrace. Marco Polo sat in his driveway and barked as Stephen ran past, and in spite of Stephen's natural dislike for dogs, he paid no attention. He pretended not to notice when Roy's car was parked on the corner, just waiting for him to make a mistake. He had no choice but to ignore everything except the fact that he was almost there, running right into the moment he had been thinking about all day, when he walked through the door and saw her, and each time he did he could not believe that men could feel this way and act as though they felt nothing at all.

The birds began to avoid the Dixons' yard; they would light on the redwood fence or along the telephone wires, but they wouldn't go any farther. The bird feeder spilled over with millet and seeds that went untouched. The blueberries on the bushes at the rear of the house were never disturbed. Patty Dixon wondered if it was the weedkiller they'd used in the spring, strong stuff that Robin had advised against, because earlier in June, Patty had found five sparrows dead on the grass, and now the birds simply wouldn't come back, and the birdhouses her husband, Lou, had made in his workshop were all empty.

Patty was known for her cheerful attitude; she was determined to look on the bright side. She conferred with Robin, then ordered bushes the birds wouldn't be able to resist: honeysuckle and winterberry, sweet raspberries and holly. One hot morning, when the birds in other people's yards had already set up a racket, Stephen dragged over the new bushes, their roots still wrapped in burlap. He dug holes all along the fence, adding lime and manure, pausing only to drink some of Patty Dixon's homemade lemonade. Sitting out on her patio with Michelle, Robin could hear him working in the Dixons' backyard.

"Stephen's all wrong for you," Michelle said. Robin made a face pretending she didn't understand, but Michelle waved her hand, as if clearing the air between them. "You're not going to tell me, so I might as well say it straight-out. You're on the rebound—that's what's going on here."

"Nothing's going on here," Robin insisted.

"Remember who you're talking to. I know you."

"And you're acting as my guidance counselor?" Robin said.

"Look, I was never one of Roy's fans, but I think he's changed."

"Please," Robin said.

"I mean it. He phoned me," Michelle admitted. "It just didn't sound like the same old Roy. He's asked me to keep an eye on you."

"See," Robin told her. "He hasn't changed one bit. All he knows is how to sneak around."

"I think you'd be making a mistake. You'd get hurt."

"Stephen is living here," Robin said. "That's all."

"In other words, shut up."

"Shut up," Robin agreed.

She offered Michelle more coffee, and Michelle raised her cup.

"I can't give my advice away," Michelle said. "Lydia barely speaks to me. Last Friday, she didn't come home till after two in the morning. There was sand on her shoes."

"You sound like a detective," Robin said. "Now there's something Roy would do, check the soles of her shoes."

"I've thought about following her," Michelle admitted.

"Well, don't. She would never forgive you."

"Excuse me?" Michelle said. "Whose side are you on?"

Robin took Michelle's hand in hers. "Yours," she said. "Always."

Michelle laughed and drew her hand away. "Right. You never let me win at anything."

And it was true: since kindergarten, Robin had stubbornly made most of the rules. It was only recently, when she'd first realized their friendship was not as one-sided as they pretended and that, if anything, she was the one who needed Michelle.

"You can win now," Robin told her.

"I think it's a little late," Michelle said. Still, she was

cheered. She threw back her head and actually laughed. The first time in weeks.

Robin held her coffee cup tightly; her fingers had begun to turn white. She looked down at the patio that she had designed and built, with the Doctor's advice, when she and Roy first bought the house. Lately she hadn't allowed herself to think about what she was doing, let alone understand the reasons why. The first time, she told herself she forgot to lock his door. The second time it wasn't so easy to pretend. She'd stood there in the hallway for several minutes, her heart racing, then turned and walked to her room.

"Just don't do anything stupid," Michelle was saying to her now. "Don't do anything you'll live to regret."

As he planted the first of the honeysuckle, Stephen could hear the women's voices, and the sound was soothing, a rhythm to which he worked. When Matthew Dixon came out of the house, Stephen felt vaguely annoyed. He didn't want to be interrupted, he was covered with dirt and sweat, but he knew enough to stop and nod a hello.

"Looks like you're doing a good job," Matthew said. He had spent the past month in his room; his complexion was pasty and he blinked in the sunlight.

"Yeah," Stephen grunted, as he shoveled dirt over the roots.

"I've been working on my programs. For my computer," Matthew added when Stephen looked blank.

"Don't know anything about it."

"Really?" Matthew said. In his shirt pocket he had two Mars bars that he was saving for later. "Computers can do anything you want them to do. If you're smart enough to handle them. I could find out anything you wanted me to, given the time and the access. I can do things people wouldn't believe."

In spite of his huge size, Matthew seemed less a college student than a little boy, one blown up with an air pump. He hadn't had much practice conversing with people, and maybe that was why he didn't take the hint when Stephen didn't answer and just kept on working, as though he were alone.

"People think they have privacy, but really, if you know how to tap into the right networks, you can pretty much get any file you want."

Stephen figured he was stuck with Matthew; he nodded to the next bush.

"Oh," Matthew said, pleased. "Sure."

He brought the honeysuckle over, and together they fitted it into the hole; then Matthew stood back as Stephen filled the dirt back in. It was an easy enough job, but on the last shovelful of earth, Stephen felt the metal hit against something. Puzzled, he stopped and crouched down.

"What is it?" Matthew said.

Stephen put his hands into the dirt. Above them the sky was perfectly blue.

"Oh, brother." Matthew came closer.

A red-and-white cat had been buried in the dirt; its coat was matted, its jaws locked.

"That's the Simons' cat," Matthew said. "Reggie."

Stephen stood up and shoveled the corpse into the earth beside the honeysuckle. "It's as good a place as any."

"Right," Matthew said, backing away.

Stephen realized that he could no longer hear the women talking. They had gone inside, and his rhythm was broken.

"I guess you don't need me bothering you," Matthew said.

"No bother," Stephen said, because that was the sort of thing men said when they didn't mean it. He turned to finish his work, so intent that he didn't hear Matthew go back inside, he didn't notice that there were fresh blisters on his hands, or that he was hearing the women's voices anyway, somewhere inside his head.

He knew Robin had stopped locking his door at night. Sleep was impossible; every sound jarred him. He heard everything. Not just the wind and the rain and the house set-tling, but Connor sneaking out, long past midnight. Connor always went out the side door and closed it carefully behind him. He carried his sneakers under his arm and shoved them on when he got into the yard. From his window, Stephen could see the radiant look on the boy's face as he bent down to tie his laces.

He knew what Connor was doing, because once he had seen the girl waiting, under the streetlight, at the end of Mansfield Terrace. She had that same luminous look, weightless and ignited. Even when they disappeared together, down the dark street, they left a pool of light behind them. And so it seemed to Stephen that everyone knew the secret he'd wanted to ask the old man about, even Connor, who was only a boy. What was this, this light that burned inside you, this thing that made you feel as though you couldn't get enough air? He knew what loyalty was, it was what made you stay together and pro-tect each other and share when there wasn't enough for your-self.

But this was different, this seemed as if it could kill you if you weren't careful. Stephen had to be careful, and he was careful all the time. He judged himself harshly. She'd forgotten the lock, that was all; anything more was simply in his own mind. There were nights when he moved the oak dresser in front of his door. He took the old black coat out of the closet and wrapped himself up, but he was much too hot to wear it. He began to burn on the coolest evenings, and the heat went up, into his head, until he thought he might explode. He believed he must be crazy or under the influence of some terrible ailment that boiled his blood, and there was no one to tell him that falling in love would make any sensible man feel exactly the same.

FIVE

ᎬACH AUGUST, STUART placed his alarm clock in a dresser drawer and slept until the white-hot sunlight woke him. He wore the same clothes for as long as he liked, and didn't bother to shave. This, the most beautiful month of the year, stretched out before him end-lessly, with days that lasted achingly long, and nights that were purple and rich. For the whole month he didn't work; he didn't set foot in the hospital. It wasn't that he didn't care about his patients, but he needed to think about simple things: Bluefish and watering cans. Fresh peaches, sliced thin. Egrets, feasting on minnows and crabs.

This year, however, Stuart's thoughts were not simple, and August brought no comfort. He had meant it when he told Kay he didn't want the house. He'd had enough of the island to last him a lifetime; he was forty-two years old and the shop-keepers still treated him like a little boy, discreetly suggesting bargain goods the way they had after Old Dick went broke. But now, facing a summer in Manhattan, he felt waves of panic. If he'd been his own patient, he would have recom-mended a strong antidepressant and intensive therapy. As it was, he watched TV around the clock and found himself growing addicted to game shows and news programs. He'd planned to rent a house out in Sag Harbor, but somehow he'd never gotten around to it. And then one night, early in August, he woke up suddenly from a deep sleep and he knew that he wanted to go home. He packed an overnight bag, which was really all he needed, and took the Long Island Rail Road to the familiar stop. He walked briskly past the willows and over the bridge, then went to Kay and begged her to take him back.

Kay wasn't about to agree to a reconciliation, but she did agree to let him stay on the third floor, which had once been his office and had its own entrance and a small kitchen and bathroom. He felt like getting down on his knees right there on the front porch and begging for forgiveness. What had happened between them, he still wasn't sure. At first, he thought it was because they hadn't had children, but the truth was, he'd grown dull and taken her for granted and now it was too late. As he carried his overnight bag around to the side of the house, Kay took his arm.

"One thing you should know," she said. "I'm dating."

He had never loved anyone but Kay, he saw that now. How had he managed to lose her?

"Well, that's good," Stuart said.

He would like to see some aging beau try to cross his path. My God, the way he was feeling, he might just be there waiting for her date with a pitchfork or an axe. Kay had taken a step back to study him.

"Really," Stuart insisted. "You've made a healthy adjustment."

Like the desperate man he was he went to her, intending to loop his arms around her. There must be hope for them, otherwise she wouldn't have agreed to maintain a friendship. But Kay held up her hand, as if directing traffic, to keep him away.

"Stuart," she said. "It's over."

"I know that," Stuart told her. "Of course it is."

He went upstairs to what had once been his office and was now a musty storage area, then stretched out full on the floor and wept. Kay went into her kitchen, which she had just painted pale pink—she was, in fact, currently dating the painter, a large-boned Russian who loved to dance and who fixed potato-and-onion soup—and immediately phoned Robin.

"Your brother's here having a nervous breakdown," Kay announced. "Or maybe it's a midlife crisis. I'm not really sure what the difference is."

"You let him move back in?" Robin asked. She herself had been avoiding talking to Stuart, since it wasn't quite as easy to lie to him as she'd imagined.

"He's up on the third floor. Let's face it. He has nothing. He's been at the hospital for fifteen years, and not one patient has ever improved. He has no social life. I don't think he even knows how to talk to a woman. He certainly never talked to me. So I'm letting him stay, but just for August," Kay said. "And I'm not taking full responsibility."

Which meant, of course, that Robin had to. She went over that afternoon, with a bag of groceries and the prescription for Prozac that Kay had ordered refilled at the pharmacy. She found the door to the third floor unlocked; bats had been nesting in the rafters and bits of plaster were sprinkled about.

"Get off the floor," Robin told her brother. "I brought Entenmann's chocolate doughnuts."

"This is clearly a generational pattern," Stuart said thoughtfully when he joined her at the dusty table. "Inability to maintain intimacy. It's no accident that both of our marriages broke up."

"Oh, really?" Robin said. She had her hair tied up with a shoelace and she wore old shorts and a white T-shirt that was smudged with dirt, and just for a second she wondered if she should have paid more attention to her appearance. Roy was the sort of man who liked women to wear short black dresses and high heels; he didn't see any good reason for a woman to wear underwear, unless it was something tiny and made out of lace.

"Gee whiz." Robin grabbed a doughnut. "And I thought my problem was Roy's ability to be intimate with dozens of people."

"You don't know that," Stuart said. "I'll grant you the one affair, but the rest was probably all for show. Narcissists prefer bragging about who they're fucking to actually doing it. They might have to relate to somebody once they're in bed."

"The trouble with you is, you're giving Kay too much power," Robin said, veering away from any explanation of her own failed marriage. "Your happiness depends on you."

"Self-help," Stuart said tiredly. "Spare me." He opened the bottle of Prozac and gulped one down. "See?" he said. "I'll bet Kay had this filled for me." When Robin shrugged, Stuart grinned broadly. "She still cares."

"You've got bats in the attic," Robin said.

"That I do," Stuart said. He tapped his head. "Right in here."

"Go to a bar," Robin suggested. "Go fishing."

"Nothing interests me," Stuart said. "It's the first sign of depression."

Robin went to the refrigerator and began putting the groceries away. She found an ancient bunch of broccoli forgotten from Stuart's last visit and, holding her nose, tossed it in the trash. Between Stuart and her grandfather, she could easily wind up as a full-time caretaker if she didn't watch out. Already she was thinking of what she needed to bring to Stuart next time: sponges and paper towels, coffee and a new mop. She might have been angry, if only Stuart didn't look so pathetic.

He was, and always had been, the best keeper of secrets Robin had ever known, far better than Michelle, whose expression always betrayed her, leading her straight into honesty, whether she wanted to go there or not. All through their childhood, Stuart had kept his mouth shut; a hundred times their grandfather had questioned him about Robin's bad behavior and a hundred times he had stared right back at the old man with his hazy expression while he knew fully well who had tied the sheets together to sneak out the window and who had shattered the stained-glass panels by slamming the door too hard. She had never once repaid him with anything more than a grin, and now, perhaps, it was time.

"I've got something that would interest you," Robin said.

"Oh, I doubt that," Stuart muttered.

"I've been wanting to tell you for weeks, but I couldn't. I shouldn't even tell you now."

"You're making me anxious," Stuart said. He reached for another doughnut, but Robin stopped him.

"Remember when you killed my parakeet?" she asked.

"Not that again." Stuart moaned.

"You insisted you knew the best way to catch him, and you broke his neck."

"Are you still holding me responsible for the death of that damned bird? I was ten years old. The door to his cage was faulty. Is this memory supposed to cheer me up?"

"I'm just reminding you. You don't always know the best way to do everything."

"All right, I killed your parakeet. Now can I have my doughnut?"

Robin grabbed her brother's arm. "I'm serious," she said.

"You certainly are," Stuart agreed.

"Come to dinner tonight," Robin said. "But you have to promise you'll keep it secret once you know."

"What are we? Six years old?" Stuart laughed. But when he looked at his sister's solemn face something happened. Although it seemed impossible, he felt a tiny sting of interest.

"Well, all right," Stuart said, doubtful as he was. "You have my word."

He arrived at the back door at seven-thirty, carrying a six-pack of dark German beer. Robin was waiting for him, and she quickly drew him inside. She had changed into white slacks and a clean T-shirt, and her hair was still wet from the shower.

"I think Kay may be sneaking out on a date tonight," Stuart said worriedly. "So this better be good."

"Oh, shut up and come in," Robin said.

"The perfect hostess," Stuart said.

There was marinara sauce heating on the back burner, and the pasta, already poured into the colander, had grown stringy and cold. Robin hadn't been able to concentrate on the meal because she and Connor had argued. What was the point in telling Stuart? That's what Connor wanted to know. Why tell anyone at all? *Because he's my brother,* Robin had shouted, *because we can trust him.* She had stopped at that, just shy of the real truth: Because he needs this.

"I probably should have gone over to see the old man," Stuart said, uncapping a bottle of beer. "But I didn't have the heart to listen to him rant and rave. And Ginny, with her cane, clomping about, dusting. I need quite a bit more Prozac before I'm ready for that."

"Actually, Grandpa's been having a visitor every day," Robin said. "It's cheered him up."

"How much are you paying this visitor?" Stuart asked.

"Nothing," Robin said.

"Oh, come on. No one in his right mind would spend time with Old Dick."

"Not that you're projecting your own feelings," Robin said.

"All right," Stuart allowed, as he put the rest of the beer in the refrigerator. "A masochist might enjoy it."

"Stephen likes going over to the carriage house. He reads to Old Dick."

"God bless him," Stuart said. "He must be an idiot."

At the counter, where Robin was cutting up cucumbers, the knife slipped and she sliced a patch of skin off her thumb.

"Jesus," Stuart said when he saw the blood in the sink.

"It's nothing." Robin held her hand under a stream of cold water when Stuart insisted. When she looked up from the sink she saw Stephen in the doorway. He was wearing the sports jacket they'd bought at Macy's. Homer had followed him downstairs and was rubbing against his legs. Blood didn't bother Stephen, but when he saw that Robin had cut her hand he winced, as though he'd been the one to feel the knife. He began to approach her.

"It's all right," Robin told him as he came near. "I'm fine. You remember Stephen from the picnic?" she asked her brother.

"The man who reads to the old monster." Stuart nodded. "You have my sympathies."

"No, Stuart," Robin said. "This is what I was talking about. The secret that would interest you?"

Stuart looked at her blankly. "Yes?"

"I took him from the hospital. He was never transferred upstate." Stuart hadn't even blinked. "The Wolf Man," Robin said finally. "Don't you see?"

"Very amusing," Stuart said. "In a sick kind of way."

"I didn't plan to take him," Robin said. "It just happened."

"No," Stuart told her. "Not possible."

Stephen's throat had become so dry that it hurt. He went to the refrigerator and got the orange juice, then took a long swallow right from the carton, the way Connor always did. Robin had asked for Stephen's permission before telling Stuart, and of course he'd agreed. What else could he do? Even if he risked being taken back to the hospital, he couldn't have said no to her. Not now.

"You expect me to believe this is the Wolf Man?" Stuart asked.

Stephen placed the carton of orange juice on the counter. "Maybe I shouldn't be here," he said.

"Yes, you should be," Robin said. She turned to Stuart. "Don't you see? He's not who you thought he was."

"You took a mentally deficient patient suffering from prolonged traumatic stress out of my ward and into your home? Is that it? Because if that's the case, I should congratulate you on not being murdered in your sleep," Stuart said. "Yet."

"Will you shut up!" Robin said. "Don't you see what this is? Don't you appreciate it? He could talk all along. He chose not to. Well, now he will. He'll talk to you, and all you have to do is agree not to discuss the case or publish before he's gone. You can't tell anyone."

Stuart sat down on a kitchen chair. The cat he had always despised rubbed against his legs, but he didn't bother to push him away. Stephen leaned up against the counter, staring at Stuart. Stuart shook his head. Still there it was, right in front of him. The face that might easily have been set among painted gold stars on a blue ceiling was the one he could have seen months ago if only he had looked at what was beneath the hair and the beard. Homer had leapt into Stuart's lap, but Stuart paid no attention. He no longer cared about the ruined dinner, or the beer he had planned to get drunk on. That wasn't what he was interested in. On this glorious August evening on this glorious island he had hated for so long, he had just received a gift even he wasn't foolish enough to turn down.

Lydia Altero grew more generous by the day. The small feral cats, which avoided people at all costs, now came to the side door of the bakery where she was working for the summer to beg for bits of butter and saucers of cream. When customers ordered a pound of cookies, Lydia tossed in extras, free of charge: buttery moons dipped in dark chocolate, raspberry hearts, sweet macaroons. Each day business was better, and the owner of the bakery, the Russian housepainter's sister, raised Lydia's salary and kissed her on the cheeks. Women on diets threw caution to the wind and ordered anything Lydia recommended. The Simons' little boys begged to be taken to the bakery after camp, and they swore that Lydia smelled like sugar frosting. Matthew Dixon, who had always loved sweets, was too tongue-tied to speak to her; instead of going into the bakery for danish and brownies, he stood on the pavement near the window hoping for the chance to watch her slice bread or brew coffee.

Even at home, Lydia's generosity seemed limitless. When she discovered that her little sister had borrowed her favorite white sweater, Lydia did nothing more than laugh, and when Jenny admitted she'd also taken several pairs of earrings, the dangling ones she wasn't yet allowed to wear, Lydia declared that the earrings should now be considered a gift. She fixed café au lait for her startled father one Sunday morning and espresso on weekdays, and although she no longer spoke to her mother and could not imagine ever speaking to her again, she was gracious enough to keep her luminous eyes downcast each time her mother was in the room, even though she could have easily announced, with a single glance, that she had possession of the whole world and her mother had nothing at all.

She and Connor couldn't hide what was between them much longer, even Lydia knew that. They tried to avoid each other in public places, where they might not be able to stop themselves from throwing their arms around each other, and when Connor did come into the bakery, as he did almost every day, to pick up sandwiches for himself and his mother and Stephen, he always got something wrong. Today, he tripped over his own feet and ordered three curried chicken sandwiches instead of one vegetable melt and two roast beefs, and Lydia just tossed her head, delighted by his confusion. Later, when Robin and Stephen and Connor had stopped working to have lunch, and were sweaty and hot and streaked with dirt, Robin unwrapped her sandwich and asked Connor why he couldn't keep their lunch orders straight. As she picked pieces of chicken off the sandwich and ate the bread plain, Stephen looked over at Connor and grinned broadly.

"What's so funny?" Connor said, embarrassed. "Cut it out," he demanded, and when Stephen did not, he gave him a shove.

Stephen laughed and shoved Connor right back.

"Oh yeah?" Connor said.

"Yeah," Stephen teased him.

Connor went to tackle Stephen, but somehow Stephen moved out of his way and Connor was the one who flopped on the grass and was pinned. Together, they rolled on the newly turned section of the Feldmans' lawn, knocking over Robin's iced tea and a burlap bag of grass seed. When Robin finally insisted they stop, they both lay in the dirt on their backs and laughed for so long Robin thought they might choke.

"You know what?" she said. "I'm bringing our lunches from now on."

Connor sat up, instantly gloomy. He thought of Lydia waiting for him behind the counter at noontime, the little bag of heart-shaped cookies she always added for free already packed up.

"Don't do that," Stephen said, slowly raising himself on his elbows. He still had that grin. "Connor doesn't mind going to the bakery."

As soon as Robin turned to wrap the remains of her sandwich, Connor gave Stephen one last shove, but he was smiling now, too. The truth was, he was actually relieved. It didn't really matter if Stephen knew about Lydia. That just made it even, since Lydia knew all about Stephen. Just a few nights before, when it was nearly morning and they still didn't want to leave each other, Connor had blurted out the truth. He had argued with his mother when she told his Uncle Stuart, but this was different: Connor simply could not keep anything from Lydia. When he told her about the Wolf Man she had listened with shining eyes, her face pale in the moonlight. Another girl might have said, *That's not true, that can't be possible,* but not Lydia.

"The people who put him in handcuffs should be locked up," she had said, which, as far as Connor was concerned, was the perfect response. "I'll never tell," she vowed.

Her solemn face was perfect as well. Why wasn't everybody in the world in love with her?

"People are such morons, they would never understand him," Lydia decreed. Indignant, she shook her head.

At this, Connor had threaded his hands through her long hair and kissed her, and then he backed away, self-conscious about his own passion, and thrilled by it as well. Now, as he and Stephen worked side by side on the Feldmans' lawn, Connor wondered whether perhaps he had made a mistake in telling Lydia their secret. It would have been better if Stephen had remained a shadow that men talked about on winter nights; he should be drinking from a clear, green stream, not from a thermos of iced tea. Lydia was right. They could not begin to understand him. They couldn't even hope to try. Goodwill was the most they could offer him, and still something awful would probably come of it.

Stephen was concentrating on turning the earth; his white T-shirt was flecked with mud. When he came to one of the holes dug by the moles whose tunnels had wrecked the Feldmans' lawn in the first place, Stephen was supposed to dig into it, then insert a packet of poison. Instead, he crouched down. After making certain that Robin and Mrs. Feldman, who were up on the front porch settling the bill, could not see, he reached in and took the sleeping mole from its burrow. Connor shielded his eyes from the sunlight. In only a few hours, he would be running to meet the girl he loved. The day was so hot and clear it seemed as if summer would last forever. But in fact, August was nearly half over. The edges of the leaves on the maples and the elms would soon begin to curl; in a month, they would start to turn crimson. Why this should make him feel like crying, Connor had no idea, but he turned his back, allowing Stephen to deposit the mole in the ivy beyond the new lawn they were putting in, even though it would surely find its way back by nightfall to ruin their day's work.

He'd promised to talk to Stuart, but now he wasn't so sure he could go through with it. He tried his best to avoid him—he'd take long showers when Stuart came to the house, he'd pretend to be sleeping—but Stuart wouldn't give up. He seemed always to be at the house, a small tape recorder ready. He was there at breakfast and again at dinner; he was out on the porch when Stephen came back from running. He sat on the couch whenever Connor and Stephen played chess. When Stephen washed the supper dishes, Stuart was right there beside him, ready to dry.

"He's driving you crazy, isn't he?" Robin asked Stephen as they sat on the steps of the front porch drinking iced tea.

It was dusk, and Stuart was stretched out in the hammock, watching them. He lifted his own glass of iced tea in a toast. His depression had lifted completely, for all the good it did anyone else.

"Not exactly," Stephen said. He took a piece of ice between his teeth and cracked it in two. "A little."

"Right," Robin said. "Go home," she called to Stuart.

"It's Kay's home, not mine," Stuart called back. "She's got that housepainter there tonight. He's fixing dinner for her."

"He won't leave," Robin sighed. Homer was curled up beside her, and she rubbed his head in the space that he liked, between his ears. "It's all my fault that we're stuck with him."

"Kay had me run out to King Kullen and pick up the sour

cream and cabbage he needed for his recipe, and I actually did it," Stuart called. "If I left here now, she'd probably ask me to wash their dishes and tidy up, and I'd have to split the house-painter's head open. You can't ask me to go."

"The funny thing is, I would do things for Stuart that I wouldn't do for anyone else." Robin was sitting close to Stephen; their legs were almost touching. "Just because he's my brother."

Alongside the house, the roses drooped and turned dusty from the heat. Stephen had never bothered to name his last three brothers. By then, words didn't mean as much, he didn't need them. He could distinguish his brothers' voices from miles away, he knew each one's scent and could identify their paw prints in fresh snow. Stephen finished his iced tea, placed the glass on the porch, then stood up.

"You don't have to talk to him," Robin said.

But she was smiling, and as far as Stephen could tell, this meant she was pleased. And she was, really, at least until Stephen and Stuart went into the house, and she was left out on the porch, with Homer as her only company. Sitting out there, watching the first faint stars appear, she realized that she was actually jealous. She wanted to be the one in that room upstairs with Stephen. Through the open bedroom window she could hear Stuart testing his tape recorder.

"One, two, three," he said, and then his words replayed back to him.

All summer long Robin had not once allowed herself to wonder what would happen next. Some people believed this was a condition to strive for: to be in the here and now. But Robin saw this could easily be just another way to lie to herself, the way she had lied to herself about Roy. The women who had asked for him on the telephone, then quickly hung up when told he wasn't home, were all delusional. That's what Roy always said. Maybe they were attracted to him, but if they were that was their tough luck. He wasn't leading anyone on. Marriage meant commitment. The words were interchangeable, weren't they? At least up until the end. Alibis were contagious little things, a way to sweet-talk yourself into believing whatever you wished could be true. Beneath those first stars, Robin wished she would have demanded the keys to the handcuffs even if Stephen had been ugly and old, even if he hadn't looked at her that way. She wished she could wash the dishes or read a book while he told her brother the story of his life and not want him all to herself. She wished she had thought to comb the knots out of her hair and change out of the soiled clothes she'd worn when they'd dug out the roots of some fallen poplars earlier in the day. Instead, she shooed the cat away and carried the empty glasses inside, and she tried to pretend that just thinking about him didn't cause her a ridiculous amount of pleasure.

Up in the guest room, Stephen was crouched down on the floor. Stuart sat cross-legged facing him, his clothes wrinkling. Between them was the tape recorder. That evening, as Robin left the unwashed dishes in the sink and searched for a comb to untangle her hair, Stephen answered every question he was asked, but that didn't mean he told the whole truth. How could he have survived, that was what Stuart wanted to know straight off. What happened when the snowdrifts were higher than his head or when ice locked his lips together? What did he wear on his feet, on his back, what did he eat, where did he sleep, did he understand fear and longing and desire? If he ever saw men did he run from them, convinced they were creatures completely different from what he was? Who, exactly, had he thought he was all those years?

Stephen told Stuart half of everything, much the way he now knew men did when they didn't want to lie outright. The other half he couldn't even say aloud. He'd never tell that ticks plucked from under the skin were always eaten whole or that blood was best washed off immediately, otherwise it caked when it dried, especially on strands of hair and under fingernails. He didn't tell Stuart that his own reflection had frightened him so badly that he took to closing his eyes when he crouched down beside a stream to drink. He did not dare mention that he'd torn meat from the bone when a deer was still warm and struggling, or that sometimes he was sent to attack not from the flanks, but straight on, quick as an arrow, but much quieter, except for the blood pounding inside his head as he pulled the deer down by the nose before it had the chance to rear its head.

He told Stuart only the half that was easy to hear, explaining how it was possible to know the hour of the day from the shadows on the ground but not how, when you were hungry enough, you could kill without thinking. How if something didn't have a name, he had named it, inside his head, and that was why language had come back to him easily. But he left out how much he hated those words he couldn't get rid of. He never said them aloud. He used only the language of his brothers and in this way he had deluded himself, and had come to believe he was truly one of them, just as he was deluding himself again, right this minute, pretending he was no different from any other man.

As he spoke, Stephen's voice was detached, but Stuart had been too gripped to turn on a lamp. He hadn't even noticed when the tape ran out and facts were escaping into thin air. Stephen's eyes, not his voice, gave emphasis to every word. They were hazel, with flecks of yellow and green, depending on the light. Look, and it was impossible to look away. As he walked back to Kay's in the dark, having gotten exactly what he'd believed he'd wanted, Stuart felt unsure. He'd been one of those to sign the transfer papers, committing the Wolf Man for life. Afterward he'd had lunch at his favorite Chinese restaurant; he'd ordered Peking dumplings and Buddha's Delight without thinking twice. He wouldn't get just an article out of this, he'd get a book, maybe even two; he should have been elated. When he returned to the house he and Kay had shared for so long, he should have thrown open the front door and walked right in. Damn the housepainter, who was probably still there, sipping the last of his coffee, his arm around Kay's waist. Damn the divorce. He should have headed for the back pantry, where Kay still kept the wine, so they could celebrate. Instead, he went around to the side of the house and up the stairs to the third-floor entrance.

He remembered when Robin first put in the clematis that now wound its way along the railing of the stairs. As far as Stuart could tell, it was nothing but a twig, and when Robin had insisted that someday the vine would be so strong it could easily survive a hurricane, Stuart had laughed. He'd never once considered that not only might this be true but he might not live here long enough to notice. Well, he noticed now. The clematis was so overgrown Stuart had to push it away each time he wanted to open the door. He went inside and put the tape recorder on the table and switched it on, then went to the sink and drank two glasses of cool, rusty tap water. He had sat across from the Wolf Man in his hospital room and never once had any idea of who he was. He'd never even looked at him carefully, and now he wondered how his own life had gotten away from him. When was the last time he had made a real decision or taken a stand? What exactly was it that he believed in? The voice he'd captured on tape was telling him what it was like to see stars beneath an open sky for the first time. Were they lamps suspended in the dark or ice crystals caught in the web of the night? Would they fall from above in a hail of fire and light, or guide you on the path home?

Downstairs, in Kay's living room, music was playing. Stuart recognized it: Stéphane Grappelli, a heartbreaking sound. The housepainter had left his bicycle leaning against the fence. It was already past midnight and the bicycle was still there. Stuart remembered that on nights as hot as these, their grandfather had allowed them to sleep out on the porch on thin cotton pallets. Robin had always fallen asleep quickly, her breathing soft and even, but for Stuart the stars had been too disturbing and too bright, and he'd often crept inside to his stuffy bedroom, relieved to be back in the house.

Now he wondered why it was he'd been so easily frightened. If he had been the one to crawl out of that plane, would he have lain facedown on the cold ground and given up? Would he have scrambled into a tree when the wolf first approached him, preferring to starve to death there in the branches? He let the tap water run until the rust was all gone and the water was clear. One month out of the year was all he had allowed himself to be who he wanted to be; except in August, he'd been so busy doing what he was supposed to do that he wouldn't have noticed if a dragonfly had settled on the journal he was reading, the shadow of its translucent wings drifting across the page. For so long, things had just happened to him that it took a moment before he fully understood what he was about to do. But actually it was a relief when he took Stephen's cassette out of the tape recorder and placed it in the sink.

With every hour the night grew hotter and more humid, the way it sometimes did late in August. This was the sort of night when everyone prayed for rain. People couldn't sleep, or if they did doze off, beneath rumpled white sheets, their dreams were not what they had hoped for. Richard Aaron dreamed he was chopping wood in a forest of a thousand trees; his back and arms were tremendously strong, he could feel the heat in his muscles. He was high in the mountains, where the air was chilly and blue, and he gasped as he woke into the hot August night to find himself in his old body, and he tried his best not to fall asleep again the whole night through.

Mosquitoes rose in clouds above the marshes, propelled upward by the rise in the temperature, maddened by hunger and heat. They swarmed through the windows of the fisherman's shack where Connor and Lydia were spending the night, both having lied to their parents. Lydia had left a note that she was sleeping at a friend's house, Connor was supposed to be at his father's for the weekend. Neither of them had felt the slightest pang of guilt, but now they wondered if the mosquitoes had been sent to harass them. When they couldn't stand it anymore and were covered with red bites, they ran out into the marsh and covered their bodies with mud. They wanted to hide nothing, and yet they continued to keep their love a secret. It was better this way, and much less dangerous. As long as no one knew, nothing could be ruined. Let the rest of the world just try to keep them apart, let anyone try to interfere.

Some things lasted forever, didn't they? Some things no one could deny. The heat, for instance, and the slugs that visited Robin's vegetable garden, traveling faster than anyone might expect as they made their way through the dark grass. Only a year before, on a night as hot as this, Robin had sat in her parked truck on Delaney, the headlights and engine turned off. Although she hadn't smoked in years, she had bought a pack of cigarettes and had already lit several; by then she was like a hunter ready to blow off her own foot just to get the rat she was aiming for. Roy had insisted he would be working, but when she'd called the station—the air conditioner in the living room had blown all the fuses, and blue sparks had shot out of the wall—George had been confused. He'd dodged around a bit and then had finally told the truth: Roy was off on Thursday nights. Apparently Roy had neglected to tell Robin that this had been his schedule for more than six months.

Wearing only an undershirt and shorts, not taking the time to bother with shoes, she had gotten into the truck and started driving. After she'd gone through town twice, she parked outside Harper's over on Delaney, not just to check for Roy but to cool down. Her clothes were drenched with sweat; her skin was sizzling. She dropped a lit cigarette on her thigh and didn't feel a thing. And just when she thought she might be crazy, and George had been mistaken or she had misunderstood, she saw them in a parked car, right across the street. He was all over some woman; she'd have to be blind not to see it. Later, Robin would realize that the car belonged to Julie Wynn, who was in charge of the drug education program, but that night the woman didn't matter. Robin got out of the truck and walked across the street. She didn't notice that the asphalt was burning her bare feet; she didn't give a damn about that. She went around and grabbed open the car door, but once she'd opened it, she had nothing to say.

"This isn't what you think, baby," Roy told her, right away, as he was getting out of the car.

His hair was messed up but aside from that he was so calm you'd think she'd discovered him picking out an inferior brand of frozen vegetables at the market. If only he had kept his mouth shut, maybe they would have had a chance. Amazing that he could say the wrong thing so quickly. It was *exactly* what she thought: There was no such thing as trust or faith. Or at least she had been convinced so at the time. Now, as she stood outside, calling for the cat to come in for the night, it seemed that last fight had happened to somebody else. Somebody else had dragged all of Roy's clothes into the driveway. Somebody else had sworn she would never fall in love again. It couldn't have been her, because if it had been she wouldn't be feeling this way. Not like this.

Somewhere there was a book of love, with all the symptoms written down in red ink: Dizziness and desire. A tendency to stare at the night sky, searching for a message that might be found up above. A lurching in the pit of the stomach, as if something much too sweet had been eaten. The ability to hear the quietest sounds—snails munching the lettuce leaves, moths drinking nectar from the overripe pears on the tree by the fence, a rabbit trembling in the ivy—just in case he might be there, which was what mattered all along. Real hunger, just to see him, as if this would ever be enough.

As an antidote, breathe in and out slowly. Don't look at the sky. Consider everyday things: toast on a plate. Laundry in a basket, carpets that haven't been vacuumed for weeks. Don't ever think, and feel even less. Take the garbage out through the side door. Tonight this was all Robin had to do: stay out in the yard near the trashcans and pretend she didn't know he was on the other side of the screen door. He had come downstairs for a glass of water, that was all. He couldn't sleep because of the heat, or the mosquitoes, or a stone he'd found beneath his pillow. All she needed was to call the cat, ignore the moon, realize that in no time he would be gone. She might have been able to do all this if she hadn't taken one more step toward the pear tree. Beyond the place where the fruit had dropped and split open there was a white circle, as if a piece of the moon had fallen to earth. Horrified, Robin staggered backward. He never would have come outside if she hadn't cried out. He would have stood his distance forever, but instead he slammed through the door and went right past her. When he knelt on the ground, all the crickets in the yard started to sing. He reached for the cat and lifted him up. Homer's throat had been slit so neatly he seemed to be sleeping, but the white fur around his neck and chest were deep red.

Watching Stephen crouched there, Robin had no idea that she had already began to cry. She should have known better than to let Homer out; the feral cats were rumored to go wild on nights as hot as this. They tore sparrows to bits and threatened house cats and clawed at the paint of cars parked in driveways. When Stephen rose to his feet, Robin came toward him, but he shifted to make certain that his back was to her. His shirt was covered in blood.

"Don't look at this," he told her.

The blood on his hands was already drying; it wouldn't be easy to wash away. His head was pounding just from the smell of it. This was only one small death in a fenced garden, nothing more. He'd witnessed a thousand acts more brutal, he'd done them himself, and yet this was breaking him apart. He clutched the cat to his chest.

"You shouldn't come over here," he said, as if he meant it, as if they weren't already lost to whatever would happen next.

When Robin took Homer from him, the last rush of blood stained her shirt and her hands. She placed the small white body in the tall grass, which hadn't yet been mowed, and it lay there curled up, like a question mark. Robin wiped at her eyes and her wet cheeks; she wouldn't even notice the blood on her face until morning. Already, he had pulled her to him, right there, beneath the pear tree, and she could feel the calluses on his hands as he reached beneath her shirt. He knew exactly what he wanted, and he wasn't going to stop now. He wasn't going to argue or justify himself or do any of those things someone who'd lived as a man all his life would have done. He wasn't going to twist this up with reason.

Wait: that's what she should have said, but his mouth was on hers and she felt too much to stop now. This was no longer her garden, was it? This was no longer the ground. The heat couldn't possibly feel this way, so deep inside there was nothing to do but give in to it. Were there neighbors out in their backyards? Were there dogs barking? Was that the rattle of a trashcan as a raccoon or one of the wild cats scavenged in the Dixons' shed for scraps of food? She wouldn't let him go. Even when he pulled off his jeans and his blood-soaked shirt, she kept her arms around him; she got up on her knees, just to stay with him. When she felt the scar on the inside of his thigh, she almost spoke, but by then there was nothing to say. She was already drowning. Her arms were around his neck and she circled herself around him until he made her let go and forced her down on her hands and knees. When he moved inside her, she cried out, but not because she wanted him to stop. He wouldn't let go of her, and that was what she wanted. And later, when they'd gone into the house, and up to her room, they still couldn't stay away from each other. They did things they could never have spoken of, or known they needed so badly. And they didn't stop until they were sore, until there was only one star left in the sky.

Outside, the first birds began to call to each other, but fortunately they didn't wake Stephen, and for that Robin was grateful. The sky in the east grew milky and pale, but she could hold on to this night just a little while longer, at least until daylight made it impossible. She could believe whatever she wanted, she could believe whatever she wished. He was turned with his back to her, and just watching him sleep made Robin shiver, although the heat was still rising, as it would continue to do until the rain came, late in the afternoon, a sudden, drenching storm that would wash away every bit of blood under the pear tree, until it was almost possible to forget what it was they'd found in the garden.

SIX

Now that it had happened to him, Stephen understood why the black wolf would have once had reason to kill him. When he was small, Stephen had hated to let the big dog out of his sight. He trotted after her and made a nuisance of himself, until at last the black wolf let him know there were times when he was not wanted. The lesson was harsh and quick: the black wolf charged and pinned Stephen to the ground, showing his teeth so close to Stephen's face that for months afterward he dreamed he was being eaten alive and woke whimpering and feverish.

That the black wolf had tolerated Stephen at all was a measure of his restraint, and now Stephen wished he had studied that restraint better, because he himself seemed to have none of it. He wanted Robin constantly; when Connor sneaked out at night Stephen couldn't even wait for the door to close behind the boy before he went to her room. When she worried that they might be overheard, convinced that Connor was asleep in his bed, it took all his control not to betray the boy and just tell her they were alone. He kissed her until she stopped talking; he kept her there in bed until she didn't give a damn who overheard. He was jealous of everything she touched: The towels she smoothed as she folded them into the laundry basket. The sweet pea vines she cut back beside the Feldmans' toolshed. The ground coffee she measured into the paper filter. One morning, when he was alone in the house, Stephen went into her bedroom and examined the clothes in her dresser. He found a photograph of Roy, an old one, taken years before, when Connor was a baby, and he tore it in half for reasons he didn't understand, and all the rest of that day he felt embarrassed by what he had done, and he tried to patch Roy back together again, using glue and tape, with no luck at all.

Whenever he went running, in the dusk that came earlier every day, he ran flat-out, so that people sitting on their front porches didn't know if they'd seen him or just a shadow cast by a cloud. He ran until his lungs hurt, hoping to extinguish some of what was burning him alive. Sometimes, when he got to Old Dick's house, he stood by the sink and drank water straight from the faucet, gallons it seemed, and still he was on fire. Instead of reading from the newspaper, he now read poems from the musty volumes no one had opened for decades; meaningless words, no sense in them at all, and yet some of those poems made his throat tighten with longing.

"What are you trying to do?" Old Dick shouted whenever Stephen began to read poetry. "Kill me?" He held up the *Tribune*'s sports page. "Here's beauty," he spat. "Here's truth."

Out of the hundred questions Stephen might have asked the old man he finally chose the one that most disturbed him. There was almost no light left; Stephen put down his book and moved his chair so that he could see Old Dick's face.

"Can what you feel inside kill you?"

"Absolutely," Old Dick said. "Bet on it. It'll tear you right up and burst your blood vessels."

"If you want two things?" Stephen asked.

"You're fucked," Old Dick said.

"That's what I thought," Stephen admitted.

Old Dick reached for his glasses. What he wouldn't give to change places with this fellow for one day, or a day and a night, a week—what he wouldn't give for that. Stephen was wound up about something, and it was exquisite to see, all that pain and emotion. By now, Old Dick often found himself waiting for the sound of Stephen running along the gravel driveway; he yelled at Ginny if she left out crackers as a snack, rather than the good chocolate-dipped cookies from England. On rainy days he found himself fretting; he was so completely out of sorts, thinking he was bound to be disappointed, that he coughed up blood. But the rain didn't bother Stephen, he ran in fine weather or foul, and if he happened to leave a pool of rainwater on the carpet, Old Dick didn't seem to care. And now, although he was enjoying Stephen's agony—almost feeling it himself, somewhere deep in his chest—there was something else he was feeling, too, and it came as such a surprise to finally have mercy in his heart that he began to cough, and he didn't stop until Stephen got up and pounded him on the back.

Old Dick caught his breath and waved Stephen away. As he struggled to sit up straight, the money in his mattress shifted beneath his frail weight.

"Love won't kill you, if that's what you're thinking," he said. "Although if you have a choice, go for sex without it. Far superior and less complicated."

Stephen looked down at the carpet.

"No choice," Old Dick judged, correctly. "Poor bastard," he said cheerfully. "I envy you."

In what the old man determined was an enviable state, Stephen ran back to Mansfield Terrace through the rain, not noticing the cars on the street or the dogs that dared to chase him, snapping at his heels as he outdistanced them. By now, he had imagined, he would have already begun the journey home, but the atlas lay on the floor of the guest room closet, unopened since the night Homer died. He could not go home and still have Robin, but he was greedy, even though he knew that if he held on to both, he'd be pulled apart, until all that was left of him was scattered, like stars, across the dark space that separated what he wanted most.

And now as he ran, he wondered if he had asked Richard Aaron the wrong question. Perhaps it was knowing you had to give something up that could kill you. Certainly this knowledge forced him to run with a fierce speed that he couldn't control, not any more than he could control his reaction when he realized Roy was following him again. This time he couldn't just go on, acting as if he didn't know he was being tracked. Instead he turned and ran toward the car, straight at the headlights, not caring, at that instant at least, if Roy ran him down.

Roy had to brake suddenly. He skidded up on the curb, then threw open his door and got out.

"Are you crazy?" he called. "Are you out of your mind?" He blinked in the rain, not yet aware that Stephen was still headed straight for him. Before Roy understood what was happening, Stephen had put both hands on Roy's chest; he shoved him, hard, so that Roy reeled backward, smashing up against the car.

"Hey!" Roy said.

Stephen approached Roy again, and again he shoved him, but this time Roy's back was up against the car and there was nowhere for him to go. They stood face to face, breathing hard, ignoring the rain that was drenching them to the skin.

"You're looking for a lot of fucking trouble," Roy said. He had bitten his own lip, and now he wiped at the blood. "Jesus," he said.

"Don't follow me anymore," Stephen told him.

Stephen turned and started to walk down the middle of the road; he could feel something roaring in his ears. He heard Roy coming up behind him, and he was ready when Roy grabbed him. Quickly, Stephen broke away; the hair on the back of his neck rose.

"You're living in my house, aren't you?" Roy said. "You're living under the same roof as my kid and my wife."

"She's not your wife," Stephen said.

Roy felt a pain in his side, just below his chest. He took a step backward. The rain was coming down harder; it could blind a man if he looked straight up into the sky, it could confuse him, too, even leave him speechless, particularly when faced with the truth, and that was why, long after Stephen had disappeared down the street, Roy was still standing there, right in the center of the white line.

A secret is always hard, a stone wedged just beneath the skin. A constant reminder that won't go away, a secret invokes longing; it takes on a life of its own. In order to keep one well, certain things have to be done backward: Laughter instead of tears, a slow walk when the urge is to run. Always deny what is most important, at least in the presence of others.

And so it was possible to be together every night and then, each morning, pretend that the night before hadn't happened. Robin and Stephen were tentative with each other in daylight, more distant than polite. If Stephen was at the refrigerator getting himself some juice and Robin had to get to the sink to wash the dishes, she'd step around him, or sometimes just forget the dishes altogether and let them pile up. When they were out on a job, she'd curtly direct him to the work that needed to be done first, then set about by herself hauling manure or chopping at twisted branches, even if it was far too much for one person alone.

"Why are you so pissed off at Stephen?" Connor asked her one night after they'd all eaten dinner in silence and Stephen had gone upstairs, to read, he'd said, although Robin knew it was to wait for her.

"I'm not," Robin told him, her voice unreliable.

"Could have fooled me." Connor shrugged.

Maybe she should have said, *Look, I'm crazy about him, I'm absolutely insane with it,* but instead she cleared the table and rubbed at her throat, as if the secret were buried right there, above her collarbone. Every once in a while she almost gave it away. The last time she'd seen her father-in-law—they'd happened to pull into the Mobil station on Cemetery Road at the same time—the Doctor took one look at her and asked if she was feverish. When he suggested rose hip tea to ward off the flu, Robin felt so giddy that she had to turn away or she'd laugh out loud. She couldn't even talk to Michelle on the phone anymore for fear of blurting it out. *This is what's happened to me,* she wanted to say. *You won't believe it.*

She took cool baths and tried not to think about the future, but she knew he wasn't hers alone. There were nights when he couldn't stand being confined, when he left her to go to the window, and the way he looked out at the yard, the way he seemed to see right through the dark, frightened Robin. Sometimes, when he couldn't bear the heat of the house and the closeness of the walls, he went out for a walk. He followed the marshes, then passed by the ginkgo trees in the center of town, going only as far as the bridge where the weeping willows grew. One night he came upon a deer that was so tame and unafraid of people she went on eating the ivy that grew beside the Dixons' driveway. Stephen stood there motionless, the way he'd been taught, but inside, his heart was pounding. In the dark, the deer's black nose looked soft and wet; it was the best place to latch on if you wanted to take her down quickly. The deer breathed out warm puffs of air as she chewed ivy, flanks shivering from the pure joy of eating.

When the wind shifted, the deer looked up at him, leaves hanging from her mouth. Stephen looked right back, not breathing at all now. If he'd been hungry, if he'd had nothing to eat but beetles and mice, his stomach would now be churning in anticipation; he would have had to keep from rushing. The deer, in her stupidity, began to walk toward him, her hooves making a sad clacking sound on the concrete. Stephen watched the deer's mild approach and was horrified, revolted by everything he had done and now considered doing again. You might lose the taste for blood and bones once you were well fed, but not your appetite for the chase. You didn't forget the way your legs felt just before you began to run, as if a spring were coiled inside, with a time clock all its own.

The moon was in the center of the sky. It was white as snow, white as the bones ravens have picked clean. Stephen waved his arms in the air. The deer stopped and studied him with eyes as big as teacups.

"Go on," Stephen said. "Run."

But this deer was used to the tone of a human voice, which sounded a little like music, and she calmly sniffed the night air. When Stephen clapped his hands, the noise echoed like a shot. The deer jumped over some azaleas and ran across the lawn, leaving small hoofprints in the grass. Stephen closed his eyes and leaned up against the Dixons' car. He put his hands on his knees and breathed deeply. Some secrets were much harder to keep than others, especially ones you kept from yourself.

Up in his bedroom, Matthew Dixon, who had begun to pack and would be leaving in only a few days for his sophomore year at Cornell, watched this whole encounter from his window. It had been interesting enough to pull him away from his computer terminal, although he had just managed to access several calling-card numbers he would soon put to good use, making as many long-distance calls as he wished without ever having to pay the charges. He felt almost as if he had caught something, the way he did when he tricked feral cats into coming right to him by setting out open cans of tuna. He was smart enough to know that something had just happened there in his driveway. He had learned a great deal about people by scrolling through their lives, as he often did when he gained entry to private files. With a few choice facts he could predict what people would do. What bills someone would hold off paying, for instance, when going bankrupt. How long it would take until a person realized his money card had been accessed—by the mysterious creature Matthew became at the keyboard in order to make unauthorized withdrawals from an account. But Matthew never would have predicted that Stephen would frighten the deer away, or that he'd stand in the driveway until he was certain she was gone.

When Stephen went home, he took the same route as the deer, but where the deer had gone on toward Cemetery Road and the woods just beyond, Stephen crossed the Carsons' lawn. Most of the neighbors were already asleep, but in the Carsons' driveway, Marco Polo faced Stephen with his great rolling bark. Stephen stopped where he was, beside the hedge of lilacs. He crouched down and called the dog to him. Still, the basset hound continued to bark. He simply wouldn't budge. Marco Polo was old, he slept on the couch and was spoiled with dog biscuits and saucers of cream, but he certainly wasn't a fool. Any dog knows the difference between a man and a wolf. And long after Stephen had gone inside the house, and had begun to walk down the hall to Robin's room, Marco Polo went on barking, his face pointed upward, toward the moon.

Kay no longer kept sugar and flour and English breakfast tea in the glass canisters along her kitchen counter. She had replaced all that with shells collected from every trip she had taken since her divorce, including that first tearful vacation to Sanibel Island, when she'd wept over each conch and sand dollar and reached out for Stuart every night for a week as she slept, out of habit and perhaps just a little regret. Since then, she'd traveled to Puerto Rico and Cancún, to Boca and Bermuda and a Club Med on a pink island so tiny it had never been given its own name. Each time she returned from a trip she filled another glass canister with mementos, although now when she searched a beach for shells she was quite systematic and not at all teary. She knew exactly what was worth keeping and what she might just as well toss back into the sea.

Kay planned to visit every damn beach she'd ever dreamed of when she was married to Stuart and he was too busy to do anything as frivolous as enjoy himself or pay her the least bit of attention. There was a beach in Hawaii with black sand where shells in the shape of children's ears washed onto shore, and another in Baja where the sand sang beneath your feet and abalones had the sheen of opals. Gregor, the housepainter, had told her about the beach of his childhood, a cove on the Black Sea where the shells were as big as cats: put one under a pillow at bedtime and it would whisper and purr all night long, so that upon awakening you might know much more than you did the day before.

Kay was in the kitchen, considering the pamphlets she'd picked up at the travel agency, when she noticed that Stuart was leaving. He came to the back door. Kay could see him quite clearly through the window; he had shaved and showered, and his clothes were clean and pressed. His overnight bag was slung over his shoulder, and he carried the bucket and mop Robin had bought him. He slipped the key to the third-floor office under the doormat, and then he did the oddest thing: he went right up to the door and kissed it, with a kiss so tender Kay found that she'd begun to cry. Suddenly, she had the feeling that she didn't have the faintest idea who Stuart was, and that she never had, and that she probably would never see him again. When he had gone, Kay took the key from beneath the mat and went up to the third floor. She was shocked to discover just how tidy Stuart had left the rooms. The cobwebs were gone, and the refrigerator had been washed with warm water and baking soda; when she went to the window she could smell the vinegar he'd used to clean the glass. He hadn't left a dirty dish or a ring around the old bathtub, and he certainly hadn't left a note.

After Stuart had been gone a few days, Kay called him, just to tell him she'd decided on a trip to Jamaica, where a new hotel had been built so close to the ocean that false angel wings and blue-eyed scallops were sometimes found in the teapots. She phoned his apartment, where the message machine didn't answer, then tried the hospital, where she was put on hold and later informed that he couldn't be reached. She had that feeling all over again, that he was gone completely, and yet every once in a while she had the distinct sense that he was near, an impression based, she believed, on the sort of radar that comes only after having slept beside someone for nineteen years. She thought she saw him out of the corner of her eye when she was on line at the market, only to discover that the aisle where she'd imagined he'd been browsing was empty. Could that be

Stuart, on the steps of the church? Was that his shadow slipping in between the library doors as they closed? Kay grew more and more edgy, but perhaps that was only because Gregor was starting to bore her—he was a crossword fanatic and had the ability to ignore her for hours while studying clues. "Alpha's opposite," he'd mutter to himself. "Hepburn's forte," he'd muse. "Pride goeth before this," he'd whisper into his beer.

After several more days of trying to contact Stuart, Kay phoned Robin, who seemed unconcerned when she heard that her brother couldn't be reached.

"Oh, he'll turn up," Robin said cheerfully. "You know Stuart."

But in fact, that was the point. Kay wasn't quite sure that she did. She began to worry in earnest: He was dead in a ditch. He was homeless and drunk, surviving in alleys on cat food and rainwater. He had ended it all by hanging himself, perhaps from the lowest branch of one of the oaks on his grandfather's old estate, and wouldn't be found until spring. Kay began to dream about him, slow, languid dreams in which he was a young man, a boy really, serious and sweet, but absolutely deaf to her whenever she called his name.

As for Stuart, he hadn't been giving much thought to his dreams. He wasn't even certain if he was dreaming at all, though anytime his patients had offered that as an excuse to avoid self-examination he'd never believed them. He was sleeping more soundly than he'd imagined possible, here, in the fisherman's shack where he'd spent so much time as a boy. Since then, dozens of other boys had made use of the shack; they'd run away from home, for an afternoon or an evening, they'd had pirate clubhouses and, after they'd turned fourteen, secret beer bashes as well. Lovers had been here, on nights when they needed privacy, and they'd listened to the wind in the marsh grass and sworn that someone was sighing.

Everyone who had used the shack, and had thought of it as his or her own, had left something behind: charred firewood and fishhooks, Coke bottles and beer cans, homework that had never been turned in, tubes of lipstick, blankets that had grown moldy over time, intertwined hearts etched into the walls with burning-hot coals. Stuart cleared most of the mess away in a matter of hours, and then set to work with his mop and dust rags. The weather was still warm and fine, so he tied one of the rags around his forehead to make certain that sweat wouldn't drip into his eyes. After all the trash was sorted and ready to be carried to the dump, and the old wooden floor was so clean it squeaked under his feet, Stuart walked through the marsh grass to the beach and threw himself into the water, and all the rest of the day he licked his lips, enjoying the taste of salt.

Why shouldn't he buy wood putty and new panes of glass at the hardware store? Why not have a mattress and army blankets and a Coleman stove delivered right to the road above the beach, even though the deliveryman insisted it wasn't a proper address? He dug a latrine and bought a wheelbarrow to cart away the trash; he used the public phone near the town green to phone the *New York Times* classifieds and place an ad to sublet his apartment, then bought fresh coffee and bread at the bakery and ate his lunch on the beach, where the sea gulls snapped up any crumbs. Now that he had all the time in the world, time itself had become a different thing. He could blink and there was a fish on his line. He could turn around twice and the sun would already be setting.

He ate one of the peaches he'd bought at the market for supper, a piece of fruit so delicious he shivered with every bite. And when the sun went down, and the air grew cool, that complicated August air that evoked both summer and autumn, he looked upward, waiting. The sky was inky and immutable, and then, quite suddenly, it cleared. When he saw the stars it was as if he were seeing each light for the very first time. What could be more beautiful? Nothing in heaven, nothing on earth. He sat studying the night until his neck ached, and still he felt he couldn't get quite enough of the sky. He didn't bother to cover the windows in the shack with pil-lowcases, as he had planned, and he fell asleep in a wash of starlight, that deep, dreamless sleep that made him smile even before he closed his eyes.

And that's the way they found him, when they rushed through the door, already tangled together, their hands all over each other. They hadn't managed to sneak out for the night in more than a week, and they were more desperate for each other than ever. Soon the school term would begin and they'd have to pass in the hallways, satisfied with only a whis-per and the promise of *later*.

"Have you missed me?" Lydia asked, after she'd pulled her T-shirt off.

Connor nodded yes; he would have agreed to anything to please her.

"Have you thought about me every minute we've been apart?" she wanted to know.

Connor put his arms around her. When he swallowed, his

head rang; he was ready to explode. Lydia kissed him, then pulled away.

"Every second?" she whispered.

"Oh, Jesus," Connor said.

When he saw Stuart in the shed he couldn't catch his breath, but instinctively he pushed Lydia behind him to protect her, although from what he wasn't exactly sure.

"It's my uncle," Connor told Lydia.

"Is he dead?" Lydia peered at Stuart. "We should check his pulse."

She was, Connor thought lovingly, the most practical girl in the world. As Lydia fumbled to slip her T-shirt back on, Connor went to kneel beside the body. Stuart was still smiling, and because Connor had never seen him look anything but anxious, he assumed his uncle was dead.

"Oh, man," Connor said. "I think he is."

Lydia came up beside Connor and took Stuart's wrist into her own capable hands. "I wish I hadn't lost my Swatch," she said.

Stuart's eyes fluttered, then opened. He looked at Connor, then at Lydia, who, in her hurry, had put her shirt on inside out. He would have asked what they were doing there, if the answer hadn't been so apparent.

"I've taken over your shack," Stuart guessed. "I've put you out."

"He's alive," Lydia announced, proudly, as though she had personally brought him back from the other side.

"Yeah," Connor said without much conviction. His eyes had adjusted to the darkness and now he could see the improvements his uncle had made—no more garbage or broken glass, no more hideaway for him and Lydia. "You're planning on staying here?" Connor asked his uncle.

Stuart raised himself up on his elbows. "Let me put it this way," he said. "I'm not planning."

When people on the island heard the news about Stuart they clucked their tongues and shook their heads and swore they'd known all along he'd wind up this way. What could anyone expect with a family like his? Of course he was now talking to bluefish on the beach and reading old novels Lydia Altero got him from the free bin at the library. Kay's travel agent was the one who told her that Stuart was claiming squatter's rights and, by all accounts from the clerks in the hardware store, was about to put a wood-burning stove into his shack. He'd ordered a set of the finest fish-scaling knives made in Bar Harbor, Maine, and bought a pair of knee-high boots for walking through the marsh. He'd started going to the AA meetings at the Episcopal church on Wednesday nights, though as far as anyone could tell, he didn't have the slightest drinking problem.

Kay drove over to the north beach the following morning. Stuart wasn't her responsibility, she knew that. Still, there was such a thing as a clear conscience. She'd just take a peek. She parked at the beach lot, then walked the rest of the way on the road, which curved around the marshes and was often filled with mud puddles. A green heron fishing in the reeds frightened her. That was completely ridiculous. She was a member of the Audubon Society; she had been to this beach a thousand times before and had no reason on earth to be nervous. The tumbledown shacks were scattered along the beach, but she knew Stuart's as soon as she saw it. There was a wheelbarrow propped against the far wall and, leading from the front door to the marsh, a path lined on either side with shells. Oyster shells, she could tell that from where she stood on the road, creamy white with purple hearts, dropped from above by gulls to split open on the rocks, then carefully gathered by Stuart. Kay stood there on the road for so long that the heron took her for a statue and came close enough for her to see its heart beating in its chest. By the time she'd turned and walked back to her car, Kay had decided to put off her trip to Jamaica, at least until after Christmas. The weather was good enough right where she was. Summer was ending with pale golden sunlight and a sky full of geese, already headed south to the Carolinas, where the beaches, she'd heard, were excellent, although not quite as fine as this one, which was just two and a half miles from her front door.

In the last week of August, Marco Polo was found in his driveway with his throat slashed. Jeff Carson covered him with a beach towel, and toward evening he buried him in the backyard, beneath the forsythia, where the dog had always hidden on days when he was to be taken to the vet for a bath. People whose backyards abutted the Carsons' yard pulled down their shades and turned away, rather than watch Miriam throw herself on the dog's grave. That was too painful to see; it was bad enough that everyone could hear her wailing, all through the night, and that they remembered how she had fed the basset hound cream and called him sweetie when she took him out for his morning walk.

For days afterward there were bloodstains in the driveway. People kept their pets inside, and George Tenney, who came to comfort Miriam and wound up with her hysterical when he told her they'd probably never find the culprit, took to suggesting that people build kennel runs for their dogs and lock their front doors. By Labor Day, tempers all over seemed to flare, perhaps because of a heat wave, a final burst of summer that often accompanied the beginning of the school term. Michelle Altero had several overwrought girls come to the guidance office on those first days of school; there were rumors that the dog had been killed by a maniac, a slasher who wandered through the marshes and along Cemetery Road looking for his next victim. Michelle gave each girl smelling salts and a good talking to, then sent her back to homeroom. But the truth was, even Michelle couldn't concentrate on her work. She had tried to discuss with Paul whatever it was that was wrong.

"I just don't feel well," she'd told him. "Things aren't right."

"Okay," he said. "What can we do about it?"

Well, she'd dropped it right then and there; he'd assumed she wanted him to fix something, but it wasn't like that. It was something inside, some kind of loneliness, a bitter thing for which there was no easy cure. She felt as if her one pleasure in life was her twelve-year-old, Jenny, a sweet, genuine girl who was still enough of a child to take Michelle's hand occasionally when they walked down the street and who often asked to have stories read to her when she was sick in bed. Jenny had been particularly helpful lately, perhaps only because she was afraid her mother's temper might be unleashed. She'd done the laundry the week before as best she could, but accidentally had mixed in the dark colors with the whites; she'd fixed macaroni and cheese one day and brownies from a mix the next. When Michelle saw the plate of unevenly cut brownies on the kitchen table she had burst into tears.

It just wouldn't do. She would have to snap out of this, ready or not. She had her hair permed; then she set about seriously to work and didn't think about the fact that her husband didn't understand her and her older daughter didn't talk to her, and it was going quite well, actually, this new regime, until the third Friday of the month, a lovely crisp day when the girls at school could at last wear their new corduroy slacks and their denim jackets. She and Julie Wynn had just led a seminar in drug awareness for interested faculty members, and Michelle was on her way back to her office when she saw Lydia and Connor beside the water fountain. Lydia's arms were around him; she had to stand on her tiptoes to kiss him, and she didn't stop kissing him until the bell for class had rung.

Connor saw Michelle first. He took Lydia's hand and nodded. Lydia stared across the hallway at her mother as if she were a total stranger.

"Get into my office," Michelle said to her daughter. "Now."

"She's only late to class because of me," Connor said, unaware that no one was interested in what he had to say. Not about this.

"You're not my boss," Lydia said to her mother. She was wearing long silver earrings that chimed when she tossed her head. "I don't have to do whatever you tell me."

"Oh, yes, you do," Michelle said.

"Technically, she really doesn't have to," Connor said. "There's a five-minute grace period after the bell."

His voice broke, but his eyes were steady and clear. He was so tall that Michelle had to look up to see how blue they were. She was the first one Robin had called, minutes after he'd been born, and she'd sat up all that night to finish the baby blanket she'd been crocheting. Blue and white, a basket stitch, and Robin had marveled over the match with his eyes.

"Don't you dare talk to me," Michelle told Connor. "Don't say one damn word to me."

"You wonder why I don't tell you anything?" Lydia said. "You wonder why I despise you?"

"This is not going to continue," Michelle said.

She left school, although dismissal wasn't for another hour, and drove to Robin's in less than ten minutes, probably ruining the gearshift on the way. Robin was out in the driveway, shoveling mulch into the bed of her truck.

"What?" she said when Michelle came tearing up the driveway. "What's wrong?"

"Your son," Michelle said. She was standing in mulch up to her ankles, and her face was so hot she looked sunburned.

Immediately Robin thought *car accident*. She leaned against her truck for support. She used to worry about that when Roy worked at night and there was ice on the roads; sometimes she wouldn't fall asleep until she heard him come home.

"*He's* the one that Lydia wouldn't tell me about. It's Connor."

"No," Robin said. "They hate each other."

Michelle took off her jacket and tried to breathe deeply.

"Don't they?" Robin said, more uncertain now.

"All this time, he was the one she was running off to meet. He's like his goddamn father. I'd bet he'd fuck anything, just like Roy. But he's not getting my daughter."

Robin took a step back. She refused to believe she had heard Michelle correctly. As a matter of fact, her ears were ringing; she could have easily misunderstood.

"It's up to you to stop him," Michelle said. "I want you to keep him away from Lydia."

Robin looked at Connor's bike, which he'd left near the back gate. Just the other night he suddenly decided he would go see his father, or at least that was what he'd told her. Robin had been so grateful to have that time with Stephen that she hadn't thought to question Connor. But then she'd happened to look outside as he was getting on his bike, and he'd looked so joyful, intoxicated almost, that she'd been thrilled by his youth.

"Did you hear what I said?" Michelle asked. "He's not to see her."

"It's not up to me," Robin said. "I can't stop them."

"You'd better," Michelle told her. "You started it."

"Wait a minute," Robin said. "Are you blaming me?"

"Because you always let Connor get away with murder? You never disciplined him, not ever. And now you're more concerned with who you're screwing than what your son is doing every night. And don't tell me you're not at it with this assistant of yours. I can see right through you."

"We'd better stop." Robin was truly frightened of where this had led them. "Right now."

"Maybe I'd better call Roy," Michelle said. "Maybe what's

going on is statutory rape. This is the sort of thing that runs in families."

"Maybe you'd better fuck yourself."

"Oh," Michelle said, "is that the way it is?"

Robin grabbed her shovel and started to clear away the mulch. Her breathing was coming too hard, but she refused to cry, and all the tears she might have shed went downward, until they formed a lump in her throat so large she couldn't have spoken even if she'd known what to say.

"Okay," Michelle said. "Fine. That's the way it is."

Robin kept shoveling while Michelle got into her car and pulled away. Once, a long time ago, they had painted a sign with tempera on a large piece of pressed wood—NO ONE ALLOWED—and hung it on the trunk of the tree they most loved to climb, the big oak at the back of the estate. For years it did not matter if anyone else in the world existed; no one was allowed past the gates of their friendship. Robin's hands shook as she finished her work, but she kept on going, pulling the hose around the side of the house to wash the last bits of crushed mulch off the driveway. When she saw Connor and Lydia approaching, she turned off the hose and wound it in a circle so it wouldn't get tangled. She knew enough to wait and let them do the talking.

"We were going to tell you," Connor said.

Robin looked at her son and saw how young he was and how little he knew, and she wanted to weep. Instead, she wiped her hands clean on her jeans.

"When?" Robin said. "After your firstborn arrived?"

"You don't have to worry about that," Lydia said. "That's taken care of."

Lydia had always been this way, serious and matter-of-fact. When she was six she had asked Robin how she could stand to touch the bonemeal she fed to her plants.

"Well, I would demand to know who those bones came from," Lydia had said.

Robin had thrown her arms around the girl, and although she felt like doing that now, all she did was nod and say, "That's good."

"My mother's just a bitch," Lydia said. Her face was drawn; she sounded much too harsh and grown-up.

But Robin knew this wasn't the truth; it was simply that Michelle refused to see that not everything made sense, love least of all. In a little while Stephen would be coming back from the market—he had gone off to do Old Dick's weekly shopping, and would drag home the groceries in the two-wheeled cart Ginny had used for marketing before the problem with her legs. Robin's grandfather was extremely pleased with this arrangement, because Stephen always bought two apple pies, the fresh ones, from the bakery aisle, and together he and Stephen had somehow managed to convince Ginny there wasn't a bit of sugar in the recipe. Nothing could be done once people fell in love, really; there was nothing anyone could say. Let a chart be printed up, predicting doom and disaster, and unfurled on the kitchen table. Let it be made out of steel and lead, and still it would burn up like an old piece of parchment. Every time she saw Stephen from her kitchen window, Robin felt some ridiculous, incurable hope inside her. Every time she set out the cobalt-blue dinner plates and the silverware, every time she kissed him, every time she saw the way he looked at her, it happened all over again. Who would choose to stop that? Who would even try?

Lydia and Connor were both staring at Robin, waiting for whatever came next. They looked so nervous, standing there in the driveway, their schoolbooks tucked under their arms, that Robin felt the lump in her throat begin to dissolve.

"Why don't you stay for dinner?" she said to Lydia.

The minute she'd uttered the invitation, she knew that if Connor had been just a little older, or a little younger, he would have thrown his arms around her. As it was, his look of gratitude would have to be enough. All she could hope for was that when it came time for him to judge her, he wouldn't have forgotten what every boy should know. He wasn't the only one who wanted something to last longer than a lifetime. He wasn't the only one who knew how that felt.

SEVEN

FORTY YEARS AGO, GINNY Thorne had believed that her life was already over, and she couldn't have been more glad of it. She'd been cleaning house for Mr. Aaron long enough that the house practically ran itself, and her girls were grown and moved away, and she could finally allow herself to consider how much she would prefer to die rather than continue with this thing that had been given her as a life. She scribbled good-bye notes to her daughters and left her gold necklaces in two white envelopes, with each girl's name printed carefully on the flap to ensure that there'd be no arguing. Every night when she lay down and closed her eyes she said farewell to the earth as she knew it, and every morning when she opened her eyes and found herself still alive she cursed whatever power it was that controlled her fate.

No one who knew her would have ever imagined the depth of her bitterness or guessed that she thought the human race horrid and evil. She played bingo every Thursday night and seemed just as cheerful as always; once a week she took Mr. Aaron's silverware out of the teak storage boxes and polished each fork and spoon, although no one had thought to use them since Mrs. Aaron had died. Had she been asked, all those years back, if she believed in heaven and hell, she would have had to say she supposed she did; at least it was true of hell, because she was condemned to it, of that she was certain.

It was the little things that set her husband off—an apple not quartered correctly, the telephone ringing at suppertime, four rainy days in a row. She never knew what would anger Donald, and she wouldn't know until bedtime—when the girls were at home he'd waited till they'd gone to sleep, growing more furious with each passing hour. He rarely left marks. Instead, he would twist her arm until the bones popped and pull her hair so that it came out in clumps. He would call her names she wouldn't dream of repeating and make her beg for forgiveness—for what, it really didn't matter. Once, he had covered her face with a pillow until she blacked out, and as she did, she assumed that the end had finally come, and she was grateful. When the life rushed back into her, she locked herself in the bathroom and wept.

She might never have fought back if he hadn't come after her up at Mr. Aaron's house. It was a cold, rainy day and she was in the kitchen; she lit a fire in the fieldstone fireplace, which was so large a pine sapling could have fit neatly between the andirons, then set about mopping the floor. Every day before she left for home, she placed Mr. Aaron's dinner on the kitchen table, since he didn't care to eat alone in the dining room. Tonight she had fixed him lamb chops and peas, and she was about to pull the dinner rolls out of the oven when she heard Donald's car coming down the gravel driveway. Only something awful, she knew, would make him come after her here instead of waiting for bedtime. Quickly, she thought of things she might have done wrong, but the list was endless, and by the time he walked through the side door, she'd given up trying to guess.

"You whore." Those were the first words out of Donald's mouth, right there in Mr. Aaron's kitchen.

He began to berate her for leaving the doors in their house unlocked; he'd found them that way when he came home from the hardware store, where he was a clerk, and maybe they'd been left unlocked for a reason. Some man, that's what he was thinking, in spite of the fact that at this point in her life, Ginny wanted nothing whatsoever to do with men. Donald was still good-looking, and he had a polite sort of voice, which made every wicked thing he said feel doubly wounding. But perhaps because the kitchen was larger than their own living room, and the wood in the fireplace popped, hard and loud, like a shotgun, his words seemed more puny than usual.

"This isn't the place," Ginny found herself saying, and to her surprise, she meant it.

"You're telling me what to do?" Donald said. "Is that it?"

This time when he went for her, she moved away instead of simply closing her eyes. Her back was to the hearth and she felt as though her blood were boiling. Years and years later she still remembered the intensity of her single thought: *I will not let him get me fired.*

When Donald grabbed her hair, she reached for the iron poker beside the fireplace; a rush of soot circled toward her and blackened her face. He was pulling the hair right out of her head, and she was thinking that if Mr. Aaron had any idea of what was going on under his roof, he'd get rid of her in a second and then she'd be trapped at home, in a house she had come to despise simply because it belonged to her husband. She was in such a panic thinking of this that she didn't notice when Richard Aaron walked through the kitchen door, drawn by the scent of dinner rolls. By that time Donald had grabbed her around the throat, as if he intended to break her neck, and that was when she hit him with the poker, as hard as she'd ever hit anything in her life.

Donald staggered backward; his head had been smashed open. As he fell to the floor he went for her one last time, grabbing out such a large handful of hair that from that time forward Ginny had a bald spot on the side of her head. By then, the dinner rolls were burned black. Ginny stood exactly where she was, her shoes in a pool of blood, as Richard Aaron went to the phone and called the police. All she could think of was that she had just mopped the floor, and now it was ruined.

"It's Donald Thorne," Richard Aaron told Sam Tenney, George's father, with whom Aaron occasionally played poker. "He's slipped on my wet kitchen floor and managed to crack his head in two."

"I killed him," Ginny said, after Richard Aaron had hung up the phone.

It was a simple self-evident fact, and Donald had always been irritated by the way she stated what was already obvious, but Richard Aaron hadn't seemed to notice there'd been a murder. He ate a blackened dinner roll, then wiped the sooty crumbs off his vest.

"The hell you did," he said. He took the poker out of Ginny's hand and held it in the fire, to burn away the blood, then returned it to its proper place. "He killed himself."

That night Ginny didn't go home. She moved into the

apartment above the garage, thinking it was only temporary, but then, when Mr. Aaron's grandchildren came up from Miami, she stayed on and sold the house she hated, dividing the profit between her two girls. She remained when it became clear that Mr. Aaron's son had lost all his father's fortune, and even after Robin and Stuart had grown up and moved out it didn't seem right just to leave. When the big house began to fall apart and there was no money left to repair the roof and pay for the heating bills, Richard Aaron moved into the carriage house with her, and the fact that he often couldn't pay her weekly salary seemed perfectly natural as well. Through all that, they never said a word about what had happened in the kitchen, even though Ginny knew that her life had started that day. She'd begun to believe in heaven. Each morning when she woke up she found herself awed by the shape of the clouds, the color of the sky, and for that she had no one to thank but Mr. Aaron.

One morning in October she woke with a headache, but she chose to ignore it. Later, when the pain spread to her arm, she knew it was another stroke. She'd had a series of little strokes that she'd failed to mention to anyone, preferring to think of them as blackouts, but this was a bad one. When Old Dick called for his tea, she couldn't answer. When her older daughter, Nancy, phoned, Ginny picked up the receiver, then could make only small croaking sounds, as if she'd been turned into a frog. By evening she was able to convince herself that she was on the mend, but when she brought Old Dick his supper he wasn't so easily fooled.

"I don't like the way you look," he announced.

"Well, that's nothing new," she shot back.

Old Dick asked for the phone, insisting he wanted to call Robin, but in fact he was calling Ginny's daughter. At seven Nancy arrived, and she and Old Dick both decided that the time had come for someone to look after Ginny. Old Dick asked again and again if the nursing home in New Jersey was good enough for Ginny, and her daughter assured him again and again that it was. Ginny's suitcases were packed and brought down to the car. Still she refused to leave. She went into Old Dick's room and locked the door behind her so Nancy wouldn't interfere.

"I'm not ready to retire," Ginny said.

"Fine." Old Dick nodded. "You're fired."

"You could come with me," Ginny said.

"To a nursing home?" Old Dick said. "What do you take me for?"

She took him for the man who had saved her life and now couldn't dress himself or get out of bed.

"I'll die right here," Old Dick said. "And don't worry. It won't be for quite a while."

Ginny went to the side of the bed. She made a funny little sound as she approached him.

"Don't think you're going to kiss me." Old Dick's voice was thin and brittle; he wiped at his eyes, which were teary all the time, just a bit more so now, making his sight blurry. He couldn't really see her face as she leaned over him and kissed his cheek.

"You're a brave girl," he said. "I forgot to tell you that."

And because Ginny knew Old Dick better than anyone else did, she never considered correcting him, although he could not have been more mistaken. He'd already told her exactly that at least a hundred times a day.

The first woman Robin hired told Old Dick in no uncertain terms that she was to have every Sunday off. Her family would be coming on Thursday evenings for supper, she'd have to have cable hooked up to the TV, and she wouldn't tolerate crumbs in the bedsheets or his nasty habit of pounding on the wall when it was time for his tea. He fired her on the spot, and when Robin arrived to see how the new housekeeper was getting on, there was Old Dick alone, munching saltines in bed. The second woman was younger, and nowhere near as bossy; she'd had experience in nursing homes and swore nothing the old man did would faze her. She lasted a weekend, and after she'd gone she sent Robin a dry-cleaning bill; Old Dick had thrown a glass of prune juice right at her, and his aim was still quite good.

Robin had no choice but to take over. She came and fixed Old Dick breakfast, and while he shouted from bed that Ginny would never have put raisins in his oatmeal, Robin vacuumed and rinsed the dishes in the sink, then sat down and phoned everyone on the island who might have a lead on a housekeeper, preferably one who didn't understand English and wouldn't have a clue when she was being baited and cursed. But Old Dick's reputation was such that no one gave her a single referral; there wasn't a soul with the right temperament to care for him, not in this hemisphere, and certainly not for what Robin was able to pay.

When she suggested to her grandfather that he come live with her—a desperate move, really, since she knew they would drive each other insane—he spat on the floor, so that was the end of that. She phoned Connor and had him come over late that afternoon, which would allow her to go see Stuart and discuss a plan of action, however temporary, for Old Dick's care.

"After you take him to the bathroom and sit him down, cover your eyes," Robin warned Connor. "He doesn't like to be watched."

"Mom," Connor said mournfully.

"And don't give him sugar." Robin had recently discovered its effects after leaving a bag of Oreos on her grandfather's night table. He had devoured all the cookies, then told Robin he'd report her to the police if she didn't go out and get him more. "It only makes him worse."

Robin got into her truck and headed for the north beach. The road was covered with fallen leaves; clumps of brilliant goldenrod lined the ditches. That her brother had come to live here, for however brief a time he might stay, still seemed to Robin some sort of joke. A long time back, during their first summer on the island, Robin had persuaded Stuart to come with her to the meadow beyond this beach, to search for earth stars, small puffball mushrooms that curled up in the palm of your hand. He had followed her dolefully, not noticing much, not the chipmunks or the moccasin flowers, not the stretch of poison ivy he meandered through. That night he had had a terrible reaction, in spite of the strong brown soap Ginny made him wash with. He couldn't sleep at all; just the touch of the sheet against his skin was agonizing. Robin had been torn up with guilt for leading Stuart through the woods, and when she heard him crying she went down the hall in her night-gown. To her, so used to the brilliant, harsh colors of Florida, their grandfather's house was particularly dark, especially at night, when she was supposed to be in bed.

Robin walked barefoot along the parquet floor in the hall-way, even though Ginny had taken her out and bought her a pair of bunny slippers, along with new school clothes, and a winter coat and warm pajamas. Robin continued to wear the white nightgown she'd brought along from Miami, though she shivered beneath the thin cotton. The door to her brother's room was open and Robin planned to go in and apologize. In an act of pure courage and solidarity, she intended to touch the raised red rash on his skin and infect herself.

But she never did get to pledge her allegiance to Stuart, or to discover whether poison ivy could be spread by human touch. When she reached his bedroom door she saw that her grandfather had gotten to Stuart's room first. He had spread calamine lotion on the worst of the rash and already Stuart had stopped crying. Stuart was exhausted; he fell asleep as soon as the itching was relieved, but Old Dick pulled up a chair anyway, and he slept beside Stuart's bed the whole night through.

Now, if the gossip Robin had heard was correct, Stuart was acting as though he'd been a naturalist at heart all his life, instead of a boy who despised mosquitoes and slugs. Robin had been down to his shack a few times and had been amazed by how comfortable he seemed; the last time she'd seen him a wasp had been trapped inside the shack, bumping into win-dows and walls, and Stuart had calmly slipped a coffee mug over it, then, with a saucer keeping the wasp in place, tossed it out his front door. When Robin had asked how long Stuart planned to stay on the island, he had hedged, insisting he was only taking a break from real life. But now when she reached the beach she saw that he'd made further improvements: a laundry line had been strung between two pitch pines, the roof had been freshly tarred. Robin walked up the path edged with seashells, knocked just to be polite, then went in to discover Stuart and Kay having tea and brownies, the kind with walnuts that Stuart had always liked.

"This is not what you think," Kay said.

"Not at all," Stuart agreed. He pulled up one of the milk crates he used as chairs and poured some tea for Robin.

"Because, you know, that's the way it seems," Robin said. "You two together. Not that there's anything wrong with it."

"Oh, no." Kay smiled.

"Not what you think," Stuart said warmly.

Robin sat down and eyed the plate of small brown snails in the center of the plank of wood that served as a table. They were moving, slithering along the edge of the china.

"Aren't they fascinating to watch?" Kay said.

"Coffee beans, we used to call them," Stuart reminded Robin.

"That was me," Robin said, indignant. "You didn't call them anything at all. You used to step on them so they wouldn't crawl anywhere near you."

"Well, we call them coffee beans now," Kay said in soothing tones. "That's what matters."

"Here's the problem that we have since Ginny's gone," Robin began.

"I talked to her yesterday," Stuart said. "Phoned her from Kay's house." He neatly cut a brownie into quarters. "She's not quite used to having people do things for her, but it turns out that she's crazy for bingo. Seems she was something of a champ in her youth."

"Did you hear what I said?" Robin cut in. "We have a problem. Old Dick."

"Just because I'm on sabbatical doesn't mean I don't have some cash flow," Stuart said. "I'll pay for another house-keeper or a nurse."

"There's not enough money," Robin said. "It has to be us. We can take turns staying with him."

"That's impossible for Stuart," Kay said. "He can't leave the shack overnight."

"Is this some religious belief," Robin asked her brother, "or just pure selfishness?"

"I'm having a dispute with the county clerk and the town council," Stuart said. "If I leave the premises for more than twenty-four hours I forfeit my rights as a squatter and they'll bulldoze the place." He clapped his hands together. "Boom."

"Never mind that there's a huge colony of coffee beans right under the shack," Kay said hotly. "They don't give a damn about that."

"You won't help." Robin looked at her brother. "That's what you're saying."

"Old Dick and I wouldn't last under the same roof for more than an hour," Stuart said. "You know that."

That it was true made very little difference to Robin. She was now the old man's sole caretaker, and all the way back to the estate she had to concentrate on the road to make certain she wouldn't suddenly turn and head in the opposite direction from Poorman's Point. By the time she got back, it had begun to grow dark, and she worried that she'd left Connor in charge for too long. She'd forgotten to mention that Old Dick liked his supper early, by four-thirty, and that whenever anyone put a plate of noodles in front of him, he'd go berserk and call whoever served him his least favorite food a horse's ass. Since boiled noodles were the one thing Connor knew how to cook for dinner, Robin parked in a hurry and ran up the stairs. Right away she saw that some sort of dinner had been made—the tray was on the hall table—and possibly even enjoyed, since no plates had been broken. The door to the old man's room was ajar and no one was shouting; there wasn't a sound, except for the pages of a book being turned as Stephen read in the chair by the window.

Connor had panicked after less than half an hour; when Stephen came by on his run, he'd found Connor pacing the floor. Old Dick had spilled a glass of orange juice, which he wasn't even supposed to have because of the high fructose, and now he was demanding a bath. Connor was terrified that he'd drop the old man, or that he'd turn for an instant and Old Dick would drown.

"I'm not ready for this," Connor confided in Stephen. "It's like having a baby. But one who curses like you wouldn't believe when you don't do things fast enough."

Connor had been so relieved when Stephen suggested he go home that he'd thrown his fist in the air.

"Yes!" he said. "I owe you," he added as he grabbed for his jacket. "Big."

When Stephen went into the bedroom, Old Dick was

pounding on the wall. He stopped when he saw Stephen, and slipped his glasses on.

"Finally," Old Dick said with a sigh, "they've sent someone reasonable."

Stephen bathed him, then fixed a can of soup for supper, which they ate together in silence as they watched the leaves of the wisteria fall from the arbor to the ground. That was when Stephen decided he would move into Ginny's old room.

"You don't have to do this," Robin said when Stephen came into the hall, closing the door behind him, but not all the way, just in case Old Dick should call out.

Instead of answering, Stephen kissed her, then pulled her toward Ginny's old bedroom.

"I can't," Robin said. "Not here."

Stephen looked at her, confused.

"My grandfather," Robin explained. "He'd be in the next room."

Stephen grinned.

"What?" Robin was flustered.

"He won't know," Stephen said.

"I'd know," Robin insisted.

"All right," Stephen said. "Then we won't."

He would have gone into the kitchen, to make them some coffee, if he hadn't wanted her so much.

"Don't look at me," Robin said. She took a single step backward.

"I have to," Stephen said.

He could look at her for the rest of his life and still not understand her, though he certainly wasn't about to ask why when she suddenly changed her mind. He followed her into

Ginny's bedroom, where the wallpaper was so faded it was nearly impossible to tell there were roses climbing up the wall. He didn't dare ask if she was sure this was what she wanted to do. But as Robin turned down the bed, which Ginny's daughter had made up with fresh sheets before she left, she didn't have a single doubt. As far as she was concerned, her logic was perfect. In order to have him, she could get used to almost anything.

There were only ninety-three days left before Jenny Altero's thirteenth birthday, and that was why she knew exactly how a caterpillar felt trapped inside its chrysalis. She knew just how hard it was to wait for that last transformation, the beating wings, the endless arc of the sky. As she sat in front of a mirror she could see that her face had begun to change: the cheekbones becoming more prominent, the mouth wider, the eyebrows raised, as if in surprise. She slept longer and longer, and often her mother had to shake her awake in the morning. She spent entire afternoons suspended in time, counting off the seconds until her birthday with exquisite precision.

And all the while Jenny waited for that mysterious instant when she would become a teenager, she was carefully studying her sister for clues. Secretly she cultivated the haughty toss of the head Lydia used so effectively when confronted by their mother. She longed to acquire Lydia's self-assured manner and often sat perched on the bathroom counter watching Lydia apply eye pencil with bold strokes.

"Aren't you afraid you'll poke yourself in the eye?" Jenny asked.

"It takes practice," Lydia said. She looked at her sister, something she hadn't bothered to do for quite a while, and was surprised to see that in no time at all Jenny would actually be pretty. "Here," Lydia said. "Let me do you."

Jenny obediently closed her eyes and tilted her head back. She could smell her sister's shampoo as Lydia leaned over her, and she thought Lydia would never notice if she started to use it, too.

"What a difference," Lydia said, when she was done. "Wow."

Jenny looked in the mirror and blinked. Her eyes looked twice as big.

"Let's really do you," Lydia said, and Jenny was so thrilled by her sister's attention that she sat motionless for nearly twenty minutes as Lydia applied lip liner and blush, then French-braided Jenny's hair in the style that Lydia herself often favored. When she had finished, Lydia made Jenny keep her back to the mirror, then slowly turned her to face her reflection.

"I'm beautiful," Jenny said, completely surprised.

"I wouldn't go that far," Lydia said. She checked her own reflection to make certain it was still superior in every way. "But you really do look fantastic," she graciously admitted, and seeing the gratitude on her little sister's face, Lydia gave her a hug.

"Better not let Mom catch you," Lydia advised. "She'll ground you for the rest of your life."

Still, Jenny decided not to wash the makeup off, not yet. It was late enough that she could sneak into her room, and before her mother came to say good night, she made certain all the lights were off. As soon as her mother had gone out of the room, Jenny got out of bed and grabbed a flashlight. She rummaged through her dresser drawer until she found a pair of dangling earrings she had swiped from Lydia's jewelry box. She pulled on Lydia's white sweater. At a quarter to eleven she heard the front door open, then close. She went to the window and watched Lydia run to meet Connor; it was a clear night and Jenny could see them perfectly. As soon as they headed down Mansfield Terrace, their arms around each other's waist, Jenny opened her window; she climbed out and dropped to the ground. She followed them all along Cemetery Road, far enough behind to ensure that Lydia and Connor weren't the least bit suspicious, but close enough to hear bits of their conversation. She wanted to know how a girl talked to a boy when they were in love. Did she reach for a boy's hand first, or wait till he came to her? When he kissed her, should she back away or throw her arms around him and hold him tight? Did she ever admit how she really felt, or was it best simply to act scornful when he swore that his heart was breaking in two?

There was a full moon that night, and the fallen leaves along the road looked as if they were made of gold. The air was cool, but Lydia's white sweater kept Jenny warm. She almost felt that she was the one who was in love; her heart raced and the stars in the sky seemed unusually bright. Before she knew it, they had reached Poorman's Point. Jenny hid behind a pine tree as Connor tried to jimmy open the lock of an abandoned storage shed. Lydia laughed when he had trouble with the lock, and Connor pretended to be angry; he chased her until she threw back her head and said she gave up, although it was clear from the look on Connor's face that he was the one who had given up. And suddenly they were all over each other; some force had pulled them together. They were kissing each other in a way Jenny had never seen before, and that was when she realized how cold she was, wearing only her sister's thin sweater. Connor turned and Lydia kept her arms around him; she pressed up against him as he fought with the lock and finally opened the door to the shed. By then Lydia had slipped her hand into his jeans, and Connor bowed his head, as if he were in pain, as if he couldn't wait.

Jenny wasn't ready to see this. She wouldn't even be thirteen for three more months. She turned right then and ran, tripping over bushes and stones, frightened by her own shadow. All at once, Poorman's Point seemed a very long way from home. There were clouds in the sky she hadn't noticed before. She hadn't paid attention to the path when she'd followed Lydia and Connor, and now it seemed to loop around in a confusing way; she kept passing the same spot, getting nowhere at all. At last she found the road. Somewhere a dog kept in its kennel was howling and a night heron answered the call. Jenny crossed her fingers on both hands. If she made it back home, she wouldn't be such a sneak anymore. When she reached Cemetery Road she should have been relieved; she always took this route in the summer on her way home from the town recreation program, where she taught kids how to weave belts and key chains out of plastic rope. But now the idea of walking past the graveyard this late at night made her stomach lurch. She held her breath and kept going; she didn't have a choice.

When some headlights came up behind her, Jenny felt herself panic completely. If she hadn't turned and recognized Robin's truck pulling up alongside her, she would have run right into the cemetery to hide. Robin swung the door of the pickup open and Jenny quickly climbed inside.

"Does your mother know you're out here?" Robin asked. She was on her way home from being with Stephen, and she felt somehow exposed, as though she were the one who'd been caught breaking curfew. Most nights she went out before supper, taking charge of her grandfather while Stephen went running, and often she didn't go home until after midnight.

Jenny shrugged and looked straight ahead; she was still shivering.

"I take it that means no," Robin said. "You know it's dangerous and stupid. I don't have to tell you that. Right?"

"Right," Jenny agreed. "Incredibly stupid."

"I thought you were Lydia," Robin said as they turned onto Mansfield Terrace.

"Really?" Jenny looked over at Robin, pleased, then saw the concern on Robin's face. She wasn't out of trouble yet. "Don't tell my mother," Jenny begged. "Please."

They'd pulled into Robin's driveway and they both looked over at the Altero house; all the windows were dark, as if everyone were safely asleep in bed.

"Since your mother's not talking to me, I can't tell her anything, can I?" Robin said. "Just don't let me catch you doing this again."

"I won't," Jenny said.

She hugged Robin, then opened the door and jumped out. She ran all the way home, and by the time she climbed in her window she was giddy with her own success. Already, Jenny couldn't remember how afraid she had been to pass by the cemetery, or why she had begun to run home in the first place. She looked at herself in the mirror and felt very grown-up; her cheeks were pink with excitement. The moon was just outside her window, as though it had followed her home. She lay down on her bed and tried her best to stay awake until Lydia came home, but by midnight she was fast asleep, still wearing her sister's white sweater, which, she had already decided, she wouldn't be returning anytime soon.

Where he came from, October was the time of frost. Twilight arrived earlier and was a deeper blue; ice crystals formed on the surface of the shallow ponds in the morning, owls called at odd hours. It was a bad time to be a wolf: men came into the woods, and they weren't there to see the sky change color or to watch the ice form. They weren't there to listen to the owls in the trees.

Trappers moved quietly and they knew what they were looking for, but in October the hunters came, ready to shoot at almost anything. They would take down deer or moose, beavers or wood ducks; occasionally, they would shoot each other. Once, Stephen found a man before anyone else could get to him. The man's friends, the ones who had shot him accidentally, were convinced they had gotten a bear, which they intended to let bleed to death before they followed its trail. So the hunter died by himself in a clearing, and Stephen watched, shivering, as he did. After the hunter had stopped breathing,

Stephen slowly approached; he crouched down beside him, even though he knew he should run. He had never seen anything like this close up before, not since he'd come here, and he had a knotted feeling inside his stomach. The face seemed too much like the one he saw when he had knelt down to drink from the clear pool. He backed away from the man; he refused to be like this thing. He didn't care what he saw. He didn't care if he needed to run on two legs, because when he went flat-out and felt the wind against him he might just as well have been running on all fours.

He had difficulty catching his breath in that clearing; there was the acrid smell of gunpowder and human flesh. It made perfect sense to avoid men; they all knew what could happen if you didn't. One October, when Stephen wasn't more than eleven or twelve, they had failed. The pack was big then, fifteen, including yearlings and that spring's pups. It was a good season for deer, and they may have been lazier than usual; the afternoons were still warm enough to lie in the sun, especially if your belly was full. The men came against the wind, but that was only one reason they were at an advantage. These hunters carried rifles with telescopic sights, expensive things they had bought in Detroit, with enough scope and power to get a hit before their scent was picked up.

The oldest wolf was shot first. He was ancient, nearly eighteen; for several years he'd had to eat the meat regurgitated for pups. Three of his toes had been chewed off by a steel trap; two of his ribs had been badly broken, years before, during an encounter with a moose. They could hear the instant of his death, and it took just another instant to know what they had to do. Before the old wolf had collapsed to the ground, the rest of them were running. They ran as one creature with a single mind, except for two reckless pups who panicked and headed for the open field and were shot straightaway. The others took off through the woods, where it was harder to be tracked and, if they got far enough away, nearly impossible for a man to see through the trees.

More of them fell before they reached the deepest part of the woods, and those who were left ran so hard and fast they barely touched the earth. One minute Stephen was with them completely, blood pounding in his ears, skin torn by brambles and low branches, and the next he could no longer see even the most awkward yearling's tail. They had disappeared right in front of him. There were no paw prints, no trail, just the trees that grew on top of each other, blocking out the light from above. The men were still coming, he knew that, and because he could not escape by running, Stephen had no choice but to go upward. This was a skill that amazed his brothers; they often ringed a tree when he climbed it, barking or making confused little yelps. Now, he threw himself at the tallest pine and hauled himself into the branches. He scrambled higher and higher, quickly, tearing the skin off his palms as he grabbed at the wood. He went farther than he'd ever been before, up where the owls nested, and he didn't stop until he had reached the sky.

They came so close that he could hear their voices: ugly, rough sounds that made him feel sick. He could smell their sweat and their smoke; they were clumsy as they navigated through the thick growth of trees, and the earth shuddered beneath their feet. Stephen was not nearly as foolish as the pups had been. He did what he'd been taught to do: he didn't move a muscle, not even when his arms and legs were riddled with cramps from hanging on to the tree. He slowed his heart-beat until it was quiet as a mouse's. Had the men thought to look up, they would have believed he was a piece of wood, a twisted branch set perilously high. Long after the hunters had gone, Stephen stayed where he'd found safety; he was there all through the night. He could see every star from where he was perched; the moon was so close he might have been able to touch it, had he been willing to let go of the branch he had wrapped himself around, even for an instant. At dawn he heard the wolves calling for him, and when he answered, the sound of his own voice sent a chill through his body. It seemed to him that a single voice was the saddest sound on earth, far worse than the thud the old wolf's body had made when it col-lapsed to the ground.

By the first light they had found him; they circled the tree, and because they had run hard they left a ring of bloody paw prints. Counting Stephen, there were only eight of them left; the bodies of the rest had been tied up and dragged through the woods, back to the men's camp, all except for the old wolf, who hadn't seemed much of a trophy once the men examined him. From the arms of the tree where Stephen had hidden all night, the ground seemed much too far away. He was afraid to come down, as if all his terror had been released now that the danger was past. From somewhere inside him he remembered pictures in a book: a long-tailed animal had chased a sparrow into a tree but then was too frightened to come back down. Men in a big red truck had to come to the rescue. *Ding, ding* went their bell. *Clack, clack* went their ladders.

The wolves started calling to him from down below, with

such clear, strong voices that he found he had more courage than he had believed. He climbed down slowly, carefully, in a hail of pine needles that smelled incredibly sweet. When he reached the ground, the wolves who were left rushed him; they bumped against him, and took his hands in their mouths, making sure the scent of the men was off before they went any farther into the woods.

By the time he came face to face with the dead man, he was a man himself. That is, he had reached his full height and weight and was as fast as he would ever be. If he couldn't quite keep up with his brothers, he could do a good job trying, so that he almost never lost sight of them. He traveled with his three brothers, the ones he had raised when the big dog died. They had broken away from the other wolves because they were an efficient team, especially now that Stephen used a sharpened rock to make up for his inferior claws and teeth. Each of them knew exactly what the others thought and felt; the biggest of them was the leader, but it was a mild leadership, since there were few disputes or conflicts. Of all his brothers, this big silver wolf was the one Stephen loved best. They slept close together on cold nights, and in the summer they pulled brown ticks out of each other's skin. Sometimes they went hunting alone, just the two of them, and they never had to exchange signals. Each knew what the other wanted, completely, as if they shared one mind.

Sitting in the clearing with the dead man, Stephen felt much too far from his brothers. It wasn't just loneliness, it was more than that: the sight of the dead man had somehow removed him from who and what he was. He couldn't take his eyes off the dead man's rifle; he reached for it, but as soon as he touched it he had to drop it again. It had burned right through his flesh. He might still have been crouched beside the body when the hunter's friends finally tracked down their counterfeit bear, if the silver wolf hadn't come for him. Stephen knew he was there before he saw him, and when he looked up, his brother was there on the edge of the clearing. His winter coat was coming in and he seemed huge, though he couldn't have been more than ninety pounds. Still, Stephen was unable to move; he rocked back and forth on his heels, grieving for something he had never seen or had or been.

The silver wolf came into the clearing then, slowly, because of the gunpowder stench. He stood beside Stephen, and although he could smell the scent of men, he began to sing. Stephen closed his eyes and leaned his head back; he heard his own voice join with his brother's. All that day, Stephen's brother kept close to him, and by evening Stephen was no longer thinking about the man he had found; although from then on, whenever he bent beside still water to drink, he closed his eyes so that he could not see what he was.

Sometimes, now, when he dressed Richard Aaron, or when he bathed him, Stephen realized that the old man was about ninety pounds, the same weight as a full-grown wolf. But Old Dick was six feet tall and so gaunt his bones poked through his skin. When he was lifted from his bed, he seemed to fold up, like a piece of paper. Ninety pounds of muscle and heart could be unstoppable, but all that was left of Old Dick was the heart, wrapped inside a miserable bundle of flesh. Touch him with one finger and he'd bruise. Leave the window open, just the slightest bit, on a cool October night, and he'd cough for days afterward. As the twilight came earlier, Stephen spent more time sitting beside the old man, but there was no longer much of a reason to read to him, and often they didn't even speak. There were times when Stephen felt certain that Old Dick was sleeping, but no, his eyes were open; he was calmly watching the shadows on the wall.

"Looks like a giraffe, doesn't it?" Old Dick said once, in such a strong, pleasant voice that Stephen was completely confused until he saw the shape the lamp cast on the other side of the room.

One afternoon, when the light was cool and bright, Stephen went into the kitchen to fix their lunch, and when he returned he found Old Dick crying. All at once Stephen realized what had been happening during those hours when they didn't speak: he had been learning how to tell what it was Old Dick wanted just by looking at him. That he should ever know a man as well as he knew one of his brothers was disturbing, but it was also a simple fact. Stephen put their plates of soup down on the night table, then bundled Old Dick in a blanket, the heaviest one he could find, and carried him downstairs. It was nothing to carry him. Stephen felt he could have gone on forever, but he stopped in the center of the lawn, where a pile of scarlet leaves was scattered on the grass. This was all Old Dick wanted, to see the sky, not through glass but as it truly was, a blue dome so brilliant it could bring tears to a man's eyes.

EIGHT

THE DOCTOR PASSED RIGHT
by his son one windy day and didn't even recognize him. He
truly didn't know him, his one and only boy, not until Roy
reached out and grabbed him by the arm.

"What's wrong with you?" the Doctor said.

"Me?" Roy said. "You're the one walking around in a daze."

"The hell I am," the Doctor said.

He was hopping mad, and the wind didn't sit right with
him; it was a foul sort of wind, with a yellow edge to it. Before
evening the thin branches of young crab apple and peach trees
would begin to snap off with sulfurous pops. Just the sort of
thing earwigs and beetles would search out in the spring, and
once they found their way into a fruit tree the damage couldn't
be reversed.

"Did you take my advice? Did you even try to get her
back?" The Doctor had to shout against the wind; the collar of
his coat flapped against his neck.

Roy grinned and cupped one hand over his ear. "What?"
he said.

The Doctor eased up and smiled in spite of himself. He clapped Roy on the back. "Idiot," he said.

They decided to go over to Fred's for coffee, even though Roy was on duty and the Doctor had been set to go home and put up his storm windows.

"You warned me," Roy said, once they were settled in a booth. "I got married too young."

"Yeah, well, you're getting divorced too young, too," the Doctor said. Then he ordered a plate of hash and a black coffee.

"I'll have a Poland Spring water," Roy told the waitress. "So?" he said, when he saw the Doctor's look of contempt. "I'm more health-conscious now than I used to be."

"Next thing you'll tell me is that you're a vegetarian." The Doctor laughed. "No," he said when Roy looked away, embarrassed. "Not you. Robin drove you crazy with all that brown rice."

"Maybe she was right," Roy said. "Maybe I was a total fucking blockhead."

"Now there you go," the Doctor said, appraising his hash as it was set in front of him. "That's something we can agree on." He began to eat, far more pleased than he'd expected to be. "The question is, what are you going to do about it?"

Roy laughed out loud. His father was a great guy, but there were some things he just didn't get. He was what George Tenney called a black-or-white man: Right or wrong. Do it or shut up about it. Not a single shade of gray. Those sorts of clear-cut choices weren't so easy for Roy, not now. He had kept on seeing Julie Wynn for a while after Robin threw him out. Why shouldn't he? Julie was pretty, and a good, easy fuck, never asking for anything like a commitment. The only problem was that as soon as he could have another woman he didn't want her. Just knowing that, that he'd been playing some kind of game with himself, unnerved him. Everything seemed suspect, including his own feelings. He hadn't even realized that he was in love with Robin until Stephen reminded him that she was no longer his wife. Then he remembered why he'd wanted her in the first place, and why he wanted her still.

"I'm not doing anything about it," Roy finally said to his father. "Pretty much what you expected."

The Doctor put down his fork and pushed his plate away. "You know what every father tells his son eventually?" He placed his hands flat on the table. "I wish you'd listened to me. Just once."

The Doctor looked so serious that Roy felt like reaching out for his father's hand. Instead, he poured himself more Poland Spring.

"That hash is going to harden your arteries, and then you won't remember whether I took your advice or not."

"Here comes your just reward," the Doctor said. "Sooner or later he'll put you through the wringer. Then you'll understand me."

The Doctor nodded out the window and Roy turned to see Lydia and Connor walking toward the diner, their arms around each other. Roy knew all about this. Michelle had called him a while ago, nearly hysterical, demanding that he do something, and quick.

"What do you want me to do?" he'd said. "Give them a term in federal prison for kissing in the school hallways?"

Michelle had then accused him of being a neglectful father

and a Casanova and a few other things, too. He'd tried his best to calm her down and promised to have a talk with Connor, but whenever he and Connor got together, he didn't know what to say.

"I hear you've got a girlfriend."

That was his brilliant lead-in, one night when they'd met at McDonald's for a quick dinner.

"Yeah," Connor said warily.

"Pretty," Roy had said.

"Excuse me?" Connor had been unwrapping his hamburger, and maybe he hadn't heard over the crinkling paper, or maybe he couldn't imagine Lydia's being reduced to one trivial word.

"Lydia. She turned out to be pretty."

"Oh, yeah," Connor had said, desperate to drop the subject. "Really."

What Roy had wanted to say, and didn't, wasn't anything that would have pleased Michelle. *Don't get hurt*. That was it. *Don't let yourself get hurt by this*.

In the past few months Roy had been floored by just how dangerous life was. Amazing that he had never noticed it before, since he was often the one who arrived on the scene first when there was a car accident or when a fisherman's boat washed up on the beach, empty except for some netting and bait. He could have blood on his hands and still calmly write out his reports. It was possible to do this by compartmentalizing everything into puzzle pieces: the skids on the road, the height of the tides, the human beings who happened to be in the way. Once someone started to think, he was in big trouble, and that's what had happened to Roy. Maybe it had begun when he started living alone and had too much free time; but whatever it was, it was getting worse.

Last Tuesday, he and George had had to go down to Poorman's Point on a miserable mission. A group of boys playing King of the Mountain had stumbled upon a mass grave filled with animal carcasses. Two of the kids were hysterical, the others appeared to be in shock. None of them was any older than nine, and they all seemed to feel responsible, the way people did sometimes when they were unfortunate enough to be the first to discover something unspeakable.

Roy gave all the boys lollipops to settle their stomachs, and after George threw a tarp over the grave, they drove the children home, then spoke with their parents, warning them about the nightmares most of the boys might be having that night. They drove back to the Point in silence, got some shovels out of the storage shed, then set to work lifting the carcasses onto the tarp so they could be taken to the animal hospital and destroyed properly. Some of the animals had been there for months and were nothing more than skeletons; others were not yet decomposed. Most were cats, but there was one that seemed to have been a large dog; some were birds that could now be identified only by the piles of feathers that were left. The birds had been strangled; everything else had had its throat slit. At the top of the pile were three baby raccoons set in a row; their paws looked so human that Roy went over behind the shed and threw up. When he came back, George offered him a piece of gum.

"The work of a sick mind," George said grimly.

"How do people get this way?" Roy wondered.

George shook his head, not understanding that Roy really

wanted an answer. Roy had been pacing, but now he stood directly in front of George. He was so wound up he felt as if he might explode.

"How the hell do they get this way?" he demanded.

"Jesus, Roy, I don't know," George said. "Take it easy."

"Yeah," Roy agreed. "You're right."

They took the whole mess over to the animal hospital, knowing as they did that they'd probably never find out who had done this. Roy wrote up the report, and that was the end of it. Except he kept thinking about those raccoons and the way their hands were closed up tight. They reminded him of Connor; when Connor was a baby he would grab on to Roy's finger and hold on with all his might. Roy and Robin used to laugh about it and call him Superbaby. There were too many things that could go wrong, too many ways a boy could get hurt. Looking out the window of the diner, seeing his son out there with Lydia, Roy felt a moment of relief. Connor, he saw, was truly happy, at least for today, standing in the wind, grinning as he listened to everything the girl he loved had to say.

"They call it puppy love," Roy said to his father as they fought over the bill, which Roy finally managed to get hold of.

"You were just about the same age when you started going with Robin," the Doctor reminded him after they got up to leave. "I'd say that turned out to be pretty serious."

Connor opened the door for Lydia, without noticing that his father and grandfather were approaching. Today, for the first time, he and Lydia had talked about their future—not just tomorrow and the next day, but their whole lives. They'd been tentative at first, both afraid to admit what they hoped for until they knew the other hoped for exactly the same thing.

They would spend their lives together; they had vowed that on the corner of the town green, and kissed each other twenty times, and then found themselves too shy to speak. Lydia finally suggested they celebrate, and they'd come to Fred's for Cokes and French fries and a warm place to hold hands under the table. Connor had turned to look for a booth in the back, when Lydia nudged him.

"Relative alert," she whispered.

"Hey there, buddy," Roy said as he came up to them. "Hey, Lydia."

Connor mumbled something no one could hear, but Lydia smiled brightly at Roy, then turned to the Doctor.

"I'll bet this wind is murder on any saplings you put in this summer," she said.

"Precisely." The Doctor was impressed. "Hold on to this one," he suggested to Connor. He elbowed Roy. "Come on. They don't want old farts like us around."

"Speak for yourself," Roy shot back.

Roy could see that Connor couldn't take his eyes off this girl. When she laughed and headed for a rear booth, Connor began to follow as if she were a magnet. The boy had it so bad Roy would have laughed out loud if he hadn't remembered exactly how it felt. And maybe that was why Roy grabbed Connor's arm, even though he knew he wouldn't be able to say what he wanted to. The best he could do was pull his son close as he handed him a twenty-dollar bill.

"My treat," Roy told Connor. He was glad that his own father was out of hearing, because he would have really enjoyed this one. "Just don't run off and get married," Roy advised his son.

In the middle of the month, when the moon turned orange and every windowpane was thick with frost, Richard Aaron dreamed he was alone in the woods. He didn't recognize the sort of trees that grew here, huge dark things with trunks large enough for a man to hide in and roots so coiled it was impossible to find secure footing. He was walking fast and his breath came hard; it was amazing that he had this much strength in his arms and legs. It was impossible, and yet it was true. Something had happened to him. He removed his thick leather gloves and discovered that his hands were no longer bony and twisted. He touched his forehead and found that the skin was smooth. He called out just to hear his own voice, and there it was: a bellow edged with the pride of a young man, a truly beautiful noise.

He walked on, over the hard earth, the frozen pine needles breaking beneath his boots. He was lost, he knew that much, just as he knew he had to go forward. The birds above him were calling, signaling the end of the day. Soon he would no longer be able to see, and he had to hurry through the woods. As he went on he grew younger and stronger; he could snap the branches blocking his way with his bare hands, he could leap over the gray rocks that littered the path. He was much younger than he had been the day he got married; his full height had come back to him and his hair was dark brown, a chestnut color the girls had all admired.

Richard Aaron went on through the woods, and finally he reached what he'd been searching for, the white horse that was waiting for him. The horse was so white his eyes hurt just to look at it, but he couldn't look away, not now, not after he'd come this far. He stopped at the edge of the clearing, out of breath and terrified. He knew he would have to ride this thing, a horse twice as big as any he'd seen before, but first he'd have to catch it. He tried edging up to the horse slowly, but the horse whinnied and backed away, tossing its huge head. Richard Aaron kept walking forward, slowly and gently, but the horse grew agitated and began to trot away. That was when Richard Aaron knew why he'd been granted these legs; he'd have to chase this horse down. He'd have to run for it one last time.

He followed the white horse through the woods as darkness fell; several times he was close enough to grab on to its tail, but the horse always pulled away. At last they came to an open field, where the grass was as high as Richard Aaron's waist, and he knew this was his last chance to do this right. The horse was galloping now, black hooves shaking the ground. It was breathing smoke in the cold, dark air, challenging Richard Aaron to race. He was as fast and as strong as he'd ever been. He ran with all his heart, and the wind followed along behind, slapping against his back. Straight ahead was an even deeper wood, with trees impossibly tangled and black; he would never be able to catch the horse once they entered that forest. He had to do it now, in this field, where the grass whipped against him and smelled sweeter than any lawn he had ever walked across. With his last, best effort he came up beside the horse, keeping pace, but that was not enough and he knew it.

And then Richard Aaron realized that there was a man running beside him, a young man, like himself, whose face was filled with concern. This young man had no trouble keeping up with the horse; he would have run right past, if he hadn't slowed his pace to talk to Richard Aaron.

"Are you all right?" the young man said. He spoke as if it were the most natural thing in the world for them to be running alongside the horse. He wasn't even sweating.

Richard Aaron was too out of breath to speak. The horse's legs were much stronger than his; in the dark the horse looked like a cloud.

"Are you all right?" the young man continued to ask.

There was the moon, shining through the window. There was the wood, looming just ahead.

"Help me up," Richard Aaron shouted over the sound of the hooves hitting against the earth. "Just help me up."

Stephen grabbed onto Richard Aaron's hand and held on tight.

"That's it," Richard Aaron called as the young man lifted him onto the horse. It was the instant before they reached the endless woods, and quite suddenly the field was green, and it went forever, forever and ever, and because the horse would now do anything Richard Aaron told it to except turn back, he never had the chance to say thank you.

They buried Old Dick the day before Thanksgiving, in the spot he'd chosen himself when he first came to the island. Nearly everyone in town came out to the cemetery, in spite of the sleet that was falling. The ice was so stubborn the gravediggers had been forced to work all morning just to loosen the top layer of dirt. Every shop in town was closed that day, except for the market—since people still had to pick up their fresh-killed turkeys—although the butcher cried as he wrapped each of the birds in waxed paper. He remembered when Old Dick had been his best customer, he remembered when Ginny Thorne would come in and smack each lamb chop before she bought it, to make certain it was fresh enough for Old Dick.

Robin wore her black dress to the funeral, the one with the silver buttons. She combed her hair and put it up neatly with clips shaped like stars. The only good coat she had was meant for spring, but it was black and would just have to do. Of course she'd known this day would come—how long could someone live, after all—and yet she could not truly believe it was Old Dick inside the coffin. The box seemed absurdly small, much too small to ever contain him. Robin stood with Connor on one side of her and Stuart on the other, with Kay beside him, her arm hooked through his. Connor's face was pale and he looked reed-thin; Stuart may have been crying, but it was difficult to tell—his shack was so chilly, even with the insulation he'd put in, that his nose was red most of the time.

After the service, they took turns shoveling the frozen earth back into the grave. A chair had been brought to the gravesite so that Ginny would not have to stand. Her daughters hadn't wanted to drive her down from New Jersey, they'd said it was bad for her health and pointless besides, but Ginny had insisted. She clutched her purse and was completely composed, gracefully accepting people's sympathies, but when they started to shovel the dirt over Old Dick's coffin she began to weep, and her grief was strong enough to chase the sparrows from the trees.

"That's the end, isn't it?" Ginny said.

Robin went to her and hugged her, then reached into her coat pocket for the tissues no one in the family had used. Ginny blew her nose, but her tears continued to fall and each tear melted a little hole in the ice on the ground.

"There won't be another like him," Ginny said, and nobody could argue with that.

Just before Ginny's daughters took her home, claiming it was too much of a strain for her to go back to Kay's house for supper, Roy walked them to their car. Robin came up beside him as he handed Ginny's daughter the bankbook Old Dick's attorney had given him. In the years before his fortune had been lost, Old Dick had set some money aside in an account he never touched, not even when he no longer had any accounts of his own. It was all in Ginny's name—thirty-seven thousand dollars. Robin was furious, not because Old Dick had left Ginny the bank account, certainly she deserved that, but because the attorney had gone over Old Dick's will with Roy. As soon as they were alone, Robin turned on Roy, even though Connor and Stuart were already waiting for her in Kay's car.

"You're not even related," she told Roy.

"Look, Robin, if you're going to argue, you're going to have to do it with a dead man. Old Dick's lawyer called me, not the other way around. It turns out he made me his executor."

"He never would have done that."

"But he did," Roy said. "Go figure."

Actually, Roy hadn't been very surprised when the attorney phoned him. Years ago, when Connor was a baby and they'd all gone over to Old Dick's for dinner, the old man had taken Roy aside.

"You're in the business," Old Dick had said. "Take a look at this."

He went through his desk and pulled out a Dade County police report that was more than fifteen years old.

"Robin's father," Old Dick had said—an odd choice of words, since the suicide the report covered was also his son.

Roy had looked the report over carefully, then handed it back. As far as he could tell, there'd been no foul play; it seemed a simple enough report, one he could have filled out in under ten minutes if he'd been assigned the case.

"I think about it every day," Old Dick had said. "But of course that's what they want you to do when they're gone. Wonder why." Old Dick returned the file to his desk drawer. "So what's your opinion?" he had asked Roy. "Why would he do it?"

Roy felt extremely uncomfortable, not only because he now knew details Robin had been spared—that her father had shot himself on a Tuesday, for example, that he hadn't even bothered to leave a note—but also because Old Dick, who Roy knew despised him, was now looking to him for an answer.

"I don't have all the facts," Roy had begun.

"Come on. Come on," Old Dick had insisted. "Your best guess."

"He was miserable," Roy finally ventured.

"You're absolutely right," Old Dick had agreed after some consideration. "He was."

It had taken all this time for Roy to figure out why Old Dick had turned to him on such a private matter. He hadn't understood until the attorney's call on the evening of the old man's death.

"Looks like he trusted me," Roy told Robin.

"Just goes to show how anyone can make a mistake," Robin said.

Kay honked her horn; the mourners would be arriving at her house before she had time to set out the buffet.

"Go on," Robin called to Kay. "I'll walk."

The gravediggers were still at work, cursing the sleet. Old Dick would have been pleased to know he'd managed to cause one last hard time.

"I never thought he'd go," Robin said. "Remember when he poured a pitcher of ice on your head?"

When Robin was sixteen and they still lived in the big house, she always refused to have sex with Roy there. Even when he begged and swore there were so many rooms—the attic, for instance, the little pantry Ginny never bothered with, the all-but-forgotten guest room on the third floor, used for nothing more than storing an old sewing machine—they'd never be found, Robin couldn't bring herself to do it right there, in the house. She would sneak out her window, climbing down the arbor meant for wisteria. Roy would wait for her, near the kitchen door, shifting his weight from foot to foot, clapping his hands together when it was especially cold, hidden, they assumed, from sight. Old Dick had found out soon enough—how, they never knew—and he stationed himself at an upstairs window with the ice water. Although they had never discussed it, Robin had always been certain she'd heard him laughing when Roy, drenched and freezing, yowled like a cat caught by the tail.

"I guess he liked your new boyfriend a whole lot better than he ever liked me," Roy said. He sounded calm, but the muscles in his jaw betrayed him; they pulsed the way they always did when he was upset. "He left him the rest of his estate. Nothing for Connor or for Stuart. Nothing for you."

"There was nothing to leave," Robin said.

"The carriage house. And enough cash to cover the taxes for the next few years. He used his mattress as a bank. I slit it open last night. No wonder he had trouble sleeping. It was the lumpiest mattress I've ever seen."

"And I'll bet you've seen lots," Robin said before she could stop herself.

"Robin." Roy shook his head and looked up at the sky; the sleet had let up, but the air was iron-gray and cold. Some things, Roy figured, still had to be paid for long after they were found to be worthless. "The cash is in an escrow account. But you and Stuart have a perfect right to the carriage house if you want to contest the will. Old Dick had it drawn up last month, and believe me, no one in town will vouch for his sanity."

Robin turned to walk down the path that led to the cemetery gates. She was wearing black high heels, which made navigating on the ice difficult; she raised her arms for balance, like an acrobat.

"It doesn't bother you?" Roy said. He had come up beside her, but he kept his hands in his pockets to make certain he wouldn't be tempted to reach out and grab her. "You don't feel like you've been cheated?"

The night before, when Roy went to the carriage house to collect the money hidden in the mattress, he and Stephen had been careful to avoid each other. But as he was leaving, Roy couldn't hold himself back.

"This place is yours now," he'd told Stephen. "Looks like you got everything you wanted. Congratulations."

Now, as he walked beside Robin, Roy still couldn't let it go. "Is it fair that it all goes to a stranger?" he asked her.

"You don't understand anything," Robin said.

She wished the weather were better; it was much harder leaving someone behind when the ground was so cold. She'd begun to think ridiculous things: that she should have left a blanket, that someone should have stayed, just so Old Dick wouldn't be all alone.

"Explain it," Roy said. There was something different in his voice, which made Robin turn to him. "Go on," Roy said. "Explain it to me."

The fact was, Robin admired Old Dick's honesty. Why should he bother with niceties after he was dead, when he'd never bothered before? He did what he wanted, always. When she was younger, Robin would have ascribed this to pure selfishness, but now she wasn't so sure. Who, after all, had made his bed and washed his sheets, cooked his supper and shaved him every morning? Who had sat beside him at the very last moment?

"I can't explain it," Robin said. "Not to you."

They had reached the cemetery gates, which opened out to the road. The gates were wrought-iron, ordered from a blacksmith in Albany.

"Well, I feel cheated," Roy said. "I was supposed to get you."

After that, there was nothing left to say. They walked down

Cemetery Road as the twilight turned the ice blue. Once, Roy almost reached out when Robin slipped on the road, but he thought better of it. She didn't want that, and he knew it. Walking beside her, on the way to Kay's, he thought that some loose talk he'd heard in a bar once really was true, in spite of its dubious source. The first person you fucked had a hold on you forever. The first person you fell in love with, you could never escape. If it turned out this was the same person, you were done for, and that was what had happened to him.

"You're not coming in for supper?" Robin asked when Roy stopped at Kay's driveway. The house was already full of people Old Dick had despised; Kay had ordered platters of cold cuts and good scotch, the kind Old Dick would have appreciated. "Are you sick?" Robin asked when she saw the look on Roy's face.

"You didn't deny it when I called him your boyfriend," Roy said.

"I'm not fighting with you," Robin said. She was shivering in her light spring coat. She was much too tired for this. "Not today."

"Don't expect me to make it easy for you," Roy told her. "That's all I'm saying."

"Are you threatening me?" Robin said. "Because that's what it sounds like, Roy."

"No, I'm not. That is not what I'm doing." He really looked at her now. "And you know it."

What he was doing was actually a hundred times worse. He was telling her that he loved her, something he hadn't mentioned and may not even have known when they were married. She used to whisper it to him sometimes, while he was fucking her, and he had to turn off his mind every time she did that. For some reason that declaration had seemed like a curse to him back then; he couldn't even hear it spoken aloud.

"Forget it, Roy," Robin said. She wrapped her coat around herself. "You can't do this to me. I'm not going to feel guilty about wanting more than we could ever have. Those days are over."

Inside, Lydia was watching from the window as Roy threw his hands up in defeat. He'd left his car parked at the cemetery just to accompany Robin to Kay's, and now he'd have to make that long walk back alone.

"Your parents are fighting," Lydia said to Connor.

"That's what they do," Connor said. "They're real good at it."

"We would never be like that," Lydia told him.

"No," Connor agreed, in love both with her and with her certainty. "Never."

Kay's house was so crowded it wasn't easy to find space to stand. There was the librarian, Sofia Peters, eating salami and rye. There was Fred, from the diner, all dressed up in a black suit he hadn't worn for fifteen years, and George Tenney, with the Doctor and a group of men who had gathered around the scotch to toast Old Dick's memory, again and again. Robin went straight to the kitchen, where she poured herself a cup of hot coffee.

"A madhouse," Stuart said as he came up beside Robin so he could collect more wineglasses from the cabinet. "Kay made the potato salad. Without bacon. You should try it."

Robin was still wearing her coat, but that didn't keep her from shivering. "I didn't think I'd feel this way," she admitted.

"Come on." Stuart left the glasses for a moment so he could put one arm around her. "He had a great life. He did exactly as he pleased."

"Right," Robin said.

"God, he would have hated this party," Stuart said.

In spite of herself, Robin grinned when she thought of what their grandfather could have done to this group with a few choice words. Half of these people would have already headed for the door.

"But he would have appreciated the potato salad," Stuart said as he took the wineglasses out to the dining room.

Still, Robin couldn't bring herself to join the crowd. Stephen had refused to come to the funeral, and she hadn't understood why until now. Now she wondered if it was really possible to mourn between bites of potato salad. Perhaps the only thing a gathering such as this served to do was separate the living from the dead. If Lydia and Connor hadn't come looking for her, Robin might have gone out the back door, with the hope that no one would notice.

"Did you have anything to eat?" Connor asked. "Do you want me to get you a sandwich?"

Robin shook her head no, but she loved him just for asking, and for being so awkward, and for drinking a Pepsi, rather than the beer or wine he could have had without anyone's noticing.

"You shouldn't be in here all by yourself," Lydia said. She'd already retrieved her red jacket from the hall closet. She reached into the wide pocket and took out a loaf of banana bread, which she handed to Robin. "My mother," Lydia explained. "She didn't think you'd want to see her, but she sent this. She said when she was little she was convinced that Old Dick was a giant."

Robin started crying right then. Lydia and Connor were both too embarrassed to look at her.

"I said something wrong," Lydia decided.

"No," Robin said, but she kept crying.

"I'd better stay with her," Connor told Lydia.

"Absolutely," Lydia agreed. She buttoned her jacket and pulled on her woolen mittens. She went to Connor and kissed him. "I'll miss you," she whispered.

Lydia went outside and slipped the hood of her jacket over her head. The sky had cleared to reveal a few stars, but it was even colder now. The trees were cloaked in ice, and some of the thinnest branches snapped. She had never met Connor's great-grandfather, yet his death, she saw, would affect her anyway. It was an awful, selfish thought, but one she couldn't get rid of. Connor's mom would no longer be going to visit Old Dick—she had often stayed until well after midnight— and so Lydia and Connor would no longer have the house to themselves in the evenings. Where would they go to be alone together? It was too cold for Poorman's Point, and the county had begun to bulldoze all the old fishermen's shacks, except for the one Stuart had appropriated. Neither of them had a driver's license yet, or use of a car, and if they checked into the one motel on the island, an inn really, run by an elderly woman named Mrs. Plant, everyone would know the news by the following morning. Desperadoes for love, that's what they'd be, searching out privacy wherever they could find it. At least for now. Someday they'd be married and then they could do whatever they wanted. Someday her mother would have to call on the phone and make an appointment if she wanted to see her.

Lydia often managed to have her own way, but that wasn't a crime. All this week she'd been working on her father, who was good-natured and hated the sound of an argument in his own house. Twice she'd cried in front of him; she'd confided that she wouldn't be able to eat a bite of turkey or stuffing if Connor wasn't invited to dinner. That was all it took, the invitation had been issued, but now Lydia worried that her mother might make a scene. Poor Connor was so nervous he planned to bring Michelle roses, although they were out of season and much too expensive. It was a long way from Kay's house to Mansfield Terrace, and Lydia had plenty of time to think. As she reached Cemetery Road she'd already decided that if her mother said one unkind word to Connor she would never forgive her, and what's more, she would consider running away, at least for a day or two, until she got what she wanted.

Lydia had begun to walk faster, although now and then she skidded on the sidewalk. She kept hearing that snapping sound. Once it was so close to her she imagined a branch was about to come at her from behind, but when she turned there was nothing, only the dark cold road and the black iron fence no child in town would dare to climb after twilight. She almost believed that there was a man inside the gates of the cemetery, but she knew that wasn't possible. She was not a girl who scared easily; she wasn't frightened by empty roads or lone crows perched on telephone wires. She went on, fighting the urge to run. Probably the funeral was what made her so uneasy; it was perfectly natural to be spooked after such an occasion. Still, when she reached the corner of Mansfield Terrace, she felt that the snapping sound was footsteps. She thought about Connor to make herself feel better; she thought about tomorrow, when he'd arrive at their door for Thanksgiving dinner, about the roses he'd be holding, the stems wrapped in green paper.

She could have sworn then that someone was following her; she heard someone breathing. Another girl would have run right then, but Lydia was too practical for that: she had to see what she was running from. When she turned and saw it was only Matthew Dixon on his way home, she stopped where she was and laughed. She had never been more relieved. If anything, Matthew was the one who looked frightened when she turned on him—in spite of his size, which seemed even larger beneath a bulky green coat.

"God," Lydia said. "You scared me." She slipped off her hood, in order to get a better look at him. "What are you doing here?"

"I'm home for Thanksgiving," Matthew said. "Vacation."

"I mean *here*." Lydia grinned. "Walking behind me." He was such a big dope, even if he did go to Cornell.

"I don't know," Matthew said. "I went for a walk. My parents are driving me crazy."

"Tell me about it. My mother's like a member of the secret police. But no one's going to tell me what to do."

"I know what you mean," Matthew began, but Lydia's attention had shifted.

Half a block away, Michelle was out in the driveway, sprinkling rock salt on the concrete. When she looked down the street she recognized Lydia's red coat. Michelle had had just about enough of teenaged antics, especially on a night as cold and miserable as this.

"Get inside," Michelle called. "It's freezing."

"Parents." Lydia shrugged, then she headed for home. She took her time, just to annoy Michelle, even though the night was so dark and cold she had the urge to throw her arms around her mother when she reached their driveway, a silly, childish urge she made absolutely certain to control.

After Old Dick died, Stephen had covered him with a clean, white sheet and pulled down the window shades. When Robin and the ambulance arrived, they'd had to persuade him to let them take the body. Robin had put her arms around Stephen; she didn't care that the driver of the ambulance happened to be Eugene Douglas, an old friend of Roy's, or that Eugene was watching them carefully from the doorway, the better to report back to Roy and anyone else who cared to listen.

"This is the way we do it," Robin had whispered to Stephen. "It's the way to say good-bye."

She could feel how upset he was just by touching him. He wouldn't look at her, not even for a second.

"You let strangers take him away? That's the way you do it?" At that moment, Stephen believed he could never belong among them. He closed his eyes, considering, then stood up. "Fine," he said, although that hardly meant he agreed. "Then that's the way we'll do it."

Stephen had insisted on carrying the old man downstairs himself, but he had refused to go to the funeral, and instead he'd spent the day gathering Old Dick's clothes from the closets, carefully folding the suits and the white shirts Ginny had always washed by hand, before putting them into cardboard boxes. When the sky grew dark, he put on his heavy black coat and went out, without bothering to lock the door behind him. Everything was still the same: the ice on the road, the bare trees, the sky above him. All of it went on, as if Old Dick had appeared in a dream that had nothing to do with the road and the trees and the evening star.

Stephen followed the route to Robin's house, but he didn't plan to go there or to the supper at Kay's. Instead, he walked down Cemetery Road, then went through the gates. It was a miserable night, but Stephen didn't feel the cold. He went to the freshly dug grave and knelt beside it; he took his hands out of his pockets and placed his palms on the newly spaded earth, which had already turned icy and hard. Two of the cemetery crows, which seemed never to sleep, circled above him, curious. This is what men did to remember the dead: They visited a place where nothing was left. They put up stones in the shape of their grief. Stephen stretched himself out on the pile of dirt, facedown, and he stayed there for so long that one of the crows came to perch on his back, and might have settled there for the night if Stephen hadn't finally risen to his feet.

If he walked along Cemetery Road every night for the rest of his life he still might not feel as if he were on his way home. But he wasn't going to choose to leave Robin, he saw that now. He'd been making this choice every day, a little at a time, until at last there was nothing to decide. Whether he belonged here or not no longer mattered. When he saw her truck in the driveway, he didn't have to think: he ran until he reached the carriage house, then went inside and took the stairs two at a time.

Stephen hadn't bothered to turn on the heat since the hour of Old Dick's death, and now the rooms were colder than the air outside. There was ice on the window ledges and along the hems of the faded chintz curtains; ice had been woven through the bands of lace on the dining room tablecloth and had left a blue veneer on the bookshelves and the floor. Robin had been waiting for him for nearly two hours. She was still wearing her coat, and although her hair had come undone, she hadn't bothered to fix it. When Stephen came up beside her and looped his arms around her waist, she wanted to stop breathing. She wanted the hour on the clock to freeze so that he could kiss her forever, until their lips were bruised, until he drew blood. He opened her coat and the buttons of her black dress. She wanted him so much that she couldn't look at him, and she was grateful that he always wanted to have her from behind. She leaned down against the table, leaving the print of her body in the ice, but that just made her hotter, especially when he wrapped himself around her. He was holding her even tighter, and his mouth moved along the delicate skin on the side of her throat; she could feel the edge of his teeth, not as if he wanted to hurt her but as if he thought she might try to get away, even now, when she was telling him not to stop.

Through each and every window Orion could clearly be seen. He'd be there until the stars shifted and he had to flee from the milky edges of the sky, or be stung, in spite of his arrow and bow. On this night before Thanksgiving, the temperature dropped quickly. Clotheslines snapped in two and car batteries froze solid and would later need to be thawed with hand-held hair dryers. A single night, nothing more, one that some people would sleep right through, beneath heavy quilts, and others would praise for each cold, clear second. When at last Robin hurried to get home, she didn't notice the position of the last few stars. She gunned the engine of her truck to keep it from freezing up on her, and when she got to Mansfield Terrace she turned off the ignition and let the pick-up roll into the driveway so no one asleep in bed would hear. She made certain not to slam the truck's door, then went to retrieve the newspaper from the frozen lawn. She felt the marks he'd left on her throat and began to shiver. She'd have to go inside and run a comb through her tangled hair; she'd have to run the water in the bathtub and wash with hot, soapy water. But for now she stood there on the lawn, for just a little while longer, as if that could stop the night from ending. At that moment, she truly believed she had everything she'd ever wanted, and she never once imagined that Connor might be watching from his window and that he had already judged her, hours before daylight.

NINE

$\mathcal{A}$LL THROUGH DECEMBER the ice stayed with them. For the first time in fifty years the water surrounding the island froze solid and children could skate the whole way around, ducking under the bridge where the willows grew, hooting until their own voices scared them. There were twelve car accidents during the first two weeks of the month; tires just skidded right off the road. People found themselves wishing for snow. At least that would be something, a change from the blue-gray ice, but even when snow was predicted it never fell.

The Doctor had taken to making models out of toothpicks because there was no need for him and his men to go out and plow, as they usually did to pick up the slack during the winter, and finally he had to let Angelo go, although he'd worked for him for nine years; the Doctor couldn't very well pay Angelo his regular salary when he himself was gluing tiny dinosaurs and ships together all day long.

During the short gray days that faded into a white twilight an hour before supper, people grew restless and were suddenly well aware that this was indeed an island they lived on. Still,

they were the ones who had chosen to vote down the mall pro-
posal and who had believed a triplex cinema would create traffic jams. They were the ones who had moved here so they
could watch the deer from their kitchen windows, and now
the poor things pawed the ice, trying to get at some greenery.
The AA meetings at the Episcopal church were more crowded
than ever; a ham-and-bean supper to raise funds for the
library drew a crowd of more than a hundred. Basketball
games at the high school were so well attended that the vice
principal considered charging admission, but of course he was
voted down by the School Board; without a few diversions like
basketball, the teenagers on the island would go absolutely
nuts.

Already there'd been several incidents: A gang of bored
high school boys had taken to hacking down mailboxes with
an axe. One ten-year-old daredevil had ridden his bike far out
on the ice, scaring sea gulls, joyfully skidding over the frozen
bay before crashing through into the water, where he would
have drowned if George Tenney, who'd taken the afternoon
off to go ice-fishing, hadn't managed to pull him out. A group
of teenaged girls, with nothing but time on their hands, had
formed a club; each morning before homeroom they met in
the girls' room to drink vodka from a grape-juice bottle. Roy
was relieved that Connor wasn't involved in any of these sort
of pranks, but that didn't mean he wasn't worried. On
Thanksgiving Day, Connor had arrived at Roy's apartment
with a gym bag filled with clothes and an armful of schoolbooks, and he'd been living there ever since. He slept on the
couch, often fully dressed, and ate nothing but pizza, washed
down with Kool-Aid. Every time Roy approached him and

tried to find out what had forced his decision, Connor would turn on the TV. When Robin telephoned, he refused to speak to her. Teenagers were moody, that was nothing out of the ordinary. But when Robin didn't come to the apartment, to argue with Connor and insist on taking him home, Roy knew that whatever had happened was serious. It wasn't like her to give up so easily, particularly when retreating meant Roy might win.

Roy went to see her the week before Christmas, when the pizza boxes in his kitchen had reached a staggering height and nearly every mailbox on the island had been decapitated, with the perpetrators still on the loose. Mansfield Terrace was one of the slickest streets on the island, though it had been dusted with salt and sand a dozen times or more. The front steps to Robin's house were downright perilous. A man could break his neck with one false move, and then where would he be?

"I don't want to talk to you," Robin said when she looked through the storm door and saw that it was Roy. Her hair was pulled back and she was wearing one of Roy's old sweatshirts and a pair of jeans.

"Fine," Roy said. He came inside even though she hadn't opened the door for him. "I'll talk."

Robin wrapped her arms around herself and stood by the door, just so he wouldn't get the idea that he'd be staying.

"What happened?" he asked. "Connor won't tell me."

"He hates me," Robin said. "That should give you endless pleasure."

"Jesus Christ," Roy said. "You won't give me a fucking inch."

"I didn't want to tell him about Stephen because I thought he'd be upset, but he figured it out and he's furious."

"Figured what out?"

Robin looked at him sharply. "You know."

Roy laughed out loud. How stupid could he be? Was it just that he didn't want to think about Robin making love with anyone else, or was he really a total idiot? Every time he even began to conjure up Robin in bed with someone else, a black curtain fell across his mind to block out the scene. Last Saturday he had actually gone shopping and bought Robin a Christmas present, gold hoop earrings that were far too expensive.

"So he knows you're fucking your little helper and he's pissed."

He really enjoyed Robin's wounded look, and he wished, just for an instant, that he'd been even crueler. Then she might have burst into tears.

"Oh, that's nice," Robin said. "I'm so glad Connor's under your influence now."

She was mouthing off, but Roy could tell how upset she was. She'd lost weight, and her eyelids were that soft purple color they turned when she couldn't sleep.

"Is Stephen living here with you?" Roy said. When Robin didn't answer, he shook his head. "It's not like I'm asking you for state secrets or anything."

"He's at my grandfather's."

"Just comes over here when he wants some?" Roy spoke before he could stop himself. "Forget I said that," he told Robin. "Forget everything I ever said."

"Connor's all right, isn't he?" Robin tilted her face up to Roy; she wasn't quite sure what she wanted his answer to be.

"No, he's not all right," Roy said.

He would have liked to get her down on the floor and fuck her right there; he could do that, he could have her begging for more. That's when he knew he had to get out. He went to the door. It was so goddamn cold, it was almost too much for a man to bear.

"Connor should be living here with you," Roy said.

Robin couldn't believe she'd heard correctly. She put her hands on her hips, waiting for the put-down she was certain would follow, but then she saw that Roy had meant what he said. For the past few weeks she'd considered giving Stephen up; maybe that was what she was supposed to do to make Connor happy. A few nights earlier she'd told Stephen she couldn't be with him anymore, just to see how it felt to say it aloud. It was awful, not just the words she'd said, but the way Stephen looked at her. She'd gone to lock herself in the bathroom, where she ran the water in the sink to make sure that Stephen wouldn't hear her crying. An hour later, when Robin came out of the bathroom, her eyes red, she found that he'd been waiting for her, just outside the bathroom door, and she knew she wouldn't be able to let him go. Not yet.

Those who kept secrets paid dearly, Robin saw that now. For six months before she'd found him out, Roy hadn't been able to sleep. She'd discover him in the kitchen, just before dawn, and each time he'd assure her nothing was wrong— indigestion perhaps, or bad dreams—and maybe he'd even believed it, at least back then, never mind that his insomnia always coincided with the times he cheated on her. It was totally disconcerting now to think that Roy, of all people, might best understand her, and yet that's what seemed to have happened. When Roy went out the back door, Robin almost regretted his leaving. He stood out on the porch, turning to face her as he buttoned his coat.

"I'll talk to Connor," Roy told her.

"That won't do any good," Robin said. "He's too angry to listen."

"Perfect," Roy said. "I'm used to that."

Robin surprised them both by laughing.

Roy grinned at her. "Don't worry. He'll listen."

He talked to Connor that night, over a pepperoni pizza that had far too much salt for human consumption. Roy lifted the pepperoni off his slice with the edge of a knife. He knew if he didn't talk fast he'd miss his chance with Connor, not just because Connor would be off to see Lydia but because Roy himself would lose his nerve.

"It's been great having you here," Roy said. "But your mother wants you back home."

Connor folded a slice of pizza neatly in half. "Are you saying you don't want me to live with you?"

"No," Roy said, a little too quickly. "My house is your house."

Connor thought that over. "Good."

"Here's the weird thing," Roy said. His hands had started to sweat. "Everybody's parents have sex. Otherwise they wouldn't be parents. They could adopt, sure." He was getting off the track, and he knew it. "But they still have sex, Connor. Even when they break up. Even if they're not sleeping with each other. That's the facts."

Connor pushed his chair away from the table.

"You're not going to say a few words on this subject?" Roy said.

Connor had already grabbed his leather jacket. Robin would have had a fit if she knew he was wearing it, rather than his winter coat. She probably would have insisted on mittens and a scarf.

"I'll be back after eleven," Connor said.

"After you've screwed Lydia?" Roy said, real easy, as if baiting Connor was the last thing on his mind.

Connor came back to the table; he towered over Roy, and Roy just had to hope his son would hold himself back.

"Just shut up. All right?" Connor said. "Who I'm with is none of your business."

"I couldn't agree more," Roy said. "It happens to go both ways."

"Are you defending her?" Connor said. "Don't you get it? The whole time they were pretending that nothing was happening."

If it had been anyone but Stephen, Connor might not have felt so betrayed. He was just a pawn, moved around at will—feel this way, feel that way, feel nothing at all. Connor saw his real mistake now. He'd trusted Stephen completely, as he would the family dog. He'd taught him tricks: how to play chess, fix a sandwich, handle a razor without slitting your throat. Someone else might have been repelled by all the things Stephen must have done just to survive, but Connor had to go and admire him. He'd kept Stephen's secret, he'd run alongside him, down to the Point, until he was too winded to keep up. In return he'd gotten nothing but lies and he'd been played for a fool, too blind to see what was set out right in front of him.

"Take my advice," Roy said now. "Mind your own business."

"You don't know anything about it," Connor said. "You don't even know what he is. Maybe you think you're talking to a human being when you're talking to him, but you're not."

Connor ran all the way to Lydia's house that night, in spite of the ice and the dread he felt inside. He took the long route, so he wouldn't have to pass by his own house. He really didn't know what he'd do if he saw Stephen face to face, and he didn't want to know. When he got to Lydia's, Paul Altero answered the door. A lucky break. Connor knew that Mr. Altero had always liked him, and now he managed to have a conversation with Lydia's father, although about what, Connor later couldn't remember. Mr. Altero insisted that he come into the kitchen for a soda, and that meant Connor would have to speak to Lydia's mother, something he usually managed to avoid.

"Is Lydia taking the car tonight?" Michelle asked her husband. Connor still had only a permit, but Lydia had gotten her license, and the Toyota was now the only place she and Connor could have any privacy. "It's so icy," Michelle added.

"She's a good driver," Paul said.

Now Michelle turned to Connor, and without thinking he took a step backward and crashed into the refrigerator.

"You moved out," Michelle said to him.

Just what he'd dreaded. An actual conversation.

"Your mother must be upset."

"I wouldn't know," Connor said. "You'd have to ask her."

That suggestion effectively ended the conversation, just as Connor hoped it would. Still, he was grateful beyond words when Lydia finally came down, already wearing her coat. She smiled at Connor, and since they didn't dare greet each other the way they wanted to, Connor looked down at the floor; he didn't want her parents to see how desperate he was to be alone with Lydia.

"Thanks, Pop," Lydia said when her father handed her the car keys.

As soon as they got into the Toyota, Connor pulled Lydia to him, even though they were parked in the driveway and Michelle could have easily looked out the kitchen window and seen them. His arms were shaking; his throat was completely dry. When he was with her he didn't give a damn about anything else. He was dizzy with wanting her; he didn't have to think about wrong and right. Lydia threw her head back and laughed, but she was a little panicked by how desperate he seemed.

"Wait a second," she said to him. "We're not in a race."

Connor slouched over to his side of the front seat. Just looking at him, hunched over and filled with longing, Lydia felt herself falling in love with him all over again. She climbed onto his lap, and she kissed him so deeply and for so long that for years afterward Connor would remember the exact thought that kept running through his head as the car idled in the driveway. *This will never change*. That's what he'd thought. *Not this*.

Christmas Day was the coldest ever recorded in the island's short history, and the next day was even worse. It was a good day to stay indoors, preferably in bed, and when evening came, suddenly, as if a curtain had been drawn, it was best to have a hot rum and some leftover turkey and go right back under the covers. Of course, some people had more important things to think about than the weather. Jenny Altero, for one—who'd gotten the hand-stitched stuffed palomino pony she'd wanted for Christmas, as well as a pair of beautiful black boots—simply couldn't sit still.

A note had been dropped into Jenny's desk at school before vacation started; Tim Lester, whose father owned the diner in town and who was a grade ahead, had a crush on her. The note was anonymous, and Jenny didn't know if it was Tim himself or one of his friends who'd written it. But it was male handwriting, of that she was certain, a sloppy scrawl that had sent her reeling. Her heart had been racing ever since that day, and tonight she planned to do something about it. She washed and dried the supper dishes; she played Pictionary with her father and kissed her mother before she went upstairs at bedtime. Then she waited for her parents to go into their room, and once she heard them turn on the TV beside their bed, she began to put on her eye makeup, with quick, accurate movements, the way Lydia had taught her. She chose her earrings carefully, the pearl ones that dropped like tears. Actually, they weren't hers at all, but she'd taken them from Lydia several months before, in the summer, and by now it seemed reasonable that they should fully belong to her.

As Jenny braided her hair, she took a certain pleasure in tonight's reversal. Lydia, after all, had come home at nine, her

French braid untangled, her lips kissed raw, contrite for the first time in ages. The Toyota had skidded into one of the Feldmans' crab apple trees, splitting it right in half. The front left fender would have to be replaced, and the headlight as well, but not even their mother had had the heart to scream at Lydia, that's how shaken she'd been by the accident. It was the passenger side of the car that had been dented, and for one sickening instant Lydia had thought Connor was hurt. He'd only been dazed, but Lydia still had wanted to go right home. Michelle had given her a few drops of whiskey and a cup of hot tea for her nerves, and now there Lydia was, already asleep in her bed, and it was Jenny who had better things to do.

She pulled on the white sweater and a pair of corduroy slacks, then tiptoed downstairs to the hall closet and grabbed Lydia's coat, which was so much more grown-up than her own pink ski jacket. She closed the front door so quietly she might have been a mouse sneaking out with some Christmas pudding in its cheeks. As she walked along Mansfield Terrace, she saw that Robin's bedroom light was on; good, there was no need to worry about being caught by her this time around. Jenny knew of at least three other girls who often slipped out after their curfews to go down to Fred's Diner, which never closed before two. They went for the vanilla Cokes and the fries, as well as the chance to flirt with Tim, if he was working behind the counter. Tonight Jenny hoped these girls would be there, in a rear booth; they probably would think she was fifteen at least. They'd whisper to each other, "Who is she?" as she leaned toward Tim, and when they finally recognized Jenny in Lydia's borrowed clothes and called for her to join them, she'd call back that she was busy, then turn her full attention to Tim.

At this hour of the night the ice along the roads turned to diamonds, and the wind shook the black branches of the trees. Jenny walked quickly, and when she reached the town green the ginkgos moaned and the telephone wires crackled in the cold. She ran all the rest of the way to Fred's, and once she was inside the diner, the sudden heat, from the radiators and the fryers, came as a shock. No one was here, at least not yet, only Fred behind the counter, cleaning up the grill. Jenny went and sat on a stool and ordered a vanilla Coke. She was extremely polite; she was, after all, addressing the father of the boy who might be crazy about her.

"I go to school with Tim," she informed Fred when he brought her the Coke. She was so casual, so cool; Lydia would have been proud of her. "Isn't he working tonight?"

"He sprained his foot yesterday," Fred told her. "Ice hockey."

Jenny thought this over. She hated to imagine Tim in pain, and she was disappointed to have come all this way for nothing. She paid for her Coke and tugged the hood of Lydia's coat over her head, in preparation for the long walk home.

"He'll be home all day tomorrow," Fred told her, as if he were a mind reader. Jenny had just been wondering how on earth she could make contact, when school would be out for another week.

"I could visit him," Jenny said. She hoped she didn't look as flustered as she felt. She crossed her fingers for luck.

"I'll tell him," Fred said.

Jenny was so excited she could barely speak. She'd wear her

new black boots. She debated about bringing the palomino pony; she knew Tim rode down at the stables, but he might think her Christmas present was too babyish. No, she'd bring him cookies, that's what she'd do. She'd stop at the bakery on the way to his house.

"Great," Jenny said. She had a big grin on her face, but even Lydia might not have been able to control that. "I'll see him tomorrow. I'll come by at ten."

Tim waited until eleven-thirty, and when Jenny didn't show he went down to the bridge to meet his friend for hockey, since his sprain wasn't as bad as his parents had thought. It was a gorgeous day and the ice was perfect, and none of the boys paid any attention to the siren that echoed across the frozen bay. And later in the afternoon they were still far too involved in their game to notice what looked like a red sack beneath the bridge where the willows grew, where you could scare yourself if you weren't careful. They played on for hours, until their toes and fingers were nearly frozen solid, and not one of them had the slightest idea that Tim's father had been the last one to see Jenny Altero alive, and that he'd been too busy wiping down the counter to see or appreciate her last beautiful smile.

The search parties were still out in the frozen blue twilight with a pack of dogs borrowed from the state police. But long before they found the body, with the throat so neatly slit, Michelle Altero knew her daughter would never come home. She knew it early that morning, when she opened Jenny's bedroom door to find that the bed hadn't been slept in. Paul had been crazy with worry and had insisted on going out with a band of neighbors to hunt through the marshes. Michelle hadn't said a word as he'd pulled on his fishing boots and grabbed the big flashlight out of the hall closet. She did nothing more than nod when he told her not to worry, and she'd let him kiss her good-bye, but as soon as he'd gone out, she went inside the hall closet and closed the door. She crouched down among the boots and the umbrellas, and cried so hard she thought she'd dissolve, right there on the floor.

If Lydia hadn't come to take her out of the closet, Michelle might have stayed there forever. Instead, she let herself be led to the couch, where she sat holding Lydia's hand, the stuffed palomino pony on her lap. She didn't move a muscle, she didn't say a word—not even yes or no when Lydia tentatively asked if she wanted a cup of tea—but at a little before nine that night, Michelle suddenly sat bolt upright and began to tear out her hair. She pulled out fistfuls and made a gurgling noise in her throat, and Lydia had to restrain her and reassure her again and again, "It's all right." But of course it wasn't. Down at the bridge, at the instant when Michelle began to tear at herself, Stuart and Kay came to sit on a wooden bench so they could lace up their skates. Stuart wore an old woolen hat Kay had dug out of a box in her basement and an ancient down parka, and Kay had on a camel-colored coat and a pair of leather gloves Stuart had ordered for her from L. L. Bean. They hadn't gone skating together in the moonlight for more than twenty years, and it was a much colder activity than they'd remembered. Once on the ice, they were clumsier than they'd remembered as well, and had to hold on to each other for support. And just as Stuart was beginning to hit his stride, and had let out a whoop, Kay signaled him over, then grabbed his arm. Out in the marshes the search dogs were barking, and the sound echoed above the frozen bay. The moon was huge and white and circled by a halo of frost.

"What's wrong?" Stuart said. His face looked healthy from racing along the ice. "Are my knees creaking? Am I too old for this?"

Kay came close to him and hid her face in his parka. As soon as Stuart looked past her he saw that something had been wrong with the ice all along and they hadn't even noticed. Blood had seeped through the water beneath the ice and turned it deep red. The beams of light he and Kay had seen in the woods weren't moonlight reflecting off the ice but flashlights and lanterns. He helped Kay back to shore, then shouted as loud as he could until at last people in the search party heard him, although once they approached, the dogs refused to set foot on the red ice, and they pulled at their leashes, then fell silent all at once. Because Stuart was a doctor, George Tenney called him over as he and Woody Preston knelt beneath the bridge. Stuart calmly examined the girl, but afterward he realized he'd been crying the whole time, and that night he went home with Kay and they held each other tight, while outside the wind grew so fierce it tore the new shingles off the roof of the fisherman's shack down on the icy beach.

It might have been Woody Preston who began the talk of an animal, one who knew exactly how to slash a throat in the most efficient manner, a predator so quiet it could come up behind its victim before she had the chance to run.

"I wouldn't write about any animals in your report," Roy advised him. "Unless you want to be fitted for a straitjacket."

All the same, the rumor grew, so that by midnight most people had locked themselves in their houses. Jeff Carson went down to his basement and got out the rifle he hadn't used for twelve years, not since he'd gone hunting with his cousins in upstate New York and shot two swans he'd believed to be wood ducks. The Feldmans set out broken bottles on their front stoop; any creature that took a step toward their door would have its feet cut to bloody ribbons.

It fell to George Tenney and Woody Preston to speak to the family, and George told Woody in no uncertain terms to keep his mouth shut, especially about his animal theory. Michelle Altero said nothing at all; she had cried so many tears that she seemed completely drained. The girl's father, Paul, was so slow to answer even the most simple questions—who her friends were, whether he'd known she had been to Fred's Diner the night she disappeared—that George felt like a heel just for being in their house.

Lydia stood in the doorway of the living room, her arms and legs crisscrossed with jitters; she could hardly stand up straight. She was in her nightgown, with her hair loose, and she'd already thrown up five times. The strange thing was, she was the one who felt like a ghost, so weightless it seemed possible that any minute she would rise up through the living room ceiling.

"You haven't noticed anything unusual in the last few days?" George Tenney was asking in his deep, sad voice. "Any strangers?"

Lydia closed her eyes. Her skin felt much too cold. She had

a curious sensation up and down her spine, as if she were growing completely numb.

"Anything suspicious at all?" George Tenney asked.

That was when Lydia told them about the Wolf Man. The secret she had kept all these months, a silly secret she'd thought, which no one would much care about, now seemed crucial. Lydia saw everything clearly at that moment. This was all her fault.

"I told you it was an animal!" Woody Preston said. "I swear there were claw marks," he managed to add before George told him to just keep his mouth shut.

"I felt sorry for him," Lydia said. The numbness was spreading, all over her body. "Connor said he'd be locked up if anyone found out who he was."

Paul Altero put his head in his hands and wept, but Michelle stood and went to Lydia. When she reached her daughter, Michelle had to lean up against the wall or she would have fallen to the floor in a heap.

Lydia didn't need her mother to tell her that the wrong daughter had been taken from her; Lydia already knew that. She knew it all night, as she heard her parents weeping. She knew it in the morning, when she heard someone knocking at the front door. Lydia found herself hoping that whoever had done this to Jenny had now come for her as well. She went downstairs in her nightgown, her feet bare, and opened the door to find Connor, his shirt unbuttoned, his hair wild from sleep. Roy had told him about Jenny as soon as he'd woken, and he'd run all the way to Mansfield Terrace.

"Lydia," he said. His voice broke as he spoke her beloved name. "I'm sorry."

He held her to him, but she was like a piece of ice.

"They'll find the person who did it," Connor said. He wished he could wrap his arms around Lydia and carry her far from this dangerous earth, someplace where it was just the two of them, where terrible things never happened and nothing ever changed.

"They already have," Lydia said. "I told them about the Wolf Man."

When Connor let go of her and stepped back, Lydia didn't move at all. The wind came in the front door and blew at the hem of her nightgown.

"You told them about Stephen?" Connor couldn't believe she would do this. "It was a secret."

"Is that all you care about?" Lydia said. "My sister's dead and all you can think about is your secret."

"He didn't do it," Connor said. "I mean, I know him. He would never do anything like that, and now they're going to think he did. All because of you."

Michelle came down the stairs just as Lydia slapped Connor. She hit him hard, and the imprint of her hand would remain on his face for hours. Even after it did disappear he'd be able to feel it, as if he'd been marked for life.

"You piece of shit," Lydia said. She was so cold she could barely move her mouth; her toes and the tips of her fingers had begun to turn blue. "You pathetic creature."

Connor blinked; she couldn't possibly be saying what he thought he was hearing. Lydia gave him a push, and he lurched back over the threshold.

"Lydia," he said. "Please."

Lydia looked him right in the eye; she had no idea that she

was shaking, or that her mother had come up behind her. Who had she thought she was to find happiness, to even think she might have a right to it?

"What a mistake you were," Lydia said. "A mistake from the very beginning."

She slammed the door, and she didn't care if he stayed out there pounding on it all day and all night. She turned and found herself in her mother's arms, the only place she wanted to be.

"Baby," Michelle whispered to her, as she stroked Lydia's tangled hair, just as if she'd been the daughter who deserved to be here on this winter morning all along.

When they came for him, Stephen was reading one of Old Dick's books, a collection of stories so lovely and strange he knew he'd have to read them again. He had learned to like coffee and had made himself a pot, fixing the French-roast beans with the hand grinder Ginny had always used. He was nearly halfway through "The Twelve Dancing Princesses" when he heard the tires on the gravel driveway. In spite of the cold, he had the windows open and his shirt off, since the temperature inside houses always seemed much too warm.

They allowed him to put on his black coat and his boots before they drove him down to the station. It was Woody Preston who tried to put him in handcuffs, and Stephen panicked just at the sight of them. He would have struck Woody, he might have gone to the open window and jumped, if George Tenney hadn't intervened. They were only taking him in for questioning, after all, it was routine after the Altero girl's murder. But when they got to Main Street, Stephen saw that a crowd had already gathered on the green; men in parkas and heavy leather gloves waited to get a look at him as he was led from the car, as if they'd be able to tell, just by the sight of him, whether he was guilty or not.

The room they took him to had glass on two sides, but the windows were barred, and Stephen didn't like that one bit. After he'd sat down, he tried not to look directly at any of the officers, since they were six and he was one. He knew when to back down and when to fight and when it was best to act as though you were already defeated. Just a few friendly questions, that's what they told him. There was nothing that officially attached him to a crime, not even a legal reason to search him.

Roy was in the back of the room. He wasn't one of the ones who was asking Stephen questions; instead, he leaned up against the wall and drank coffee. It was impossible to tell whether he was enjoying this, although Stephen believed he must have been. Here were his buddies, his friends, demanding to know where Stephen had been the previous night between ten and two, and Stephen was at their mercy. When he said he'd been reading, some of them exchanged a look, although Roy didn't blink. After that they wanted to know strange things: how many times he'd spoken to Jenny Altero, whether he'd been to Fred's Diner, whether, when he'd lived in the woods, he'd killed deer with his bare hands or maybe used a knife to slit their throats. He accepted a cup of bitter coffee and answered as best he could, but he stopped talking to them when Woody Preston asked if he'd ever tasted human flesh. They'd already decided something for themselves, with or without his answers.

George Tenney went to get himself some coffee, then stood next to Roy.

"The stuff those kids found over at Poorman's Point," George said. He had his back to the rest of the guys to make certain that they wouldn't overhear. "Those animals. Their throats were all slit. Maybe that was him, too."

Roy narrowed his eyes and nodded. His stomach was a mess and his head was pounding.

"Nobody will think anything if you want to get out of here," George said. "Considering him and Robin and all."

Roy was about to say something, but now he looked at George.

"He asked me to call her," George said. "At the moment, we can't keep him, not yet, and that means she'll probably come get him. Go on," George advised. Roy's skin was ashy and there were dark circles under his eyes. "Take a break."

By the time Robin came down to the station, Roy was sitting on a stool at the bar at Harper's and the group of men out on the green had grown to more than two dozen. Robin went right up to the desk where Woody Preston was filling out his report.

"What's going on out there?" she asked him.

"I guess they think we've got a killer in here," Woody said. "And now you're going to take him home with you, after what happened to Jenny Altero?"

Twice Robin had gone over to see Michelle, and both times Michelle had refused to see her.

"Don't ever come here again," Lydia had finally told her.

When George phoned he'd informed Robin that Stephen had been brought in for questioning; now she understood why. She understood why Lydia had slammed the door while Robin was still standing out on the porch, just about to ask if she could bring dinner over for them in a wicker basket.

"Do you have some proof?" she asked Woody now. "Or are you just going on your own stupidity?"

She waited on the bench in the hallway until George brought Stephen out.

"I'll take you home," Robin said.

Stephen nodded but he didn't look at her, not even when she took George aside.

"You know it wasn't Stephen," Robin said.

"Are you sure?" George said.

"Yes, I'm sure," Robin said. "Was this Roy's idea? Is that it?"

"Look, we know all about him. I had a long talk with the director at Kelvin, so we know his history. He lived like an animal, Robin. Face it."

Robin tilted her chin up; her lips were tight and dry. "Am I supposed to give you bail or something?"

"He was just here for questioning," George said. "But it's not the end of it."

"Can I go, or am I being charged with something, too?"

"Robin," George said sadly. "You know you can go."

Robin headed for the exit. "We can leave," she told Stephen. He followed her, then put a hand on her arm to stop her. He nodded toward the green, where the men were still gathered.

"Fuck them," Robin said as she pushed open the door.

No one said a word as they walked to the truck; there were

no shouts or catcalls, although one rock was thrown as Robin made the turn onto Cemetery Road. She drove as though there were no ice, and when the tires skidded, nearly off the road, she didn't seem to notice. She'd decided it would be better to take Stephen to her house, because of that crowd on the green, and as soon as they were in the kitchen, she double-locked the back door.

"Did you have dinner?" she asked Stephen.

Stephen came up behind her and put his arms around her.

"Hamburgers?" she said, and then she started to cry. "It's nothing," she insisted, but she let him kiss her, softly, the way he did when she was upset, before she moved away. "Let me have that awful coat," she told him, and at that they were both able to smile.

Stephen took off the coat and handed it to her.

"They didn't even give you time to put on a shirt?" Robin said.

"I didn't think of it," Stephen said.

"Those bastards," Robin said.

She went to the closet in the living room, and as she reached for a hanger the black coat fell from her hands. When she bent to retrieve it, she felt something sharp in the pocket. She reached in and found the carpenter's knife. Stephen was making coffee in the kitchen; his back was toward her as she approached him.

"What is this?" Robin said.

Stephen turned to her and blinked. "I found it up in the attic," he said. "A long time ago."

"Have you used it?" Robin asked.

Her voice sounded very sharp and strange. Stephen knew

219

that when people sounded like that it was best not to speak to them directly. He shook his head. No.

"Not once?" Robin said. "Not ever?"

She had come up close to him. He could almost feel her.

"Tell me the truth," she said. Her face was white and drawn; it didn't even look like her. "Not ever?"

She was whispering now, in a funny way, as if she might hit him or run away. There was no clear answer, not one he was certain would please her.

"I kept it just in case," Stephen said. "That's all."

Robin quickly went to the cabinet beneath the sink and took out a spade. A box of detergent had toppled and a stream of soap powder fell onto the floor, but Robin paid no attention.

"Robin," Stephen said, but she didn't seem to hear him. Instead she went outside, not bothering with a coat. Stephen grabbed one of Connor's old sweatshirts left on a hook by the door and pulled it on, then followed her. She was out behind the pear tree, down on her hands and knees.

"They could have found this," Robin said. She attacked the ice with her spade until she could dig up some frozen earth. "Well, they're not going to find it now."

Her hair kept falling over her face, so that it was difficult for Stephen to see her.

"There," Robin said, satisfied, when the hole was big enough. She placed the carpenter's knife in the hole, then began covering it up until Stephen stopped her. He had knelt down beside her, but she hadn't even noticed until he touched her. "What?" she said. Her voice was still sharp and she was out of breath.

"You don't have to do this," Stephen said.

"Oh, really?" Robin said. There was frozen dirt caked under her nails and streaks of black earth were on her face. "What do you imagine Roy and his friend would think if they found this knife on you?"

"What do *you* think?" Stephen said.

Robin pulled her arm away and stood up. She looked at him for a long time; her breath turned to smoke in the air.

"I'm going to bed," she said.

She started toward the back door, but Stephen stayed crouching beneath the pear tree. The night was so clear he could almost believe those were the same stars he'd always seen, far away from here, in a place where it was impossible to hear a man or a woman cry.

"Are you coming?" Robin asked.

All she wanted at that moment was to be alone, and Stephen knew it.

"Not yet," he said.

After she'd gone inside, Stephen went to the rear of the yard, away from the branches of the pear tree, to have a better look at the sky. He knew from a book he'd taken from Old Dick's shelf that stars died, but he found this hard to believe. *Make a wish,* that's what his mother had said to him once. *Close your eyes.*

Matthew Dixon, who was home for Christmas vacation and wouldn't have to return for the spring semester until the end of January, had come outside. He was supposed to drag the garbage cans out to the curb, but instead he'd been watching Stephen. Now he zipped up his parka and came to his side of the redwood fence. Stephen heard him approach, but he kept on looking at the stars.

"I hear they're really after you," Matthew said. "I knew you weren't like other people. I could tell right away."

Don't tell your wish, Stephen's mother had said. *Or it won't come true.*

"Wolves," Matthew said now. "I think it's fantastic. Of course they're going to go after you. It makes perfect sense to a small mind."

Matthew leaned his elbows on the fence; he was chewing peppermint gum and the scent was sweet every time he breathed out.

"You're going to have to get out of here," Matthew said. "I mean, you can't sit around and think they're going to treat you fairly, because they won't."

Stephen thought this over.

"You see my point," Matthew said. "You've got to outwit them. You've got to go back."

"I don't know where it is," Stephen said.

"I could find out for you," Matthew told him.

"No," Stephen said. "I've looked in the atlas. The maps don't mean anything. I knew my way because of the way things were."

"Rocks? Mountains? Landmarks like that?" Matthew was grinning. "Topography. I can get that."

Stephen looked over at him.

"I'm serious." This was just the sort of thing Matthew found exciting. "You give me the information, and I'll tap into the USGS and do the graphics. It's simple."

From where he stood, Stephen could see Robin's bedroom window.

"So should I?" Matthew said.

"Why would you?" Stephen said.

"Because I know how it feels," Matthew Dixon told him, "when they all hate you."

The night was filled with so many stars it would have seemed impossible for the streets to be dark, but the road to Poorman's Point was filled with shadows. That was where Roy had headed after he was done drinking at Harper's. He'd gone directly to the old estate; every tree that had been planted here had been chosen by his father, yet Roy couldn't have given the correct name for more than half a dozen varieties. He regretted that now; it would have been so easy, if only he'd paid some attention.

He parked on the grass in front of the entrance to the driveway. Through the trees he could see the dark carriage house; the windows had all been left open, even though no one was home. He turned off the car headlights and settled back in his seat; he was wishing he'd thought to stop at the 7-Eleven for a six-pack of beer, when he saw the men from the green making their way along the black, looping road.

There were more than a dozen of them, and although it was difficult to distinguish one man from another in their down jackets and parkas, Roy recognized Jeff Carson and Fred Lester from the diner and several others. Either they didn't see his parked car or they were so outraged and bold they just didn't care. Roy grabbed the steering wheel and sat up straight. They were much too silent for such a large group, and when they turned into the driveway the gravel made absolutely no noise beneath the weight of their boots.

Roy realized that he was sweating; his shirt was drenched and his hands were too wet to keep hold of the steering wheel.

He sat there and didn't even think to try to stop them as they threw bucket after bucket of red paint on the carriage house, on the stucco walls and the mailbox and the arbor where the wisteria had always grown. One of the men, perhaps it was Jeff Carson, dipped his hands into the paint and drew a five-pointed star on the door, as if a sign like that could ever ward off true evil. By the time the men had finished, Roy had stopped sweating, and his skin had turned clammy. He had a siren under his front seat, and he could have radioed in to the station, but instead he just watched, exactly as he had the previous night when Jenny Altero was murdered, when he'd followed Stephen all the way back here from Robin's and parked in this same place, watching through the open window as the Wolf Man read a book with a leather binding, and not turning for home until at last those few birds that could tolerate winter on this island began to sing.

TEN

*I*T MAY BE TRUE THAT marjoram sprinkled onto the earth helps the dead sleep in peace, but it does nothing at all for the living. The living can pick wild garlic and place pots of clover on their windowsills and still not be able to rest. They can cut down a larch and huddle around it on a cold winter night as it burns and smokes for hours, down at the Point, where the fire ignites the black sky, yet continue to be afraid of the dark.

For the next three days, as soon as the sun went down, the main street of town became deserted, all at once, as though a curfew had been set. There were no customers at Fred's Diner, and Harper's began closing at six because even the regulars had taken to staying home and drinking gin or beer in front of their own TVs. Boys stopped playing hockey long before dusk, even when their mothers hadn't yet called them home. Dogs went unwalked, and scratched at front doors. Every single cat had a bell around its neck, and even the toms had to wait until morning before going out on the prowl.

The only ones who ventured out after dark were the men who had formed the patrol, and they always went out in groups of no smaller than five or six, unless one of them had a gun. Sometimes people were already in bed when they heard the patrol round their corners. The sound of those men, whose only mission was to protect their neighbors, should have been comforting, but it wasn't. Flashlights made shaky white circles on the lawns and the front porches, garbage cans were rattled and turned upside down as the men searched for anything suspicious, though at this time of year, on nights such as these, almost everything was suspect.

Whenever Stuart heard the patrol inspecting Kay's street, he went down to the kitchen for tea and Alka-Seltzer, and then he would never get back to sleep. As soon as the board of Kelvin Medical Center was informed by the police that their patient had never been transferred, Stuart was asked to resign. There was no proof to tie Robin to Stephen's escape, and no evidence that Stuart had been an accomplice, but the board had already tried Stuart and found him guilty of gross negligence. He dutifully composed his letter of resignation and mailed it to the medical center; in return no criminal charges would be filed against him. A request had already been placed to return Stephen to Kelvin, where he would be reevaluated and most probably sent upstate to the locked ward that had been his original destination. The hospital would wait until the criminal investigation on the island was completed, and this time they would send not only three attendants but two armed guards as well, just to make certain there wouldn't be any trouble.

Stuart had never suffered from insomnia before, and now he understood why his patients who did often felt persecuted, as though sleep had somehow singled them out and denied them their rightful rest. Kay begged him not to go back to the shack, at least not for a while, and he'd thought she was over-reacting, until he went to his usual AA meeting and discovered that no one would sit on the same side of the room with him. No one would wait on him in the hardware store or the bait shop. Sofia Peters, down at the library, indexed an entire tray of the card catalogue before finally checking out his books, and then she wouldn't look at him, not even a glance.

Robin was having an even worse time of it. Some people actually spat on the floor when she walked into the market. She'd left without buying anything, and when she phoned and asked Max Schaeffer, who'd known her since she was ten, if she could have her groceries delivered, he told her that the delivery boy would refuse to come to her house and that he himself wouldn't walk up the front steps for all the money in the world. The Doctor had come over and sadly informed her that five of her clients had phoned to hire him, and spring was still almost three months away. He'd turned them down, of course, but that didn't mean they would be coming back to Robin.

"This is all Roy's fault," the Doctor said as he drank the tea Robin served him, made from the peppermint that grew in her yard, since she'd used up her last tea bag and had intended to buy more at the market. "If he hadn't screwed up, you wouldn't have divorced him, and this wolf fellow would never have come here."

After the Doctor left, Robin found five hundred dollars under his teacup. She knew he could ill afford the loan, and she would have run after him and forced him to take it back if she hadn't been so totally broke. She and Stephen had taken to

eating Minute Rice flavored with coriander, and winter potatoes from the vegetable bin. At night, when they slept in
Robin's bed, they didn't touch each other. In the morning,
when the wind howled down the chimney, they sat drinking
the last of the coffee at the kitchen table, but they didn't dare
talk. Suspicion grows that way, between the sheets, in the
teacups, with every word that isn't spoken. One day, while
Robin was at the sink washing out soup bowls, Stephen came
up behind her, and she jumped. She tried to blame it on too
much caffeine and the awful sound of the wind, but Stephen
knew that wasn't what had frightened her.

He moved out that afternoon. When he put on his black
coat Robin didn't try to stop him. He ran all the way to Poorman's Point. It was almost dusk and the patrol always began
its rounds as darkness fell. The sky was as gray as stone when
Stephen reached the carriage house; the oaks and the Russian
olives no longer cast shadows across the lawn. He saw the
pools of red paint in the driveway and the ruined stucco walls,
but he walked right past them. Stephen refused to be stopped
by the mark on the front door. He went inside and locked the
door behind him before he went upstairs. He left the lights off
and closed all the windows, then sat down in the overstuffed
chair beside the bookcases to wait. They weren't about to let
him go, not when they had every advantage. That's what men
called a fair fight, when they were a dozen strong; not one of
them would have approached on his own, except for Jeff Carson and a few of the others who had guns, and even they
might have turned and run when the branches of the oaks
shifted in the wind.

They didn't come up the driveway until a little before eight, and they stayed for more than an hour, huddled around a fire they made in one of Old Dick's garbage cans, after they'd chopped down the wisteria for kindling. The wood gave off a sour scent as it burned, and yellow sparks shot out, so that several of the men's coats were singed. The carriage house looked abandoned, and after a while the men guessed that Stephen hadn't come back, that he wouldn't have dared to, and they left to patrol the town green, throwing a few rocks at the windows just for good measure.

Stephen didn't bother with the broken glass. He didn't sweep it away, although there were shards of it on the table and all across the orange-and-black Persian rug Old Dick had had carried across the bridge by two strong men whose knees buckled under its weight. He didn't get up and light the stove to boil water for coffee or tea, or fix himself supper, although there were still cans of vegetables and soup in the pantry. He didn't have to make a choice anymore; the choice had already been made for him. Robin had watched him put on his coat, and when he'd left she'd locked the back door. At that instant, when he heard the turn of the lock, he knew he had lost her. It was as simple and quick as that. One way open, the other closed.

All that night Stephen listened to the wind through the broken windows. It was a sound he recognized, and it made him feel homesick in some deep, awful way. In the morning he changed his clothes; he showered and shaved and took some scissors to his long hair. He might as well look like other men, at least until he was gone. He ate half a package of crackers, the kind Old Dick preferred, even though they tasted like sand. It wouldn't do him the least bit of good to get sick or weak now, not when he had so far to go, not when the snow along the ridgetops would already be deep and thick, slowing him down, it was true, but also covering his tracks.

"You let him go back to the carriage house?" Stuart said when he came to see Robin. He'd brought along a basket of corn muffins Kay had baked and two bags of groceries they'd shopped for off the island, at a Grand Union on the North Shore. "With the way feelings are running around here? You don't think that's dangerous?"

Robin had been up since dawn, but she hadn't bothered to dress and was still wearing the T-shirt and sweatpants she'd slept in.

"He's not my puppet," Robin told her brother. "I don't tell him what to do. Was I supposed to throw myself across the door and force him to stay?"

"He shouldn't have left," Stuart insisted. "There's something wrong with these people. They want a monster. They won't be satisfied until they have one." He grabbed a corn muffin and ripped it in two. "Kay could sell these. They're better than the ones at the bakery."

Stuart reached for a pot of jam and happened to see Robin's unguarded face. She was so pale it almost seemed possible that the monster he'd spoken of had just appeared at the back door.

"Robin," Stuart said.

"I'll make coffee." Robin went to the stove for the kettle, but Stuart followed her.

"You think he might have done it," Stuart said.

"You've always liked to tell me what I think," Robin said. She filled the kettle and pleated a paper towel into quarters. It was cheaper than using coffee filters but for some reason folding it made her feel like weeping.

"Stephen doesn't fit the profile."

"There you go," Robin said. "You do know everything."

"He is not obsessive-compulsive, he has absolutely no violent history, no sexual perversions—unless you want to correct me on that—no abnormal aggression."

"And no alibi," Robin said.

"They're wrong about Stephen," Stuart said. "He didn't kill that girl."

"You're so sure of yourself," Robin said. "Aren't you the person who lives in a shack and has a nervous breakdown at the drop of a hat?"

Stuart put his corn muffin into the sink, uneaten. "I don't deserve that."

"No," Robin said. "You don't."

"I was fired," Stuart told her. "Asked to resign."

"That's it," Robin said. "I've ruined everything." She turned, so that Stuart wouldn't see her cry.

"Stop it," Stuart said. "I wasn't certain I was ever going back. To tell you the truth, I'm not quite certain of anything."

Stuart put his arms around Robin, then politely busied himself with pouring hot water over the ground coffee, while Robin wiped at her eyes and blew her nose. People really could be one way outside, when inside they were torn to shreds, a fine white powder of grief and regret replacing blood and bones, and no one even noticed. Robin and Stuart had their coffee, lightened with evaporated milk, but they were careful to speak only of the weather, which the meterologists swore would be warming in less than twenty-four hours. They'd done this when their father died and they'd sat on the living room couch in their Miami apartment, knees touching, as they waited to hear their fate. They'd done it on the plane years later, returning to Florida for their mother's funeral. They'd become experts when it came to cold fronts and cumulus clouds, novices still when it came to speaking about real pain. Stuart had once had a patient, a teenaged girl who refused to eat anything but small portions of mashed potatoes. When he'd realized she thought of them as clouds, and that she was obsessively listening to the radio for weather reports, he felt such tender affection for her that he'd asked to be taken off her case. He didn't have the heart to make her face her pain; he'd spent most of his last session with her discussing the lack of rainfall in the Southwest. As it was, when Stuart was leaving Robin's he suggested that she wear a scarf if she went outside, since the wind-chill factor was high, and that advice alone nearly made Robin burst into tears. She knew what he'd meant by it, and she kissed his cheek before he left.

"Maybe you're the one who shouldn't be alone," Stuart said, considering her through the storm door.

"Stop worrying about me," Robin told him. "Thank Kay for the muffins."

After Stuart had driven away, Robin stored the groceries he'd brought her, then wrapped Kay's corn muffins in foil. She made buttered toast and sat down at the table, but she couldn't bring herself to eat breakfast. She carried her dishes to the sink and told herself she'd be absolutely fine, but that wasn't the truth, and she knew it. It wasn't just that she missed Stephen terribly or that she felt she'd betrayed him, for reasons she still didn't understand. She was sick to her stomach, as she had been every morning for the past three weeks. Only, this time when she went to the bathroom to vomit, she stayed there on her knees for a long while, just as she had when she knew she was pregnant with Connor, and she didn't get back on her feet until she was certain she'd be able to stand.

They met just before dawn, when the birds were still asleep and the men in the patrol had all gone home to soak their frozen toes in tubs of hot water and crawl into their beds. Stephen got to the cemetery first. He stayed crouched down low until he heard footsteps, then he quickly rose to his feet. Matthew Dixon was having a hard time climbing up the hill. When he reached the top of the incline his face was blotchy and he'd just about run out of steam.

"I wasn't sure you'd really show up," Matthew said. "When I was a kid I wouldn't even walk through the gates, let alone do it in the dark. It still kind of gives me the creeps."

They were standing in front of Old Dick's grave. The sweeping view of the island, from the beaches to the bridge, was nothing now but a black blanket, except for the cluster of lampposts set around the town green.

"Did you find out anything for me?" Stephen asked.

All fall semester Matthew had made certain that he had no classes before ten; he wasn't used to being awake this early in the day, and his eyes looked swollen. Still, he grinned as he pulled a disk from the inside pocket of his parka. Stephen looked away when he saw that Matthew had printed WOLF-MAN across the disk.

"It's all here," Matthew said. "You know, I really envy you."

"Don't," Stephen told him.

"No, really, I'm serious." When Matthew spoke, great puffs of smoke rose into the air. He moved his weight from foot to foot and turned up his collar. "I'll bet the cold doesn't even bother you. I'll bet nothing bothers you." Matthew sat down on a wrought-iron bench that Old Dick had ordered from England during his first year on the island. Black swans were coiled along the back of the bench. "Do you mind if I ask you something personal?" Matthew had lowered his voice. "I'm just interested in knowing what your most frequent prey was."

Stephen looked at him, confused.

"What you killed most often to eat," Matthew said.

"Beetles," Stephen said.

"No way." Matthew grinned. "Not little squiggly bugs."

"You found out exactly where I came from?" Stephen asked, impatient. From this vantage point on the hill he could see that the lights around the green were growing dim; by sunrise they'd have turned off automatically.

"I pretty much have it pinpointed. I rolled the graphics in three-D from every single angle till I got it right. Information is a dangerous thing in the wrong hands, which is why I'll keep this file."

Matthew put the disk back in his pocket and unrolled the printout of the map. For an instant he hesitated, perhaps only to see the craving on Stephen's face; then he handed it over. Stephen folded the map, placed it in the pocket of his black overcoat, and shook Matthew's hand.

"I really owe you," Stephen said. "I know that."

"Let's have the truth," Matthew said. "It wasn't just beetles."

"No," Stephen said.

"I saw you that night with the deer. I know you wanted to kill it." Matthew pushed his hair out of his eyes, then shook his head. "You really held yourself back. I wish you hadn't."

The birds in the quince bushes around Old Dick's grave began to wake with their first tentative songs. To the right and the left grew hedges of boxwood, and in the spring there would be daffodils and sweet ivy.

"When you first get them and they're too surprised to fight back? That's the best part. You understand that," Matthew said. "I can tell."

Stephen didn't move, but inside his coat, inside his skin, he felt as if something were crawling along his spine. This was the moment when he began to pay attention to everything: the movement of the wind in the branches, the last star disappearing above them, the way Matthew chewed on his bottom lip when he grew excited. It was easy to tell what men wanted to hear, even Matthew, who was breathing too hard, the way he had when he first climbed the hill.

"I understand," Stephen said.

Matthew threw his arms up to the sky and made a noise deep inside himself. "To talk to someone who knows how I feel is incredible. It's like a relief or something. You know?"

Stephen nodded, just the way Matthew wanted him to. Today would be warmer, Stephen could feel it already, and when the ice began to melt, the air would turn foggy and white. There was often a thaw at this time of year, and the turn in the weather could surprise some people and catch them off guard.

"You were taught," Matthew Dixon said. "I had to learn it all by myself, step by step. And I did everything right, until the mistake at the end, when it was the wrong girl."

The wind shifted slightly. Stephen kept his hands in his pockets; he didn't take his eyes off Matthew.

"I can control it," Matthew said. "I know I can. Lydia just messed things up. That won't happen next time."

Next time, Matthew confided, he wouldn't leave anything to chance. He'd go get Lydia. No one would suspect someone with the courage to knock at her door. He'd ask for her help with a dog who had been hit by a car, and since she liked to pretend she was generous, she wouldn't deny him. He would guide her to the cemetery.

"The perfect place," he confided to Stephen.

When they arrived, and there was no dog to be seen, he would tell her it must have crawled into the bushes. It was injured, too desperate to fend for itself. And she'd call to the poor thing, and she'd whistle for it, and that was when Matthew would get her.

He came a little closer to Stephen now. "You choose who you're going to kill carefully, don't you? You plan it all out."

Stephen didn't blink. "Whatever runs," he said. Stephen's voice was thick, but Matthew didn't seem to notice.

"Whatever asks to be chased." Matthew had whispered, as if afraid that the birds might overhear. "Just the way she's asking for it."

There was a thin line of light at the bottom of the sky. The footprints Matthew had left as he climbed up to Old Dick's grave were already disappearing as the ice melted. Matthew was talking softly about Lydia, how she thought she was too good for everyone, how she stared right through people and thought no one could ever tell her what to do, but Stephen was thinking about another set of footprints he'd once overlooked, tracks through the woods that were set much too close together. That's what rabies could do, make it more and more difficult for a wolf to walk straight, because its rear legs would wobble. But it had been spring, and the tracks had been left in the damp earth, then covered with the moss that grew overnight, and Stephen hadn't spotted them until it was too late. It hadn't been a hard winter, and the spring had been even easier. Stephen hadn't been hungry for a while, and he may have grown lazy, but whatever it was, he'd been careless enough not to pick up the scent of the lone wolf who had come into their territory. Or maybe the wolf had been extraordinarily silent, as if his sickness had given him the power of deceit with one hand as it stole away his life and health with the other.

Stephen was at the stream when he felt another presence. He raised his eyes, slowly, the way he'd been taught, and there was the wolf, right in front of him, a male who was all gray, except for his black muzzle, and who was already looking at something that wasn't there. Lone wolves had come into their territory before; some they'd chased away easily, some they'd had to fight; one female had remained with them until she died of old age. Stephen stayed where he was, waiting for a sign of what was to happen next. The lone wolf's ears were already flattened close to his head and his tail was raised. He licked at his lips, though he couldn't have been thirsty; the stream was right in front of him, and all he needed to do to drink was lower his head. The sickness was the only thing that drove him; a wolf tied up in such agonizing knots was capable of anything. It was as if he had swallowed a bolt of lightning whole and was now electrified from mouth to tail.

The wolf began his charge slowly, through the ferns that grew alongside the stream. Stephen felt his own fear rising up through his skin, but he'd forced himself not to run, to keep his fear in check to make certain that the lone wolf wouldn't smell it. The sick wolf's mouth was open, so wide it seemed the jaws had been forced apart by wire; his breath was hot and foul. Beneath his unsteady feet, the ferns broke in two. When he made his attack, Stephen was ready, but the lone wolf was propelled by the lightning inside him. Stephen knew that if he rammed his fist into the wolf's throat, it would be nearly impossible for him to bite down with full pressure. But the lone wolf clawed at him so savagely he cut right through to the bone; Stephen's thigh was split open. Right then, he began to see the white light in front of his eyes.

Stephen called to his brothers with a voice he'd never used before. His fist was being crushed inside the lone wolf's jaws, and the white light was growing stronger, urging him to follow it. He didn't hear his brothers approach; all he heard was their teeth and the sound deep in their throats, and he didn't open his eyes until they had managed to drive the lone wolf off. That night, after Stephen had thrown himself in the cold water of the stream and washed off his own blood before it congealed, he wrapped a doe's skin around his thigh, so that pieces of himself wouldn't fall off. He would feel the pain from this for a long time, and it would serve to remind him of his own carelessness. His brothers licked at their own bloody legs; they circled around him, and together they listened to the sick wolf's call. He was just on the other side of the ridge, their territory still, and that wasn't nearly far enough.

Stephen looked at his favorite brother as he listened to the lone wolf's call. The silver wolf's throat trembled; he may have wanted to answer, but he did not. That was when Stephen knew what his brothers would do, and that it couldn't wait another night. A rabid wolf cannot remain in the same territory, not ever. They would never know when he would return, they'd be listening for him always, frightened by a breaking branch, an owl's call, more and more edgy, perhaps even turning on each other. One day he'd come back, he'd be driven to it. Together or alone, near the spring on a morning when the air was foggy or deep in the woods where it was always night, he'd find them. Stephen's leg was throbbing and he was feverish and hot, but he went with his brothers to the other side of the ridgetop, following behind, leaving a trail of blood. They were as silent as the stars above, the ones the lone wolf howled at as he stood high on the ridge, condemned to his aloneness.

They moved in on him so quickly that he never had the chance to bite. And as he was dying, the wolf looked at them, with the eyes he had seen through before he was rabid, before he was cast out again and again, as though grateful for his release. Then Stephen saw the lone wolf for who he was. He knelt beside the body and grieved for him, not the agonized thing they had killed that night, but that other wolf, the one who'd been lost long ago.

Men think about right and wrong, they have to debate it, discuss it, draw upon possibilities and statistics, laws and codes. Wolves have to know. They have to know in an instant, pure instinct, not thought, because they can never be wrong. If they're wrong, the ice they walk upon cracks, and they drown, their lungs filled with cold water and crystals. If they're wrong, their brothers and sisters starve and their pups are shot as they run. If they're wrong, the rabid wolf comes back, and he always comes back, only this time they're sleeping, and they can't even put up a fight as he splits them apart.

Stephen should not have even been on the hill where Old Dick was buried, because the sky was now pearl-gray, opening into light all along the shore. In only a few hours, the trucks would be out, sanding Cemetery Road, and the men who took the train to work would kiss their children and wives good-bye and walk across the bridge to the station. Stephen had been among them too long, he was slowed down by pity, something no wolf can afford. But he hadn't been among them long enough that it lasted.

"I wish I'd known about you from the beginning," Matthew was saying. They had begun to walk down the hill, and Stephen paced himself; he couldn't go too fast with Matthew beside him. "We could have been in it together," Matthew said.

"I stay alone," Stephen said. "It's better that way."

While Matthew thought this over, he slipped on the ice. Stephen reached out to steady him. Matthew was heavy, and Stephen had to hold tight so he wouldn't fall.

"Thanks," Matthew said. "This damn ice."

They were near the boxwood hedge, where rabbits liked to hide in spring.

"I'll get her next time," Matthew said. "You know I will, don't you?"

Matthew was about to head for the gate when he felt Stephen grab him again. Thinking there was a patch of ice ahead, Matthew grinned, grateful for the help. It never occurred to him to defend himself. In the end he was quite certain that the birds that had been chirping, signaling the close of night, had quieted all at once, when in fact they continued to sing long after Stephen had reached Mansfield Terrace, long after he'd climbed over Robin's fence and used the hose to wash the blood from his hands.

All that night Robin had been dreaming about him, and when he appeared in her yard at the first light of day it seemed like a miracle. She brought him inside and kissed him for as long as she could. She'd made a mistake: she told him that immediately. She'd been wrong. That she'd ever thought to doubt him now felt like a crime; every kiss begged his forgiveness. She wanted him so badly it hurt, but he moved away from her and asked for a glass of water.

He was out of breath; Robin could see that. He'd run all the way, just to see her. How selfish she was, how crazy for him. She got them both glasses of cool tap water, and Stephen gratefully took the water and drank it in one long gulp. He wiped his mouth with the back of his hand. He looked at her carefully, memorizing the angles of her face and the arch of her neck.

Robin laughed. "Don't look at me that way," she said. He

was making her nervous. He'd looked at her a thousand times before, and yet she had the urge to hide her face in her hands. "Stephen," she said. "Don't."

At last he turned and went to the window. He could see the rosebushes that were always the first to bloom on the island; he could see the redwood fence that circled the yard.

Robin came to stand behind him. Somehow, what they'd had was already over, and she hadn't even been aware of the end. This happened with roses: it was possible to take them for granted all summer as they wound along fences and gates, and then in September, when they faded, how beautiful they'd once been suddenly took hold. That was when people began to yearn for them, and all winter long they'd watch the bare branches for buds, vowing that this time they'd be grateful for all that they had.

"I did something," Stephen said.

"Whatever happened, it doesn't matter." Robin knew she sounded frantic. "You don't have to tell me anything."

As soon as he started to explain, Robin put her hands over her ears. But that didn't stop him from telling her that Matthew Dixon hadn't made a sound, he'd made certain of that by crushing his windpipe quickly.

"Stop it," Robin begged him.

It was an act of mercy. He couldn't have walked away before that moment when Matthew fell into the hedge of boxwood, where his parka caught on the branches and the low sticker brambles that grew wild all over the island.

"I had to do it," Stephen told Robin.

"You had to! You couldn't tell the police? Or me? Or Roy?

Don't you understand? You don't just kill someone because you think he's guilty."

"He was guilty," Stephen said.

"Because you *think* it!" Robin said. She had begun to cry, and that just made her feel more helpless. "And even if he was, that is not the way we do it! You can't just kill someone. You can't just decide that."

This was not what Stephen had come here for. He reached for Robin, but she wrenched her arm away.

"Who are you that you could do this? Who are you?" she cried.

Stephen didn't flinch, even though Robin raised her hand as if to strike him. But she didn't hit him. She knew exactly who he was. She had from the very start.

"All right," Robin said. "This is what we'll do." She wiped her eyes and tried to concentrate on every word, not on what she felt inside. "We'll explain that you didn't understand. You didn't know the way things work, no one ever told you. We'll tell them that."

Stephen knew that he would change things. Later, when he remembered, her eyes would not be filled with tears, her face would not be so pale. Robin had already gone to the phone and had begun to dial Roy's number. Stephen took the phone away from her just the way she knew he would. She didn't have to turn to him to know he was looking at her as though he'd never see her again. He had never once said he could believe what men believed in; he'd never pretended that. She'd known him all along; she'd been locking the doors in order to keep him, praying that he could get used to the easy chair, the dinner hour, the pillows on her bed.

"You'll leave," Robin said. He had both arms around her now. "That's what you'll do, isn't it?" He rested his cheek against the base of her neck.

Robin locked the doors one last time and took him to her bedroom. She led him up the stairs and along the hallway. She would never love anyone again, not like this, not ever again. She wanted him in her bed. She wanted to always remember this one morning, when the shades were drawn against the morning light and he told her that there would never be anyone else. She didn't have to cry when she felt this way, that's what she had discovered. She just had to hold on tight, because before she knew it, it would be over and she'd have to watch him reach for his clothes that had been dropped on the floor. She'd have to make up the bed so that it might look as though he'd never been there at all.

All that day the thaw continued, and by midafternoon most of the ice had melted, bringing the level of the water beneath the old bridge dangerously high. Streets flooded, forsythia was nearly tricked into budding, children who'd been forced to stay inside for weeks pulled on their rubber boots and splashed through the mud. By afternoon, it was nearly sixty degrees, a record high, yet when they went out to the truck, Stephen continued to wear his old black coat. Robin had given him the five hundred dollars Roy's father had left on her table; she would drive him out of New York, to a bus station in New Jersey, and be home by midnight. She had her hair tied back and she wore her boots and her old work jacket, stained with mud. Stephen didn't offer to show her the map Matthew had given him, and she didn't ask to see it. She might have torn it in half; she might have been tempted to follow him. She had to think of everyday things: how much gas they would need for the trip, whether the truck might stall out, as it often did on damp days such as this. The truck was idling roughly, and Robin had to concentrate so that she wouldn't flood the motor. She didn't even realize they were being followed until the bridge was right in front of them. Stephen reached out and put a hand on her arm, then nodded to the rearview mirror. Roy's car was behind them.

"Damn him," Robin said.

She pulled over, and the wheels on the right side of the pickup sank into the mud.

"I'll talk to him," she told Stephen. "You'd better stay here."

Robin got out and slammed her door shut. If pushed, she just might explode, but then Roy was used to that, he wouldn't find it the least bit unusual.

"You're fucking doing it again," Robin said to Roy. He'd parked behind her and was now rolling down his window. "You have no right to follow me."

She leaned down, the better to curse him, and that was when she saw that it was Connor who was behind the wheel.

"I didn't know it was you," Robin said, flustered. "What are you doing with your dad's car?"

"I got my license last week," Connor said.

As Connor got out of the car and leaned up against it, Robin could have sworn he'd gotten taller and thinner since she'd seen him last. He was wearing his leather jacket and jeans, and he'd had his hair cut shorter than usual, so his neck was exposed.

"Your dad doesn't mind you driving with all the flooding that's going on?"

"Mom," Connor said.

"All right." Robin backed off. "Fine."

When Connor was a baby, Robin would count his fingers and toes, and each time she did she was counting her good fortune. He was all in one piece; he was hers. She'd never liked babies much, never begged for a closer look or asked to hold them in her arms, until she had Connor. Even Michelle had laughed at her because his whole first year she didn't want to put him down for an instant. *He'll never learn to walk,* Roy teased her. *You'll still be carrying him when he's a grown man with a family of his own.*

"Is that Stephen in there?" Connor nodded to Robin's truck. "I've been wanting to talk to him."

"He can't talk now. We're going to the mall," Robin said, just a little too quickly. Connor looked at her. "He needs some clothes. Sweatshirts, things like that."

"I should have told him right away," Connor said. He looked much more angular, Robin saw that now, as if he'd grown up overnight. "I know he didn't do anything to Jenny."

"No," Robin agreed. She kept pushing her hair away from her face, the way she always did when she was upset.

"You're not taking him to the mall," Connor said.

Stephen opened the door of the pickup, then stood beside it, there on the side of the road, where the mud was so thick a man could easily get stuck in it. He waved to Connor and Connor waved back.

"You're not taking him shopping," Connor said to his mother.

"No," Robin said.

Connor smiled and ran a hand through his hair. "Yeah," he

said. "That's what I thought." From where he stood Connor could see the bridge and the willow trees that had grown there for a hundred years, longer than anyone could remember.

"You'd better go," he said. "You don't want the mall to close before you get there."

Connor got into his father's car and watched his mother walk back to the pickup. Stephen was still by the side of the road, and even after Robin started the truck, and exhaust filtered into the air, he didn't move. Connor grinned and flicked his headlights on and off.

"Go on, you jerk," Connor called.

Stephen got into the truck then, and as soon as he did Robin headed for the bridge. Connor leaned his head back and closed his eyes. He listened to the beat of the truck's tires until it was replaced by the low rustling echo of the willows, which could sound exactly like crying to anyone who didn't understand that their branches formed a wind tunnel through which even the slightest breeze could spin itself into a moan. Connor headed toward his father's place, since he'd promised to get the car there before dark. He drove slowly, because the roads were indeed flooded, and when he reached the end of Cemetery Road he thought maybe the sewers had backed up. Several police cars were parked at the gates and traffic was a mess. When he saw that it was George Tenney who was directing the detour, Connor parked up on the grass and went over to talk to him. By now, Connor knew, his mother had already pulled onto the Long Island Expressway; still, it couldn't hurt to tie up George Tenney with conversation.

"I'm legal," Connor said when George looked shocked to see him. "I got my license last week."

"Then go on and drive yourself home," George said.

Connor saw that there were several officers beneath the hill where Old Dick's grave was, his own father among them. Roy was over near the boxwood, and Connor had a strange feeling inside his throat, as if Roy had been hurt.

"I'm just going to see my dad," Connor said.

George Tenney blocked his way.

"Hey, George," Connor said. "Come on."

"There's a corpse up there, and you're not going to take a look," George said.

"Who is it?" Connor asked. "I'm going to find out sooner or later," he added when George hesitated.

"Matthew Dixon," George said. "It looks like he fell down and broke his neck. Happy now?"

"Not exactly," Connor said. "I think I'll just wait for my dad."

Several people had gathered around the gates, and when Connor went over he heard that Patty Dixon had called the police when she realized Matthew wasn't home early that morning. He'd never gotten out of bed before ten, let alone dressed, fixed himself breakfast, and just disappeared. What was more, she had found one of Matthew's old shirts covered with blood in the garage, stuffed under some old newspapers. Connor broke away from the group at the gates and went along the fence until George couldn't see him; then he climbed over and made his way up the back of the hill. From here he could look down and see his father, along with Woody Preston and several other men who were waiting for a forensics team from the state police to arrive. Julie Wynn, from drug education, had brought them coffee in a thermos and some paper cups. Roy drank his coffee. Then he must have made a joke, because everyone laughed, and they were still laughing as Roy walked back to the hedges. He had a green tarp over his arm, which he was supposed to place over the body, but before he did he knelt down, placing his coffee cup on the ground.

Connor watched as his father quickly went through the pockets of Matthew's parka. He took out some candy wrappers, and then a photograph that seemed to jar him, because he slowed down and stared at it, before reaching into Matthew's other pocket. He pulled out a computer disk. Connor moved closer to the edge of the hill, brushing against some quinces. Roy looked up, but he saw nothing, and he replaced the candy wrappers and the photograph of Lydia that the forensics team would find in the next half-hour. The computer disk he put in his own pocket.

Watching his father kneeling there, Connor had a peculiar feeling, and he almost called out, but he didn't. And later, when the sky was growing dark, Roy found Connor standing at the cemetery gates.

"What are you doing here?" Roy said. "You're supposed to have the car home by dark."

Connor shrugged. "I felt like waiting for you."

"Oh, yeah?" Roy said, pleased.

"Yeah," Connor said. "Let's go home."

Roy thought about that moment for a long time, the way it felt to see his son, who was now taller than he was, waiting for him by the car. He thought about it as they had pizza together in front of the TV, and later as he walked through the living room after Connor had fallen asleep on the couch. He went out at eleven and drove over to Mansfield Terrace and sat in his parked car. He hadn't been a particularly good father. Not that he'd done anything spectacularly wrong, but he felt, all at once, that he was about to be granted a second chance. He'd never say it aloud, but he was sorry, not for the things he'd done, but for all that he'd left undone. He could have managed a hell of a lot better, he saw that now. He could have tried his best. It wasn't just Connor whom he'd failed. Out of jealousy, he'd refused to give Stephen his rightful alibi, and if Roy wasn't careful he'd wind up ruined by his own spite. It would lead him around by the nose and take over his life, until finally he wouldn't even remember who he'd been before that night when he sat in his parked car and did nothing at all.

Robin didn't come home until twelve-thirty. She had cried all the way back through New Jersey, then taken the wrong exit off the expressway, and wound up on the old road that was once the only direct route to the end of Long Island. She drove for miles, past doughnut shops and gas stations, calmed by the blue-black puddles on the asphalt and the wavering neon signs. At midnight, she had found a road that cut across to the North Shore, and by the time she reached the bridge she felt better.

Twice she'd almost told him. Once when she'd had to stop to fill the truck with gas and then again when they turned off the New Jersey Turnpike. But she knew enough not to. A baby could turn into a trap, its fingers holding fast, the sound of its milky cry bringing him back to someplace he'd never intended to go. Maybe that's what she'd planned once, without even knowing it, since she'd been especially careful not to get pregnant all those years after Connor. It was possible, after all, that this was no accident, because as it turned out, this baby was exactly what she wanted.

She got out of the truck, carrying the black coat over her arm. She was actually hungry, always a good sign in the first three months. Her plan was to go inside and make herself a pot of oatmeal, flavored with cinnamon and raisins, and perhaps some buttered toast if she still wanted more, but Roy had met her in the driveway and he insisted on coming in to fix them both scrambled eggs, which were far more nutritious.

"We're not going to fight?" Robin said as he broke four eggs into a bowl. "You're not going to say, I told you so?"

Roy rolled up his sleeves, then searched through the drawers for a whisk.

"Tabasco sauce?" he asked, considering some bottles on the spice rack.

"I think you've gone crazy," Robin decided. "I truly believe you have."

But that wasn't it at all; it was only that he was so sure of what he had to do. After they'd eaten, he stayed long enough to wash the dishes, since Robin was clearly exhausted. Roy should have been tired as well, but he wasn't. He had the oddest feeling deep inside, and he had the urge to stay up all night. This time he wasn't about to make a mistake, and he knew it. When he gave Robin the disk, which she would later put up in the attic, along with the black coat and all of Stephen's books, he had simply set them all free.

On the morning of his twenty-sixth birthday, Connor Moore left his apartment in Boston, kissed the woman he loved good-bye, and got onto the Mass Pike, heading west. He had a lump in his throat for the first three hundred miles, and he pulled off the road for coffee so often he began to wonder if he was stopping in order to give himself a chance to turn back. He drove for two days, getting off the highways each time dusk fell, searching out inexpensive motels, still wondering if he should reconsider and head back east. But on the third day of his journey, he suddenly felt light-headed and clear. He pulled over at a truck stop and telephoned the woman he would marry in only a few months just to tell her that the trees here in northern Michigan were huge enough to put the pines in the White Mountains to shame. The sky was so blue it hurt just to look at it.

He'd become, of all things, a doctor, something he'd never planned or imagined he'd be. As it turned out, he was good at it; he inspired confidence and actually listened when his patients spoke. His father liked to joke that most traits skipped a generation in families, and now they had two doctors, one for trees, the other for people. The tree doctor would have liked the upper peninsula of Michigan, Connor thought as he drove, off the highway now, over winding, rutted roads, because there was nothing but trees here; he had to get out of his car and stare upward through the branches when he wanted to know what the sky was like, otherwise he would have sworn it was dusk around the clock.

His mother and sister had moved at the beginning of the month, and he'd gone down to help with the packing. Robin had finally gotten the carriage house into shape. The renovation had taken much longer that it should have, since she did everything with such care. There was a new kitchen, and a shower had been installed beside the claw-footed tub; the roof no longer leaked and the chimney had been rebuilt. But there were also details no one else would have troubled with: she had spent an entire summer laying out the bluestone patio, and had interviewed several furniture-makers before choosing the right one to restore the dining room table. As the work on the carriage house had progressed, deer had ventured closer and closer; by the time the painters had arrived, the deer had grown so brave they trotted right up to the windows to have a look inside. Finally, twelve rosebushes were planted beside the arbor where the wisteria had once grown.

During the move, Connor had found Stephen's black coat in the attic. When he brought it to the carriage house, Robin buttoned each button carefully, smoothed out the wrinkles, then hung the coat in the hall closet. There had never been any question that she'd ever want anyone else; even Stuart and Kay had stopped trying to fix her up. But Connor still could not understand how his mother had accepted what had happened. He took loss personally, he fought it so hard that in medical school his friends had called him the ox behind his back; he just couldn't give up the burden of his patients. There were times when he didn't see his own apartment for weeks on end, when he stayed at a bedside long after a last breath had been taken.

And so, when he discovered the disk in the attic, there beneath the black coat in the bottom of a box, he felt a wild sort of hope. He'd kept his find to himself, then went off to the library at noon. After he'd printed out the map, he rushed back to the carriage house, certain that his mother would be overjoyed. But when he presented Robin with the map, she refused to take it. She led Connor outside, into the garden where the roses would grow, so that his sister wouldn't overhear, and told him it would be best to throw the map away.

"Why?" Connor had said. "Don't you want to find him? Isn't that what you want?"

"What I want?" Robin had been surprised. "What does that have to do with it?"

Connor had stalked away, confused, and Robin had followed him. She'd put her arms around him and told him to do whatever he wanted with the information he'd found, and that was what he was doing now. When he got to Cromley he bought a backpack and some cans of food, as well as some overpriced oranges and apples. It was the last week of April, warm enough to wear jeans and a sweatshirt, but as Connor drove farther north he could see there was still snow in the mountains.

He stopped and had his lunch sitting behind the wheel. Peeling an orange, he felt a wave of homesickness, not for Boston but for the island. He usually went back four or five times a year, and he always visited during the first week of August, for his sister's birthday. Last summer, when she turned nine, they'd had a party at Stuart and Kay's, since the heat was brutal and the little cottage Stuart and Kay had bought near the beach, after selling their old house, was always breezy and cool. Connor had given his sister a charm bracelet, and she loved it so much she hugged him and swore she would never take it off, not even if she lived to be a hundred. Roy had just arrived with the cake, and he'd tried hard not to laugh at this vow. He'd been a much better father to this little girl than he'd ever been to Connor. She stayed with him every other weekend, and on Wednesday nights he drove her to ballet lessons. They'd gone to Disney World together twice and were already planning another trip. When she ran to him to show off her bracelet, Roy had put the birthday cake down on the picnic table in order to give each charm his full attention.

After that party, Connor had gone off by himself. He'd had coffee at Fred's Diner, then walked back through the town green and along Cemetery Road, which now had sidewalks and streetlights and wasn't nearly as dark as it used to be. When he got to Mansfield Terrace, he went to stand outside the Alteros' house, although they'd been gone for years. They had moved to North Carolina the summer after Jenny was killed, and occasionally Robin got postcards from Michelle, brief cheerful notes without any substance. The year after they'd moved, Connor had received a postcard as well. *Having a terrible time Wish you were here* had been scrawled on the card, but the postmark was fuzzy and he was never certain whether or not Lydia had sent it. Lately, he found himself wishing that he could see her, maybe because of his impending marriage. But the truth of it was, he and Lydia could have been in the same room and not known each other; they'd be searching for people who no longer existed. If they ever shook hands they'd have to pretend they knew each other; they'd be puzzled and then embarrassed by all they might have expected.

Now, as he traveled north, searching for the trapper his uncle had told him about, Connor kept one eye on the twisting dirt roads and the other on his map. An hour after lunch he found the place, a wooden house with a wide porch, a small barn, and a fenced-in kennel for the two dogs, which barked like crazy when Connor drove up. He got out of his car and waved when the old man came out to see what the ruckus was about. His nephew had up and moved to Detroit, where he'd worked in a factory and bragged about his great benefits until the place went and closed down on him. The old man's wife had died and he was living on his army pension. He'd had a huge dish put up so he could get TV stations he couldn't even believe existed: movies all night, talk shows where people said things the old man wouldn't have even confessed to a priest.

"Hey," Connor called to him, "do you mind some company?"

The trapper waved him over and Connor walked past the barking dogs and up onto the porch, then followed the old man inside, where there was a pot of coffee already made. They talked about the weather, something Connor was completely comfortable with, considering the family he came from, and the difference between the rutted dirt roads the trapper was used to and the traffic in Boston, which could send any sane person around the bend. When it came up that Connor was a doctor, the trapper showed him two lumps on his wrist, which were probably benign tumors, although Connor suggested he make himself an appointment at the hospital in Cromley to have them looked at. At last, Connor asked about the man they had found years back. The old man put down his coffee cup and rubbed at his face.

"You don't remember?" Connor said.

The trapper smiled, and Connor made a note to himself to suggest a visit to the dentist as well.

"I remember it every day," the trapper said. He was now so old that ten years gone often seemed quite a bit closer than the day before. "I wish we'd never caught him. Or we should have left him there. Maybe he would have bled to death and maybe he wouldn't have, but I never felt right about sending him back to people when he'd never learned to defend himself from them."

He agreed to take Connor into the woods, but it would be slow going, and they'd have to put it off until morning. Connor spent the night on the couch where the dogs usually slept, and at dawn his cramped muscles woke him. They set off early and still didn't get close until after a lunch of crackers and cheese. The trees were so thick and so tall Connor actually felt dizzy; it seemed a sin to speak in a place as deep and green as this.

"This is probably the spot where we found him," the trapper said, but in fact he was certain of the place. He'd come here quite often. He always had a gun with him, but he rarely went after anything these days, just like those old men he used to scorn, who swore that deer could cry.

"Are there still wolves around?" Connor asked. Now that he was here, he wasn't sure what he wanted the answer to be.

"Nobody sees them unless they want to be seen," the trapper said. He pulled off his gloves, slowly because of the lumps on his wrist, and reached into his jacket pocket for some chewing tobacco. "We had some fellow here from the National Park Service who reported back to Washington there wasn't a wolf left in Michigan, and just that morning I'd seen tracks, so you tell me who the fools are."

If there were birds in these woods, they weren't singing

now. The ground was still covered by a few inches of snow, although the ferns were already unfolding. The trapper picked some fiddleheads that he'd cook with butter for supper.

"Do you ever see him?" Connor asked.

The trapper looked up and considered the patch of blue sky through the branches above them.

"Would I tell if I had?" he said.

Connor smiled and listened carefully. He held one hand above his eyes and gazed north. Up on the ridgetop nothing moved, at least not anything he could see. That was just as well. In no time the sky would be growing dark, and it was a long way back home.